EXILE

EXILE

Kevin Emerson

KATHERINE TEGEN BOOKS
An Imprint of HarperCollins Publishers

Katherine Tegen Books is an imprint of HarperCollins Publishers.

Exile

 PC STUDIO

Copyright © 2014 by PC Studio, Inc.
All rights reserved. Printed in the United States of America.
No part of this book may be used or reproduced in any manner
whatsoever without written permission except in the case of brief
quotations embodied in critical articles and reviews. For information
address HarperCollins Children's Books, a division of
HarperCollins Publishers, 10 East 53rd Street,
New York, NY 10022.
www.epicreads.com

Library of Congress Cataloging-in-Publication Data
Emerson, Kevin.
Exile / Kevin Emerson. — First edition.
pages cm
Summary: As band manager for the up-and-coming Dangerheart, seventeen-year-
old Summer Carlson navigates a relationship with the lead singer and decides
whether to act on information that could rocket the band to stardom.
ISBN 978-0-06-213395-3 (hardcover bdg.)
[1. Rock groups—Fiction. 2. Bands (Music)—Fiction. 3. Dating (Social
customs)—Fiction.] I. Title.
PZ7.E5853Ex 2014   2013021526
[Fic]—dc23   CIP
                                    AC
Typography by Carla Weise
14 15 16 17 18 LP/RRDH 10 9 8 7 6 5 4 3 2 1
❖
First Edition

For the moment between
the last stick click
and the first downbeat,
when anything can happen . . .

EXILE

15 Years After We Pledged Allegiance

—posted by ghostofEliWhite on August 28

As all true music fans know, this year is the fifteenth anniversary of one of rock's greatest triumphs and tragedies: the release of Allegiance to North's seminal second album, *Into the Ever & After*, which dropped one year after the death of lead singer and songwriter Eli White. There is no bigger *what-could-have-been* than this phenomenally talented group out of Mount Hope, CA. From the moment they burst onto the scene with their first EP, *Forests in Cloudlight*, through the worldwide smash success of their full-length, *The Breaks*, it seemed like Allegiance was sure to be the greatest band of the new millennium. But that was before White redefined the cautionary tale, ending a downward spiral into drugs by drowning in the dark Pacific at the age of 22.

And as we all remember, it was on this date fifteen years ago that Candy Shell Records leaked the now-infamous track list for *Into the Ever & After*, three months before the album's release. Why infamous? Because the list included three songs that did *not* appear on the album, when it was finally released after

Eli's death. Those lost songs . . . did they ever get written? No recordings have ever been found. I'll admit, it makes me sad every time I think of what they might have been. Here's the list:

**Allegiance to North: *Into the Ever & After*
Official Track List**

1. The Here & Now
2. Infinite Starling
3. The Sound of Your Smile
4. Deadfall
5. Last Chance
6. Roll the Credits
7. On Dreams That Seem Like Silent Movies
8. Exile*
9. Encore to an Empty Room*
10. Finding Abbey Road*

*Unreleased

Just after dinner on the night before the start of senior year, Dad polishes off his guacamole garden burger, looks at me seriously, and asks, "So, now what, then?"

Tonight is also my eighteenth birthday, which means that I've known my dad for six thousand five hundred and seventy days, and so I probably should know that he means this question to sound supportive. Concerned, but supportive.

But my heart races, and all I can hear is *I told you so.*

"I don't know, yet," I reply, shoving the last chunk of burrito into my mouth.

"Honey, it's senior year," adds Mom, whom I've presumably known for about nine months longer, and who I know means to sound supportive, too. But Mom wears her worry on every word.

"I've heard," I say around food.

Now what. . . . Senior year is supposed to be the culmination, the big finale of an epic journey, but given our surroundings, I wonder if I'm going in circles instead.

We sit in a red-vinyl booth, hunched over a linoleum table decorated with a cliché painting of the Mexican desert. Around us blink the jalapeno-shaped lights and other assorted kitsch of La Burrita Feminista. Freshman year, I brought my five closest friends here for a birthday party, complete with poppers and present bags and personal piñatas, but invitations for this year's celebration went only to my parents and my aunt Jeanine. Maybe I'm not just going in circles. Maybe this is actually a downward spiral, like into a black hole.

My parents normally prefer something a little more sanitized than a radical feminist burrito bar, especially when it means driving all the way into Hollywood. And normally I'd prefer not to be spending my birthday with my parents. But I think they sensed that I had no other options, and found it in their hearts to make the effort, even if Dad defiantly ordered a garden burger at a Mexican joint.

Also, Aunt Jeanine loves this place. My parents think it's because she's secretly a lesbian. I'm more inclined to think it's because: a) she knows a good burrito and a fun atmosphere, two things my parents couldn't possibly comprehend, and because b) regardless of her orientation, she knows that men are vermin.

Dessert arrives before my parents' line of questioning can continue. Feminista has this crazy cake that you're supposed to split called the *Orgasmo de Cacao*. Any other night, I'd share one, but anticipation about tomorrow and a series of tweets I've been getting all evening have me wolfing down a whole one myself. Mom and Jeanine are sharing one, and Dad got, for dessert—I kid you not—a side salad.

As we dig in, I read tweets on my phone from all the people over at the Hatch, the best all-ages club in Silver Lake. They're seeing a band called Postcards from Ariel. Tonight's show is their North American tour kickoff. Thirty dates, coast to coast, celebrating the release of their new album, *Dispatch*. Postcards is from my high school. They graduated last year.

And they used to be mine.

I was planning to spend tonight at that show. Back when it was just the next show on the calendar. Back before Postcards got signed by Candy Shell Records, who subsequently rerecorded the album we'd been working on all spring, booked them a nationwide tour and, oh, fired their former management company, Orchid Productions, aka me.

One could argue, if one wasn't busy eating a two-pound skillet of chocolate cake, that I was the reason Postcards got that record deal, the reason there was big interest in them even after only one EP last fall. Those awesome rocket-ship mailbox T-shirts? Yours truly.

One could also argue that their lead singer, Ethan Myers, and I had something special.

Oh, seventeen-year-old Summer, I tell myself yet again, over bite after bite of molten chocolate, *you were a sucker.* Which is maybe true, maybe not. True that I thought Ethan Myers was the real thing. I could have watched him strum that guitar and croon those sweet high melodies forever. It seemed so real. We met at the Spritz, a coffee shop back in Mount Hope, just after Postcards had played an acoustic set. I was a sophomore and so into music. He was a junior with a cool new band. I couldn't believe he was actually into me.

I mean, I could believe it a little. I clean up nice, and when he asked me what I thought of the set, I said, "I like that fourth song you played. The one with the line about the tides inside us? That was a cool idea."

Apparently, most people respond to Ethan Myers with phrases like, *Oh. My. God. It was uh. Mazing!* Or: *You guys . . .* [insert crying].

Apparently, it was completely novel for a girl to have a thought about a specific thing in a specific song, and to articulate that thought coherently.

"Oh, nice," he replied, adding, "'beneath the surface of the photograph.'" At the time I should have caught this finishing-his-own-lyric move as a sign that he was a self-gratifying nematode, except then he said, "Thanks for noticing," and it sounded sincere, and also he smiled, and

4

yowch, the way his eyes lit up was sort of amazing. Then he asked, "What about the other songs?"

Then, apparently my response, "Oh, they were fine, too," came off as a little indifferent (even though at the time I was whirring inside)—and apparently, telling a musician their songs are "fine" is basically like telling them you think they suck.

And then finally, this level of indifference is apparently completely irresistible to men. Guys dig when women fall all over them, but what they really love is a chase.

We started dating. I sincerely loved the band. Their sound was one part folk, one part rock, but with a melancholy thing that occasionally turned dark. I helped out: spreading the word about their shows and videos, designing their website and BandSpace page. And it worked, so Ethan thought I should become their official manager. There was some Yoko danger there, and the other members were skeptical, but then I was good at it.

One rainy Sunday in January, Ethan and I printed up my first business cards for Orchid Productions at Expresso Mail. We drank medicis, like mochas with orange, a drink that Ethan had discovered while visiting Seattle, and we took a self-portrait, me with a bit of foam on my nose, the attendant frowning in the background because we insisted on drinking them with the tops off so we could enjoy the froth even though there was a big sign that said NO BEVERAGES NEAR MACHINES. It was my profile picture for over a year.

5

What I'm good at is spreading buzz, fanning flames, setting up great gigs. But most important, it turned out that I have an eye for what really sets a band apart. What their greatness truly is. Bands have a hard time seeing that from the inside. Lots of times, they care too much about sixteenth notes and egos, and which girls in the audience are checking them out.

After two years of work, Postcards was really taking off, but then along came Candy Shell Records, with a studio and a tour and a marketing team, and one more thing: a contract with a clause stating that the band could not have any *third-party* management.

Suddenly, so long, Summer. But that wasn't even the worst part. Because only then did I learn that Ethan Myers was also not what I'd thought. Those pretty melodies and guitar chords he spun . . . it turned out I wasn't the only heart he'd ensnared in his web.

"Nothing bonds two people as deeply as music," Ethan said to me once. (I know: in hindsight, SO LAME!). And I was the fool who assumed he was only referring to the two of us, when actually, Ethan had felt that deepest of bonds quite a few times during our relationship: like with a blogger named Alice he met in San Diego while on a tour I set up but couldn't go on; with freakin' Missy Prescott at Todd Forester's house party a few hours after I'd left; even the night they got signed, with a Candy Shell intern named Royce.

And the poetic wordsmith's excuse for all this? "I couldn't help it. They were so into me. It was hard, you know?"

"I bet it was."

I managed to fire that little zinger before the stupid tears and the storming out and everything else.

And then of course, after the breakup came the regret. I am still sorting out where on the scale of being played for a fool I fall. There's the embarrassment, too. For two years, I'd hung out with Postcards all the time: at lunch, before and after school, sitting in the back row together at assemblies. They were my band of musician pirates. I felt like I'd finally found my tribe. I knew some people mistook me for a groupie, but I also believed they didn't get it. Turns out they sorta got it.

My phone buzzes again. One of my blogger associates, *FreakyLizzy*, has checked in to tweet a "SQUEE!" in support of Postcards's next song: "You're My Forever."

I remember when Ethan Myers first strummed that song idea for me last fall, after fish tacos on Venice Beach. I remember thinking, *Damn*.

"Have you had any more thoughts about colleges?" Dad asks. "Applications are due in a few months."

"I don't know," I say. "Maybe I'll major in pre-law."

"Law?" It's hilarious watching Dad try to suppress his excitement. He works for a major construction firm downtown, managing the books. Concrete numbers, pounds of cinder block, foot lengths of two-by-four. The kind of guy who wears a tie even to a rainbow-colored burrito joint on a Sunday night. He doesn't say anything more, but I know exactly what he's thinking: *Finally.*

Of course I can count on Mom to say it. "Well, that would be a relief." Mom's use of pearls (on a Sunday! Eating burritos!) is like Dad's tie. They're like a law firm of their own. Carlson Squared, Parental Attorneys.

"Yep," I say, still behind a sarcasm shield. And yet . . . would law be so bad? It sounds like about the furthest thing from art and passion, but where have those gotten me? I could stop going by my middle name, Summer, and switch back to the ol' parent-conceived identity: Catherine S. Carlson.

What's the "S" stand for? a striving jock attorney might ask me over cocktails in a mahogany bar off-campus where all the cool pre-law kids go.

It stands for "Settle out of court," I'd reply. And everyone would laugh expensively.

"You could do entertainment law," Aunt Jeanine suggests, also missing my sarcasm, or maybe not. She's the only adult at the table who seems to actually empathize with my current plight. Maybe the only one who's actually noticed who I'm really trying to be. "You could work to protect artists' rights."

"Meh," I say, "I was thinking corporate law. You know, taking down the riffraff, those troublemakers like

Greenpeace and MoveOn. Fight for the rights of the poor shareholders."

Normally I'd revel for a moment in my parents' total lack of response to that comment, but that old satisfaction just isn't there, not even with the glycemic bliss that the *Orgasmo* is providing.

My phone hums with more updates from Silver Lake. Postcards has started their encore with "Never Leaving You." I had to admit, it's the perfect choice. Ethan has that lyric in there:

I'll stand with you, as long as you can stand it—

And suddenly I seize up. *Dammit!* My breath catches and my eyes spill.

"Cat?" says Mom, using her old pet name for me. No matter what I do, I'm still Catherine to my parents, always have been, always will be.

I hate nothing more than having my parents see me cry. I try to hide my tears. What I want to say is, Please, no sympathy, no hugs, if you want to care just shut up, because anything you say will just sound patronizing, like my pain validates your worry, and yet your worry makes it worse . . . and around we'll go!

But I never say things like that to them. Instead, I dab my eyes with my napkin. "I think there was some cayenne in my *Orgasmo*," I wheeze.

"Have some Coke." Aunt Jeanine pushes my soda toward me. There's a tissue between her fingers.

I snatch it and flash her what I hope is a thankful smile.

"I'll Google colleges with the best pre-law programs," says Dad, my tears only further motivating him. "We can plan some trips."

"Dad . . ." but I can't finish, have to beat back this feeling, the overwhelming sense that life is already over, that I've missed the one best chance I had for doing what I really love, and that, in a beat-up rock club across town, the life I want is moving on without me, leaving me here in the same burrito joint, on the cusp of the future—

So, now what, then?

—with no idea how to answer the question.

Mount Hope High School

POPARTS FALL KICKOFF CONCERT

Lineup

FRESHMAN

We Still Play with Joysticks

Bait

SOPHOMORE

Brain Food

We Salute You

The Progress Reports

JUNIOR

The New Past Lives

Supreme Commander

The Theo Alvin Four

SENIOR

BeatKillaz

Android Necktie

Fluffy Poodle and the #'s of Doom!

2

Formerly Orchid @catherinefornevr 1hr
Senior Year existential sandwich. Me = the Tofurkey between
slices of whole grain Optimism and Oblivion. Pass the Baconnaise!
#Iworkedhardforthatmetaphor #stilllame

Seen from above, Mount Hope High looks so random: a
spill of blocks, a bad joke of architectural trends, cost over-
runs, and budget shortfalls. Every five years it has to be
added on to in order to support the town's widening belt
of sprawl and spawn. It looks like a slow flow of geometric
lava. A five-year-old could do better with Legos.

Safety regulations have made it bulletproof, earthquake
proof, heatproof, smog proof, nuclear fallout proof. It has a
greenhouse that's used for calculus classes, and the painting
club has to meet in the chem lab. It has seven stairwells,
twenty-two locker rooms, sixteen supply closets, and yet

the only safe place to hook up during the school day is the vice principal's office.

[pause for laughter]

The school has graduated 96 senior classes. Five hundred forty-eight kids per class, give or take an asterisk.[1] That's 52,608 human beings with hopes and dreams and wishes that have passed through its halls. I am some number between 52,609 and 53,156. And more will come after me, over and over, for as long as the antibiotics stay ahead of the bacteria and the sun doesn't throw a supernova tantrum. Someday, long from now, when California is a desert island and humans are halfway back to dinosaurs, archaeologists will unearth this structure, read the inscriptions on the cockeyed bathroom doors and try to figure out who we were, and what we were thinking, and they'll get it all wrong.

Of course by that time, myself and the rest of my senior class will have joined the entire current population of the earth in a fingernail-sized sheet of sediment.

Okay, maybe that's a little extreme.

Formerly Orchid @catherinefornevr 3sec
There is no more avoiding this. #timetofacethemusic #orlackthereof

"Summer!"

I turn from where I've been rooted to the steps, watching the minnows file in through the barred-window doors

---

1 drop out, suicide, attempted suicide, pregnancy, pregnancy with faculty, rehab, teen acting contract

of school. Contemplating the meaninglessness of my existence feels easier than going inside.

No one's said hi to me. I've spotted a few people I could have greeted, but didn't. Every now and then I get a glance that says, *Oh yeah, her. She hung out with that band all the time. Too cool for the rest of us. Then she got dropped. Who knows what will become of her now?*

Nice to see you, too.

I should've made a sign to wear around my neck: "It takes a lot of hard work to manage a band. I was also maybe in love. It happens. We're all nice people. Can't we just talk about this?"

Or maybe just: "Don't look directly at it! It burrrns!"

"Hey!"

But there is one person who seems to be holding nothing against me: Maya Barnes, a sophomore and someone who is as serious about music as I am. She zips up the steps, dressed in a professional black skirt and tights, white shirt, thick platform shoes, and a lime-green scarf, even though it's going to be in the eighties today. She has thin oval glasses over giant almond eyes, her streaked-blonde hair pulled back in a big clip. Her look is so hardworking and optimistic compared to my lazy ponytail, slouchy jeans, slate-gray hoodie, and faded denim jacket. The only flair I'm sporting is all the shiny band pins on my jacket pockets.

Oh, to be young.

"Happy new year!" she says, breathless with perk.

14

"Your senior year. Are you excited?"

Maya is a fan of mine. My only fan, I think. She manages a band called Supreme Commander. She can be a little clingy, and I can be sullen. Still, most of the time it's nice to have an ally.

"Excited . . . ," I say. "On a molecular level, I suppose. I was just standing here thinking about how by geologic timescales, nothing we do here will amount to anything more than a sliver of sedimentary rock."

"Jeez, and I still had my will to live . . ." Maya makes a cartoonishly glum face.

It makes me smile. A smile! Feels like the first time all week. "I am a little excited," I admit. "Not for econ, or Mr. Salt's World Cultures class, but maybe . . ."

"To find a new band, right?" says Maya. She starts walking and I fall into step beside her. Cool to be entering senior year with a sophomore? Who even cares?

We pass through the doors and it hits me: the smell of First Day optimism. Well, that and the overwhelming odors of body spray and perfume, and also that strangely sour fear BO that wafts off the skittering freshmen. Oblivion be damned, everyone here still thinks they can make that enduring mark, a game-winning catch, the ultimate yearbook candid, the perfect song. A memory that will cheat time, viral and immortal. Senior year. Five hundred forty-eight dreams, one hundred and eighty days of possibility. Maybe I can't resist it.

And so even though I feel like Maya's question deserves an answer in a grizzled, smoked-too-many-packs, seen-too-many-things voice, the veteran taking the shine off the newbie, I allow myself to be upbeat instead. "Yes, to find a new band."

"Just don't steal mine!" she says with a nervous laugh. We reach a main branch in the halls. "So, I'll see you at the kickoff concert today?"

"Definitely."

"I'll save you a seat!" She's a touch too loud, a touch too eager. It's going to get old, but it hasn't yet.

"Cool. Thanks."

I slog my way through the morning: Economics (suck), Survey of World Cultures (information not-suck, teacher mega-suck), Twentieth-Century English Literature (infini-suck). My brain is barely able to perform that dual trick that is the key to high-school success: moving fast enough to keep up with everything being said, and yet also being fine with how severely dull it all is. I don't know how some kids do it.

Actually, I do. Academically, I'm ranked seventh in our class, a fact I tell no one. The part I don't understand is how some kids thrive on it. My performance has everything to do with maintaining a cover story so my secret identity can flourish. My parents, while they know I'm into music and "that managing bands" thing, still have no idea how real it is for me. Things like the grades keep them happy. They'd probably like some athletics, a student senate seat, too, but all shall fall subservient to the great letters A and B (well, B as long as it comes with a +).

I get a second wind as I head to lunch. Today, we're allowed to eat out in the east courtyard, where the kickoff is happening.

At Mount Hope High, most things—econ classes, cafeterias, athletic fields—look like the ones at any other budget-strapped public school. It's when you enter the east courtyard that things start to look different. You walk out of doors off the cafeteria and find yourself in an actual stone amphitheater: curved seating that steps down to a half-moon stage. It looks like something out of ancient Greece, but aside from the yes-these-are-actually-stone seats, the stage and lights and sound system are all state of the art.

Welcome to the Don Henley performance stage. Yes, *that* Don Henley. His kid went here a while back. But that kind of thing is normal at Mount Hope High.

Fifteen years ago, Mount Hope was a normal high school, but then a band from here called Allegiance to North happened. There was all this press, including a big article in *Spin*. In that article, the members of the band, Eli White, Kellen McHugh, Parker Francis, and Miles Ellison, happened to mention a curious fact: their assistant principal, Mr. Abrams, had allowed them to practice after school in a classroom, and even gave them credits for a class he invented called Applied Popular Art, to make up for their less-than-model academic performance in virtually every other area.

Next thing you knew, Mr. Abrams was the principal, and parents from all over LA, especially former rockers, started moving to Mount Hope so their kids could go here. Now, PTA meetings are like a leather fashion show. And the money pours in for Mr. Abrams's brainchild: Popular Arts Academy.

As a result, if you play football at Mount Hope, you can be part of one of the lamest programs in Southern California, but if you play guitar, you can take a class called the Physics of Volume, which is held in the Amp Lab, an acoustically perfect room that houses a wall of classic and modern amplifiers worth so much money it requires a twenty-four-hour guard. And there's just as much for bass, drums, vocals, keyboards, songwriting, recording, video shoots, and management. This school literally rocks.

One of the annual traditions is the kickoff concert, held during the lunch periods in the amphitheater. The bands have been playing for probably an hour already when I arrive, working up from freshmen to senior. As I head in, there's a decent group with a girl singer on piano called the Progress Reports.

"Summer!" It's Maya again, up in the back row, waving two notches more enthusiastically than she needs to. We're both in the industry track of PopArts, which has classes and its own student-run record label called Lion's Den. (Our school mascot is a lion, and the label's logo is a lion in a cave kicking back, paws behind his head with big headphones on. Corny? Yes. Kinda cool? I think so.)

You can also get internships at real labels. I was all set to have one last summer at Candy Shell, but after things happened, I backed out. Maya took my place, and she was cute and asked my permission, which I obviously gave. I even managed to do so without offering her any dark jaded comments like *Watch your back*.

As I make my way to her, I pass within orbit of a group of five girls. There is a lull in their conversation, but not one long enough for exchanging hellos. I suppose I could have forced it, but Callie, Alex, Beatrice, Melanie, and Jenna resume talking before any of us has a chance. Once upon a time, three years ago, they all shared a birthday booth with me at La Burrita Feminista. Now they sit in a pentagon across two steps, all long legs and perfect hair.

We were thick as thieves back in middle school, and even into the breakwater of high school, but out in the deep, I lost them. By the end of sophomore year, we barely spoke. There were serious riptides pulling us in different directions: athletics, boys, and student senate for them, and music and then managing Postcards for me.

But something bigger happened, too. If we check the records, we'll see that technically, I stopped calling first. Partly it was an accident of being really busy with Post-cards. But maybe it was also a little bit because I sensed this

19

slow-motion way that all of them were morphing into their parents: the looks, the gestures, the *beliefs*. I started to feel like I could see the future versions of them, someday pulling up to Mount Hope in a woefully fuel-inefficient crossover SUV, dropping off their kids while dressed for morning yoga. It's the version of me that I refuse to let happen.

Of course lately I've wondered: What exactly will I be doing? If you'd asked me last spring I would have said sitting in a cool loft office in New York City, managing my small but visionary roster of bands. Now? I might avoid your question.

I'm just past them when there's a unison peal of laughter, and I think, *Don't look!* because I don't want to know what they're saying except dammit I look back anyway but none of them are looking at me. They're laughing too hard at their own thing. It makes me wonder if maybe I was the curse, the hex of the hexagon. Look out! Geometry joke! They wouldn't have laughed at that. Ethan would have. He was secret smart, too. Bastard.

"So, which band are you excited about?" Maya asks me as I sit.

"I'm not sure," I say, looking over the program I was handed on the way in. "Definitely not Supreme Commander."

She smiles, but also nods seriously. "Good."

"So, hey, how was the internship?" I think to ask.

Maya sighs. "Oh, you know, it was okay."

"Maya." I try for my most professional smile. "You can be honest."

Maya's face collapses into a big grin. "Okay, it was so excellent! Candy Shell is such an amazing place! Well, you know, not *all* of it, but I was in publicity, not with the sharks who stole Postcards from you—"

"It's fine. I get it. I'm glad it was good."

"They're actually keeping me on this fall, a couple afternoons a week."

"Oh, nice." I keep my smile up for as long as I can, and turn back to the band. I am maybe a little jealous. Would I want to be at Candy Shell? No way. Well . . . no, but would I like to have done so well at an internship at a record label over the summer that they asked me to stay on? Yes.

The Progress Reports finish and there is a quick gear switch. Black-clad members of the Tech Squad scurry around, moving instruments, running new cables, and wielding gaffer's tape with ninja-like speed, their Chucks scuffing and their oversized key rings jangling.

The next band up is greeted by a barrage of screams from the gaggle of freshmeat girls crowded on the grass up front. They're all legs and shoulders and smiles, like sacrifices waiting to be gobbled up by the music gods. I think, *You'll learn, girls*, but also make a mental note because having enthusiastic fans is a key to getting your band off the ground.

"Hey, everybody," says the singer, an awkward

underclassman, slouching at the mic with an oversized guitar and too-tight flannel shirt. "We're the New Past Lives."

Okay, candidate number one. For the first time in too long, things feel like business. I pull out my graph-paper notebook and flip to a new page. I prefer the grid to normal old straight lines. It might seem rigid, but I actually find it freeing. Any direction is in play. Up, down, left, right, or a diagonal against the perfect squares. That's how you have to think in this business. Lined paper has only one direction, the acceptable one. Lined paper is so Carlson Squared.

Four stick clicks and the New Past Lives are in. It's edgy guitar, busy drums, and within moments I know the verdict: decent, but not polished enough. The singer is too unsure of himself. Sometime in the future, his third or fourth band will probably be pretty excellent, but by the time the New Past Lives finish their fifteen-minute set, I can barely remember anything I just heard.

Next up, Maya's band: Supreme Commander. I liked this band last year. Dreamy, sci-fi pop. They've gotten better. I'm ever-so-slightly jealous of this, too.

"Good job," I say to Maya.

She beams. "Why thank you."

After them is a band called the Theo Alvin Four. I think I read online that this is the new version of Square Pets, one of last year's decent bands. Maybe they'll be the one? But then the lead singer begins with, "Hey, we've had a mind-blowing summer, and our sound this year is going to be a little . . . different. This first song is dedicated to one of the masters: John Scofield."

I should have known by the new interest in facial hair and the hipster hats they're all wearing: Square Pets have been bitten by the jazz. And it's not the good melodic kind, like they made a half century ago. Ethan and I used to study to *Kind of Blue*, the Miles Davis record. The good kind of jazz seems to be all about vibe, mood, and feel. This is the bad kind of jazz, where the music feels like a math problem. After a minute, I've totally lost track of the song, and when I look around, most everyone is talking among themselves except for two uber-fans down front, both wearing suit vests, one in a fedora, bobbing their heads wildly and waving their fingers like the music is a cloud of moths they need to swat out of their eyes.

I spend their set working on my econ homework. The band I'm really waiting to see is the one that comes on next. A senior band: Android Necktie. What I remember from last year: edgy, indie, with really cool melodies. In fact, they'd been widely considered the heir apparent to Postcards from Ariel. As I remember it, they have a pretty great lead singer. They were terrible at promotion though. Which could be where I come in?

But I can tell immediately that there's something different about them as they take the stage. Where's that singer boy I remember them having?

"Hi," the bassist says softly. "We're Android Necktie.

23

Well, most of it."

Most people probably miss it, but I catch the glare he gets from the keyboard girl. Bassist has just violated a sacred rule onstage: Never show your dirty laundry.

They start, and the song is pretty catchy: cool bass-and-keyboard unison riff. But when the keyboardist starts to sing, her voice is shrill and grating.

"Didn't they have a boy singer?" I ask Maya.

She nods. "Caleb. He quit over the summer, kinda out of the blue. It was quite the scandal. The band name was the bass player's idea, though, so they're trying to press on. I saw fliers up for new singer auditions."

"What happened to Caleb? Does he have a new band?"

"Nah. He's been basically exiled at this point."

Well, we'd make a pair. I feel a stir at this, but then remind myself that what I need is an actual, functioning band. And about the last thing I need is to take my already shredded reputation and pair it with another that's equally tattered. But still . . .

"Wasn't he good?" I ask.

"He was hot," Maya replies.

"Hot and good?"

"Hot and hot. And yes, good, too. I saw him down in the Green Room before I came up here."

"What's he up to?"

"How would I know? I could never talk to Caleb . . ." Maya blushes at the thought. "But I did Twitter-stalk him and I remember him saying something about how everything had changed, and that he needed to start fresh. That was right around when he left the band. Actually then I think he disappeared offline, too."

"Hmmm . . ." As Necktie drones on, I search Twitter. Caleb Daniels. Easy enough to find. Interesting. He has only seven followers, and four tweets, starting in August. Classic signs of a fallout and reboot.

The first three tweets are from the same night.

Caleb Daniels **@livingwithghosts 14 Aug**
Out with the old, in with the bold . . . or maybe just out. / What we had was great but I'm different now.

Caleb Daniels **@livingwithghosts 14 Aug**
Now I wear you on my sleeve / waking from a silly dream / Where I find you, alive and well / And your smile erases all the hell. . . .

Caleb Daniels **@livingwithghosts 14 Aug**
. . . I've been through without you

The fourth is from last night.

Caleb Daniels **@livingwithghosts 16h**
Tomorrow the charade begins anew. Can somebody please tell me the point?

Whoa. This is all some major drama. It feels like there's more going on with him than just a band breakup. What's between these dark and lyrical lines, Caleb?

Stop it. Caleb is damaged goods! Of course, but . . . so am I. And I know things need to happen, fast, but if he's talented . . .

And besides . . . I look down at my notebook. My pen is tapping, not writing. Because it's not happening here. In fact, I've totally forgotten Android Necktie is playing. I focus in on them again—

"It would be so good, to get back at you good," Trevor warbles weakly—

This is not the band. I just know it. And the only band left to play today is Fluffy Poodle and the #'s of Doom! and I've seen them, with or without the foam hashtags they wear around their necks and the pink poodle tails, and while they are certainly something, they're not what I'm looking for.

I close my notebook. "You said he's down in the Green Room?" I ask, gathering my things.

"He was," says Maya. "Why?"

"Gonna go try to find him."

"You are?" Maya sounds awed. "I can't come, can I?"

"You have your band," I say. "Besides, it probably won't lead to anything."

"If it does, I will be so completely jealous."

I half smile. "I will do my best."

I make my way across the top row of the amphitheater. For a second, I catch the eyes of my former friends. But they keep doing their thing, and I'm off to do mine.

Formerly Orchid @catherinefornevr 6m
This gumshoe is off to chase a lead.

The Green Room is kinda excellent. It's a long rectangle with yes, green walls, except for one, which is a sound-proof window looking out on the main auditorium stage. There's an actual espresso bar in the corner, surrounded by little tables and chairs, and, in the other corner, a long table covered in art supplies beside a copy machine for making old-school flyers and zines. Everywhere in between there are musical instruments on stands, in cases, stacked, hanging from the walls. The room smells like coffee beans and rubber cement.

I love being in here, with all the creative energy of the place. Sometimes it bums me out a little, though, because for as much as I love music, I'm not a musician. There were piano lessons briefly when I was a kid, but when I didn't seem to "excel at classical instruction," preferring instead just to bang out chords and sing, Carlson Squared deemed them not vital to my education. They thought my after-school time was better suited to science clubs and math labs.

I've always had the voice of a crow, at best, but there were years when I could have gotten somewhere with piano, or tried drums or guitar or something, when my parents could have noticed the Summer waiting to bloom in their Catherine, but those years have passed. People always say you have all the time in the world to do whatever you want, and that may be true for some things, but not if you really want to get to the highest level. And what other level is there?

Don't get me wrong. I love managing. I love perfecting the potential of something, of teasing out greatness. But sometimes, when I'm in the Green Room watching everyone noodling happily on their instruments, I do think it would have been cool to be a band kid instead of a "suit." That's what the musicians sometimes call us (not all of them, just the jerks). It's a natural rivalry, though, mainly because it's the role of those of us on the production side to be critical of what the musicians are doing. And yet the very personalities who are adept at creating music are also deeply sensitive, and they get defensive easily. A lot of times, with artists, it's not what you tell them, it's how you tell them. And this understanding is maybe what I'm best at.

It's quiet down here now; everybody's at the show. Wherever the mysterious Caleb is, I must have missed him.

I'm turning to leave when I hear something muffled, distant. I move toward the far end of the room, and look through the door into Mr. Anderson's office. He's the PopArts coordinator, but we call him Coach. He's not here either.

The sound reverberates again: guitar.

Now I notice a bright orange extension cord leading from the wall out the back doors. I follow it, leaving the Green Room and entering a hallway of practice spaces. Each officially recognized band at Mount Hope gets one.

The extension cord slithers past these, connects to a second one, then takes a left at the next intersection. The guitar is getting louder, but it's not coming from any of the practice spaces. There's maybe singing, too.

The cord drops down the back stairwell and out an exit door, holding it a sliver open. I stop at the door. It occurs to me that whoever is out here is seeking precisely the kind of privacy that I'm about to interrupt. I peer out anyway.

Outside is a concrete landing. There is a ramp on one side that leads down to the back parking lot. The other side is bordered by a high cement wall. The smell of garbage is ripe on the warm afternoon air. The guitar amp is right in front of me, aimed toward the wall. Overdriven chords burst from it, but the volume is set pretty low, just loud enough to feel and sing along to, but not loud enough to carry around to the front of the school. A rainbow-colored cord arcs up, seemingly into the sky.

I edge around the door . . .

And find a boy standing on the top of the cement wall. He's kinda skinny, wearing a navy-blue T-shirt and jeans. He has a cherry-red Les Paul slung over his shoulder, and he's strumming and singing. His eyes are closed, half hidden by a mop of brown hair, the tendons in his neck straining. I push out a little further, to get a better look.

Caleb Daniels, standing on a wall, playing a rock show all his own.

He sings. It's a ballad:

You never knew what you left behind
Never cared to come back
No matter how much light shined on you
You took it with you into the black

I find my breath getting short. My heart accelerating. Not just because Caleb's got a great voice, or because his melody is catchy, no, *triumphant*, or even because Maya was right about the hotness. But because . . . all together, it's doing that thing, *he's* doing that thing that a song can do. Do you know it? When a song inhabits you, possesses you, and moves you like a marionette to its will?

His voice is high and easy, confident but also with a

slight sandpaper edge to it. He's in a trance as he launches into the next part:

But I still wear you on my sleeve

Oh wow, this melody is huge. This melody is going to cause death-by-swooning.

Always waking from a silly dream
Where I find you, alive and well
And your smile erases all the hell
I never knew was . . . was—

There is an off-key whine and Caleb stops, the spell broken. His hand missed a chord. He looks accusingly down at the guitar. Then his eyes snap up, right at me.

I duck back but I know it's too late. The last thing I see is him starting at seeing me.

And then from beyond the door I hear, "Ahh shit!"

Silence—

Then a crash.

I lean back out. Caleb has vanished. The guitar cable has pulled out of the amp and is draped over the wall. I hear a long, pained exhale from the other side.

"Oh!" I rush out. "Are you okay?"

I run to the wall and try to hoist myself up, but it's been

a long time since those Saturdays at gymnastics, so instead I sprint down the ramp and around to a line of Dumpsters. I peer over the lip of the one nearest the wall to find Caleb lying on a pile of black trash bags, his cheek resting against an unidentifiable pile of something like dust or hair, it's hard to tell. The smell is unreal but the bags seem to have held. He's holding his guitar up above his chest.

He stares blankly at the sky, blinks, then finally takes a big breath. He examines the guitar. "Okay, it's fine."

"What about you?" I ask.

Caleb sits up, taking in his surroundings. "I suppose it would be a pretty lame cliché to say that this fits my current situation."

A little laugh slips out before I can stop it. "Yeah, please don't."

He unplugs the cable and holds out the guitar. "Can you take this?" For a moment, his eyes lock on mine. Dark brown, like murder-mystery dark, especially in the shadow of his shaggy hair. Soft features that just seem to get out of the way of those eyes . . . oh, boy.

I take the guitar carefully. "Got it."

Caleb pulls himself out and brushes off. "How do I look?"

"Less like you just Dumpster dived than you could have."

"I didn't think anyone would hear me out here," he says, coiling the guitar cable as we walk back around.

"I almost didn't," I say. "Why weren't you up at the concert?"

"Long story." He turns off the amp, unplugs it from the extension cord, and stuffs the amp's power cord into the back.

"You mean the long story of how you blew up your old band and now you're Least Likely to Get a Hug from a PopArts Kid?"

Caleb looks up at me. "Word gets around, huh?"

"That's the point of words. They get around." I hope that sounds witty. Then I worry it sounds dumb. But then I hate that I'm worried or trying to sound witty just because I'm around some band boy. Okay, a hot, dreamy, great-singing, possibly-with-a-deep-dark-side band boy. But still.

Caleb lifts the amp in one hand, takes his guitar back with the other, and starts toward the door. It seems like he might just walk off, but then he pauses for me to catch up. "So why aren't *you* at the concert?" he asks.

I smile. "Long story."

We head inside. He bends, straining to grab the extension cord around the bulk of the amp, but I step in front of him and start looping it around my palm and elbow as we go.

"Very professional," he says.

"Thanks."

"So, long story like the band you totally broke to the world dumped you and now you can't stand being around bands?"

"There go the words," I say. "Getting around. But, actually, I came looking for you."

"It's Summer, right? We were in chem lecture last year. I'm Caleb."

"I know. And yeah, I think we were."

"No, we definitely were. And in Spanish class sophomore year. You sat in front."

This is impressive and maybe has me a bit with the fluttery nerves. "*Sí, señor.* Aren't you going to ask why I came looking for you?"

We arrive back in the Green Room. Caleb slides the practice amp into a closet and locks it. "No," he says, moving to the case racks on the far wall. "I don't want to spoil it."

"What do you mean?"

Caleb pulls out his case, kneels and lays his guitar on the bed of burgundy fur inside. "Because you'll say that you're wondering if I'm going to put a new band together, because the ones you just saw up there weren't good enough. . . ."

"Which is just past confident and maybe slightly cocky of you to think."

Caleb shakes his head. "Just being honest. I used to care what sounded confident or cocky . . ."

"But now?"

"But now I'll just tell you that I'm not going to put a band together. No one would have me anyway."

"Well, that might be true, but . . . why not? I heard you

34

out there just now. It was good. Though I guess you know that."

"Really?" Suddenly he sounds like my opinion matters. "No, I mean, sure I can sing and play and stuff, but that song just now, I was out there because I didn't want anyone to hear it."

"Why not?"

"Same reason I'm not forming a band."

The bell rings. End of lunch. Time for sixth period, which for me is calc.

Caleb stashes his guitar. We start out the door just as the first PopArts kids are pushing in and they all have a glare for Caleb, and by extension me.

Out in the hall, Caleb stops before heading in the other direction. Streams form on either side of us.

"So," I say, "you're gonna do the loner thing."

Caleb frowns and glances away. "Not that simple."

"Okay. What happened then? What happened on August fourteenth"—just the mention of his Twitter-nuking date makes his eyes flash back to me and they've cooled and I can tell we've entered shark-infested waters—"that turned you into an—"

"Exile," says Caleb. He just looks at me.

A second passes and it's weird. "What?"

He looks at the ceiling. Back to me. He's not smiling, exactly, more like studying, but . . . damn those eyes. "You want to know?"

35

I give him a courtesy eye roll. "We covered that topic already when I asked *what happened*."

"I'll tell you, but you have to go out with me."

"What?" I wonder if I heard him right while knowing of course I heard him right and thinking this is one of the most backward pickups I've ever heard of, but also I think my pulse just hit a hundred. "You're asking me out?"

"Yes."

I don't want to say yes, but I don't want to say no, and then just to say something I hear myself ask, "When?"

Caleb's eyes stay dead on me. "Now."

I probably kind of gape at him. "Now."

"Now." He glances at the pair of doors that lead out toward the parking lots.

"I have class," I say.

Caleb sighs. "So do I. Everyone has class. There will always be class. Come with me anyway. And I'll tell you why. I'll tell you everything." He steps closer. It feels dangerous, like maybe he's being too forward, or like maybe I might just reach out and touch him, and I'm having no luck figuring out which, because my senses and my heartbeat and my thoughts are all a blur.

"I thought you were going with the nobody-understands-me thing."

"I was, until five minutes ago. But one thing I learned this summer is that life can change pretty fast in five minutes."

I remember a five-minute stretch in July where I learned the same thing. "I'm not gonna lie; you're making a good case here."

"Summer," he says.

What is it about someone calling you by name? How rarely does that actually happen? To hear your name in close confines.

"Um . . ." None of this is what I'm used to people saying to me. *Summer* . . . but what the hell? I just spent the vast majority of two months rehashing and regretting all things band boy! Did I not just do this? Is this not just me going in another circle? The cute singer boy who says the big things, all mysterious and poetic? And we remember how that turned out and yet, YET, *Caleb isn't Ethan*, I find myself thinking, and I want to know. I want to know.

Dammit dammit dammit.

I need to know.

It's my turn to glance at the doors. This probably lets him know he's almost got me. Maybe that's my point. "When you say tell me everything," I say, "do you mean like tell-me-you're-secretly-a-psycho-killer-with-a-plan-to-add-me-to-your-petri-dish-collection everything? Or—"

Caleb laughs. "We'll walk to Taquitas. There is nowhere along that route for me to dice you up with a scalpel."

I stare at him. Six thousand miles away, the bell rings.

We're late.

And it is like that bell has somehow severed me from

the universe. The hall has emptied. Life has gone on, just like it did last night in Silver Lake. Everyone is somewhere and I am in this other place, a bubble out of time. Only this time it's not in La Burrita Feminista, though the similarity in prospective restaurant choices does hint at a larger plan to a universe I was calling out as an empty void just a few hours ago. We are in our own time line now, that's how it feels. Like life has left us behind but maybe also like we are free. We could do this. I could leave school *on the first day back*. . . .

Somewhere, Carlson Squared is calling "Nooo!" in slow motion.

Somewhere else, Postcards from Ariel and Ethan Myers are on the road doing God-knows-what.

Here, now, I am saying:

"Okay."

Caleb smiles. I thought it might be victorious, but actually, he just looks relieved.

"Come on."

Formerly Orchid @catherinefornevr 3m
So bummed to be in calculus right now!!

For the first few moments after leaving school, across the sidewalks, through the main parking lot, I keep looking over my shoulder, expecting alarms to go off or for someone to come running out after us. Another part of Catherine's cover story is her near-perfect attendance, and so this feels like breaking cover.

But nothing happens; the sky remains blue; the birds chirp; the school's doors stay closed.

"You know seniors are allowed to go off campus for lunch, right?" says Caleb.

Actually, I'd forgotten that. We've only been seniors for four hours. "This isn't lunch period, though."

"Well, no, but, since we missed lunch, we're now

applying critical thinking to a situation. Isn't that what they're always telling us to do?"

I smile. "Sure."

Neither of us adds anything, and then ten seconds go by . . . then thirty . . . and then, uh-oh, somehow we've been walking for almost a full minute in silence. For someone who just invited me on a school-skipping date, I expect Caleb to be chatty, but now it's getting awkward. We've exited the school parking lot and still nothing. One of us will need to say something *important* to justify breaking the world's longest silence—

"What bands do you like?" Caleb finally asks.

Phew. We talk bands, comparing notes as we weave through the labyrinth of strip mall that stands between us and Taquitas, which itself is part of an outdoor food court. My parents have described a time when Mount Hope was a quaint town with something called "charm." At some point, though, the town decided to allow a series of factory outlet stores in. The kinds of places that have last season's seconds perpetually on sale. The kinds of places that make you think: Does the world really need this much *everything*?

After that it was like a zombie breakout, one block affecting the next. There is still one strip of downtown that's "historic," with a single art-house movie theater and an old Spanish mission and a chrome diner called Smackie's, but—no joke—if you want to meet your friend to shop for sweaters at, say, J.Crew, you have to specify which one (there are three).

It's far too hot to be wearing my denim-hoodie combo. I push up my sleeves and redo my ponytail, feeling sweat breaking out on my neck and forehead, my cheeks getting red. Nice look. A skirt would have been good. Sandals. But dates were not on the first-day-of-school schedule! And besides, manager Summer doesn't dress up for business. Then again, I'd vowed never to let my heart hammer again during business hours, and here it is, hammering away.

We find common ground on Arcade Fire, Death Cab, Particle Board. Our first big disagreement comes as we wait in line to order from the window, over Radiohead. "They haven't made anything good since *OK Computer*," I say.

"Tuh," says Caleb. "Everything they've made that's good has been since *OK Computer*. That's when they started acting like a real rock band, not giving a crap about what anyone thinks."

"But they don't write songs anymore." As I say this, I wonder if it's my opinion or Ethan's. Radiohead was a band he got me into. Now here I am acting intelligent about them. Except I do know them. Except it feels like I'm faking it. *Oh my God, stop worrying!*

"They already wrote some of the greatest songs in music history." Caleb runs his finger through the air. "Check.

Their newer music is like a trip into a postapocalyptic future, into the ruins of their own success, but in a good way." He glances sideways at me. "Did that make sense?"

"Maybe you're like Radiohead and you don't need to."

"Touché."

We order. Caleb gets a burrito and I waffle and settle on fish tacos, and instantly regret ordering the same thing I so often ordered with Ethan. Both band boys like Mexican. Is that a sign? *Stop it!* Most people like Mexican. Ugh. I'll be lucky to make it through this without driving myself crazy.

We get our paper plates of food and then turn to face the array of metal tables surrounding a modernist fountain. It's like a coral reef, dotted with brightly colored yoga moms and strollers, and the occasional barracuda with his or her jacket off, crisp white shirt glaring.

"Want to go eat at the center of the solar system?" Caleb asks.

"You mean this isn't it?"

Thankfully, Caleb gets that I'm joking. "Not even close. In fact, there's Venus."

I follow his pointing finger to a little pedestal off on the side of the dining area. It's cone-shaped and at the top is a tiny model of a planet. "Ahh, right."

Back when we were in elementary school, the town arts council installed this scale model of the solar system all over town. Each planet is represented by a model on a pedestal, all at their exact relative distances from the sun. They printed maps, and I remember thinking it was so cool, how you could travel the solar system, but somehow I never got around to seeing them all. The inner planets are all in this mall, but then Jupiter is like a mile away, and Saturn even further, and so on.

We weave back through the strip mall, passing the pedestal that holds Mercury outside J.Crew number two (the one that sells only cardigans, belts, and sandals) and reach the giant yellow sun. It stands ten feet tall in the center of another consumer courtyard, surrounded by a ring of grass, which is then enclosed by home decor shops.

We sit in the oval of shade off to the star's side. The grass is immaculate, like no one's ever touched it, let alone dared to risk staining their khakis on it.

"Center of the Mount Hope universe," says Caleb.

"All the upscale housewares you could ever want," I say, looking around. I rub my hand over the painted metal curve of the sun above our heads. It's bumpy with sunspots. There used to be a big solar flare arcing out of the side, but it's been broken off, its two endpoints sticking out with jagged edges.

"Have you ever been to them all?" Caleb asks after his first bite of burrito.

"No. I've always wanted to, but who has time with all the dumb movies to see and Facebook posts to read?"

"I went once," says Caleb. "My fifth-grade teacher loaded us in a bus and we drove all around town and saw every one—well, except Pluto. It had been downgraded to dwarf planet that spring—"

"An unspeakable injustice," I say. "Pluto will always be a planet."

"Always and forever," Caleb agrees. "But we skipped it."

"Was it cool? Seeing the others?"

"I guess? I mostly remember eating Cool Ranch Doritos and getting harassed because I sat next to a girl named Lin Yee and everybody said I loved her."

I grin. "Obviously because you did."

Caleb shrugs, but smiles too. "She was good at kickball and didn't mind playing Bionicles at recess so, obviously. Anyway I guess I learned that if space travel is anything like a school bus trip, it's too long and too cramped. Still, the models are worth seeing."

"Why?"

"Because they're there, and, like you said, you don't have to buy anything or 'like' anything to see them. Also, even though they took Pluto off the map, people say it's still out there somewhere, because the town couldn't afford to send a welder out to remove it."

"That I'd like to see. The lost ninth planet. I feel for it."

And I feel Caleb looking at me. "Maybe we will sometime."

"Maybe." I meet his gaze. It's a quick thing, a passing of eye contact, half smiles, as we both move to our next bite, but suddenly in that moment I feel a little quake in my heart, and realize I'm probably done for. No! Too soon! I tell myself to calm down. Jaded, professional, unflustered. This isn't a date, it's a job interview, for *Caleb*, not me. But oh, I am probably lying to myself. Still, I am not going to let him see it.

We eat for a bit. The small talk is done. Now my tacos are, too. I'm not sure what to say next.

"Back to Radiohead," I try. "That new song you were playing before sounded like a real song, like well-crafted in the . . . you know, pre-post-*OK Computer*-way, but not like wannabe Radiohead, just . . . the . . ."

Caleb grins. "I'm curious to see how you pull this out."

I am a flushed fool. "What I mean is that it might be a really great song."

"Well, thank you."

Annndd . . . back to silence! But this time I wait. It's your turn, Mr. Caleb.

Finally: "It's kinda personal."

"Do I get the big story now?"

He sees my hopeful gaze, but his face darkens. "I don't know why I want to tell you this."

"But you're going to. That was the deal. I come space traveling with you, you spill the beans. Besides, you've turned me to a life of crime. Now pay up."

"Right . . ." Caleb shifts. He wraps the unfinished half of his burrito back in foil. "I live with my mom. I never knew my dad. She always told me that he didn't want to stay around. That she didn't want him around. I asked her sometimes if I could meet him, or contact him, but she said she didn't know where he was. I could have called BS on those excuses but our life has been fine. Mom's a social worker and she makes enough money and it's cool. She supports my music. We could live even better if we weren't in Mount Hope, but Mom tries to keep up with rent here so I can go to PopArts."

"She sounds pretty great," I say.

"She is, definitely." He half unwraps his burrito again, his fingers jittery, then wraps it right back up. "What's your parent situation?"

"Oh, I got the standard package," I say. "Two, mixed gender, mostly annoying, but admittedly making some good points now and then, and providing me with the material necessities and then some."

Caleb nods. He takes a deep breath. "So, August fifteenth was my eighteenth birthday. I had a party planned, but my uncle Randy came over the night before. That's Mom's younger brother. She wanted to have a birthday dinner, just the three of us. And so we're at the dinner table and Mom's been acting strange all day and I know something's up."

He pauses again. Tears off a corner of foil and crinkles it into a tiny ball.

"She told you something about your dad," I guess.

Caleb nods. "Mom decided that now that I'm eighteen I

should know that my dad was the lead singer for Allegiance to North."

"Whoa." I can barely believe what I just heard. "Really? *Your dad* was Eli White?"

"The one and only. Guess he and my mom had a fling one summer, hot and heavy, but then it didn't work out. I mean, I worked out, but they didn't. And then . . . you know."

"He drowned."

Caleb flicks the foil ball, a little shooting star. It lands in the grass, gleaming in the sun. He starts making another. "At first, I almost felt like, whatever. I mean, he was never a part of my life. They both wanted it that way, and he sent money. We still get money from his royalties or estate or whatever." Caleb shakes his head and glances up at the sky. "But I think I liked it better not having a dad."

"Why?" I ask. "Doesn't this make you the son of a rock legend?" I can't keep my band-manager brain from spinning ahead. "I mean, just from a publicity point of view, that's—"

"No," Caleb snaps. "That's exactly what I don't want." Before I can even react, he's getting to his feet. "Shit. What was I thinking? I shouldn't have told you. You, of all people . . ." He spins and walks off.

"Caleb . . ." I hurry after him. "Why *did* you tell me?"

He stops and stares at the ground. "I felt like I had to tell *someone*."

"FYI, telling a girl she's just *someone* is not the best way to make her feel special."

Caleb throws up his hands. "That's not—look, I'm not good at saying things right the first time. You just seem, I don't know, not that you like me, but that you're *like* me in some way. Both of us have ended up alone for a reason. And I needed someone to trust. I don't know—"

"It's okay." I touch his shoulder. "I get it. Now listen, I promise I won't tell anyone, but why are you keeping this a big secret?"

"Because," says Caleb, "I don't want to be Eli White's kid. I don't want *that* to be the reason I get anywhere in music."

We start walking again, weaving back through the mall toward school. I can barely keep up with his pace. "I get that, and for the record, I loved that song you were playing on the wall before I knew who your dad was. So why did you nuke your band? Was it because you were afraid of them finding out?"

"That was part of it. And . . . well, it'll sound dumb."

I grab his arm. We're right near the doors to a children's clothing outlet store, so there is a traffic jam of strollers around us. New moms eye us suspiciously, like we're threats, or like they fear that if they don't use the right kind of sippy cups or buy the right wooden toys, their little trophies might someday end up like us.

"Tell me." When he hesitates, I remind him: "Life of crime."

"I know." Caleb searches the sky for words. "It's just that, Eli might have been some kind of musical genius, but he was also a self-centered asshole, by all accounts. He treated my mom like crap, totally bailed on any responsibility to me other than cash, hooked up all the time, was into heroin . . . I just . . . I don't want to be like that."

"Not even the hooking-up-all-the-time part?" I hope that sounded like a joke.

It nearly makes Caleb smile. "I mean, I want to transcend. I want to do the big things, get all the way to the top, write the biggest song ever, but Neil Young was wrong."

"About what? Aside from muttonchops."

"He said it's better to burn out than fade away. Kurt Cobain quoted it in his suicide note. But they're wrong. I want to do all those things and then still be around later, like, get old, get a lifetime achievement award fifty years from now, to still be . . ." He throws his arms up as if to indicate the world. "In it. Does that sounds silly?"

Silly or possibly painfully romantic. "No," I say.

"But now I find out that my musical genes come from someone who did his best to be out of it, who couldn't survive his own success."

I find myself taking his hand, and buzzing at what he's saying, so much like the thoughts I'd had this morning, sandwiched between oblivion and optimism. And I'm thrumming with the idea of this boy, this dark, busy mess of a boy, and how both of us have ended up exiled together. . . .

So, now what, then?

"Caleb." I see his eyes snap down, just as affected by the use of his name. "I know what you're talking about. Well, not totally. My dad works at a concrete company and is home every night at six. But the rest . . ."

An absolutely screaming baby is wheeling by us, the mom shushing it. I want to get us to a more private spot but I don't want to lose this moment. And also Caleb is taking my other hand. Now we are two people holding each other's hands facing each other, which makes people notice us and give us a wide berth, and I am determined to finish what I was going to say.

"If you don't want to burn out, then you need to stop deleting Twitter accounts and alienating everyone in PopArts, and playing guitar alone."

Caleb looks away and shrugs, a touch sulkily. "I guess."

From a business point of view, what I can feel myself about to say may not be a good idea. The grizzled, veteran me knows better. Throwing in with the mercurial head-case singer type? Never good. But maybe Caleb is just a singer of the average head-case variety who happens to be going through a really rough patch. I heard that song behind the school. Nobody at the Kickoff Concert had anything like it. I feel as certain as I can that I've found my next project.

"I can help you," I say. "You can put together a band, and I'll manage. I know what to do. Your job is to get"— before I can consider stopping myself, I reach out and touch his chest with my index finger—"*this* out into the world. Then everything you're talking about can happen."

Caleb shrugs, but then he takes my hand. "Maybe this is why I asked you out. How do you make everything sound so *possible*?"

I want to ask Caleb if this is a line he's used before. But no, I don't really want to know. I don't care to know. Maybe he's another band boy but so what so what so what? Sometimes things happen and we feel things because we are who we are and we can't control it.

"Because it is possible," I hear myself saying, and I'm leaning forward, my body seeming to have already made up its mind about what happens next, and suddenly I'm terrified: am I really thinking about him as my next project or am I thinking about him as this cute, wounded beautiful soul, so honest on the surface, no games, no quoting his own lyrics at me, and getting hotter by the second? *Slow down! It's too soon! Remember last time*— And I know, oh I know, this is so . . . Not. A good. Idea. Where's one of those fortune-tellers made out of folded paper, a silly *Seventeen* magazine quiz, a flower to pluck petals, anything that would give me a sign that could make me feel certain about what to do next—

But I tip up on my toes and kiss him anyway.

I think it surprises him, but then he responds and, has it really been three months since I felt this feeling because, oh, kissing, hello! And this is exceptionally good and it makes me wonder if we're made to think each new kiss is the best one we've ever had, or if it's possible that there are just frequencies between people, wave vibrations that align in a perfect hum. Maybe it's our relation to the magnetism of the planet, or the specific arrangement of our molecules, or maybe we both just so happen to have slightly elevated levels of some mineral, let's say manganese, in our blood. Who knows? But there is something, something more than just the simple physics of lips and tongues at work here, and it's vibrating me like a kite string and it's almost like I don't need to know any more. We've only talked for half an hour and yet I don't need to know what cereal he likes or what his politics are or which Kurt Vonnegut novel he read first. None of it matters because of this frequency that is making me long to slide my cheek slowly down his neck to his shoulder and feel his arms at my waist pulling me close so that my lungs can't fully expand.

Except I pull back. Take. A. Deep. Breath. "Okay," I manage to say. "Wow."

"Yeah," Caleb breathes. "Um, thanks."

"We should probably get back to school," I say. "Either that, or . . . never mind."

"What?" He takes me gently by the shoulders. "What were you going to say?"

"Nothing. It was silly—"

He kisses me back. "Tell me."

Woozy. "I was just going to say that we either go back

52

to school or instead we head to Long Beach and stow away on a cargo boat headed to Palau."

"Two solid choices." Caleb hugs me. "Probably school. For now."

"We'll need degrees in Palau. To start a music school."

"And we should learn Palauean first."

"Palau-ese?"

"Wait . . . we should get this right."

I check my phone. "Palauan."

"We'll learn Palauan."

"Yes."

We walk, drifting along. He takes my hand. "That was definitely not in my plan," says Caleb as we go. "I mean, I thought about it."

"You thought about what?"

"Well, I mean I'm a guy . . ."

"Right." I don't bother telling him that girls have those thoughts, too. We're just better at poker.

The end of our walk is as silent as the start, and yet, this silence is a whole other world, nearly bursting with possibility. I expect the school to be empty. But when I look at my watch I see that barely forty-five minutes have passed. Last period will be starting soon.

We stop in the same hall outside PopArts, the circle complete. The last moment before returning to the real time line, and I'm almost sad. "So," I say.

"So," he replies.

This makes me want to kiss him again, but the halls feel like they have eyes. "So . . . that."

"That."

Before we can say any more, the bell rings, and the hall begins to fill.

Caleb takes a step back. He motions like he's going to head to class. So I take a step back, too. We both smile. We both turn away. But he is the only thing on my mind for the rest of the afternoon.

You Can Take It with You

—posted by ghostofEliWhite on September 17

More from the anniversary of *Into the Ever & After.*
Here's something interesting: I was reading through
On the Tip of Your Tongue, the anthology of interviews,
letters, and journal entries from the band, and I
noticed a quote, the significance of which I'd totally
missed before. When asked by KNBC's Hollywood beat
reporter Sherrie Pine how the new record was coming
along, Eli said:

*"Slow slow slow, but the end is in sight. I think we've
got seven tunes tracked. Kellen's are all done, as usual.
I've gotten a few of mine down, but it's these last few
that I'm most excited about. I think they're my best
work, and I can't wait to lay them down."*

You do the math, friends. If they'd recorded seven,
then doesn't that mean that Eli is talking about the
LOST SONGS? Is it possible that he had those songs
sketched out, at least in his mind?

It just makes his passing all that much worse, knowing
that his best work went with him into the ever & after.

55

MoonflowerAM @catherinefornevr 1h
Now hear this: Introducing Dangerheart! Mount Hope's astonishing new band feat Caleb, Jon & Matt. Say you knew them 1st. #youllthankmelater

It takes two weeks to get things rolling. Two weeks to make flyers and BandSpace ads, to find a drummer (Matt, a freshman) and a guitarist (Jon, a junior transfer), neither of whom knows or cares about Caleb's baggage. Two weeks to try out six bassists, all of whom are worse than me, and I've never played bass.

All the school rehearsal spaces are taken, so Caleb, Jon, and Matt pool money, with help from Caleb's uncle Randy, to get a tiny spot over at the Hive, a warehouse that's been converted to practice spaces.

Caleb comes up with a list of names, and on a Sunday we meet for coffee and commence the Sad Googling, which reveals that after sixty years of rock bands, ALL OF THE GOOD NAMES HAVE BEEN TAKEN. The only two names left from Caleb's list of twenty are the Lonely Clones and Dangerheart. Nobody really likes either, but they dislike the Lonely Clones more. Dangerheart it is.

We also do a search for my list of new management names. That's a little easier, and I am officially reborn, from Orchid Productions to Moonflower Artist Management.

During the coffee-and-naming session, Caleb and I sit close, hips and shoulders touching as we lean over his tablet. There was no kissing for the first week after our date at the center of the solar system, and it was just starting to feel difficult, like something exceedingly special would need to happen for us to kiss again, and besides, shouldn't Caleb be the one who initiates this time? Of course, at the same time, I didn't mind that no one has witnessed us kissing. I felt almost paranoid after our sun date, the excitement of our connection dampened by my concern with how the world might cheapen it.

Except then right in the middle of a search, while page results are loading, he just reaches over, turns my chin with his finger, and our lips meet again. This one is quick. Familiar, the kind that is meant to be just one of many. Like a habit. A good habit. And at least for this moment, I couldn't care less what anyone might think.

"What was that for?"

"Um, for search engines? Does it matter?"

"It really doesn't."

"Good," he says. "'Cause I think I'm going to have more kisses than reasons."

And I melt. And we kiss more.

With the terrible task of naming settled, what the band really needs next is a goal.

A gig.

And so on Tuesday morning Caleb and I meet up at the front doors of school and prepare to split up, Special Forces–style.

"Remember," I say to him, "Operation Swordfall is going to be bloody. But it's vital."

Caleb takes a deep, queasy breath. He's been more quiet than usual this morning, ever since I met him in the parking lot by his car. His face gets blank when he's nervous. I call it Fret Face. I know he's not looking forward to this operation, but when I asked him if anything else was wrong, he said he was fine.

"I know," he mumbles. "Do I really have to?"

Caleb's mission is to make amends with the members of Android Necktie. "We're going to be playing the same gigs as them," I remind him, "moving in the same circles. We won't have them on our side, but if we can at least keep them from actively rooting for our failure and telling everyone that Dangerheart sucks, that would be good."

Caleb sighs, but he nods in agreement. "Your mission

almost sounds worse."

"Operation Tater Tot? Yeah, it's going to be ugly. But it's equally vital." I punch him in the shoulder. "Godspeed, man."

Caleb almost grins, but Fret Face is strong.

I bound back down the steps and head around the side of school. As I go, I can't help glancing anxiously at my binder, where I have etched twenty capital T's across the top. This is the number of "tardies" you can get in a class without losing credit. They're like player lives for Catherine. I've already pre-crossed out Number Three for this morning. At this rate, she may need to find the hidden cache of medical supplies if she's going to survive this level of the High School game. Summer, meanwhile, is doing great.

I round the corner and arrive at the Armpit, an awkward triangular cement area in the crux where the south wing of school meets the auditorium. A high hedge shields it from the office. There are windows up on the second floor, but if you're close to the wall, this is one of the very few spots on school grounds where you can be nearly invisible. Thus the concrete is littered with cigarette butts and dip cups and wrappers. It's too early in the year for a single gang to have claimed it, but there are a few clumps of boys standing around in clouds of smoke and testosterone, sizing each other up.

The person I'm looking for is sitting on the short wall beneath the hedge.

"Ari." Ari Fletcher doesn't hear me through his donut-sized red headphones. He's bopping his head and slapping drumsticks against his thighs. His two friends are hunched over an iPad, arguing about how best to proceed in some video game. It whines with trebly sounds of shrieking females and chainsaws.

"Ari." Ari is the son of Jerrod Fletcher, who happens to be the head of Candy Shell Records. But more importantly, Ari throws a yearly back-to-school party out at their beach home called the Trial by Fire. Invitation only. For most guests, the Trial involves surviving Ari's patented punch and making it home with your dignity. For bands, it has a different meaning. Getting an invite is a big deal, and the best bands in school are always there. Jerrod is usually also throwing a party up the dune in their ridiculously lavish house at the same time, so there is the bonus potential of star sightings. Last year, Hatchet from Ninja Harem came careening down to the beach with her action figure of a boyfriend and they tore off their clothes and went skinny-dipping right in front of everyone.

More important than what you'll see, though, is that your band might be seen. Ever since Allegiance to North and PopArts, the scouts at Candy Shell know to keep an eye on Mount Hope's latest bands, and the gig has gained mystique: play here, and you might get noticed. Postcards is the latest example.

Which means the Trial is also the place where I began

to lose my last band, not that I knew it at the time. Part of me wants to avoid this gig, to keep that from happening all over again with Dangerheart. And yet, I know it's the best gig they could get to start out, and the best way to introduce themselves to the scene.

"Ari." I give him a friendly kick in the shin.

His eyes finally snap up and when he sees it's me, his peeled-and-mashed face quickly reforms into a smirk. He puts his sticks between his legs, pointed straight up, and slips off his headphones.

Ari looks kinda like somebody built him out of potatoes, lumpy beneath his wide, baggy jeans and hoodie, his face blotchy with acne. He barely looks like a senior. And yet in spite of this, he has a sort of amazing record of scoring with girls. He's one of those rare cases where his self-confidence can, in moments—especially involving alcohol—overcome his appearance. Part of it I know comes from the fact that he's the son of a big record-label exec at a school full of aspiring bands (though Ari's own thrash-hop bands have been notably bad throughout our years here).

"Hey, Summer." He flashes his patented smile, but luckily, I'm immune. The stick erection isn't helping. Also, he's looking me over. I imagine punching him in the face, like with a flat palm to the nose, so his head would snap back and slam the concrete wall. Mmm, so nice. But sadly, bad for business. I settle for crossing my arms and his eyes finally return to my face. "How you holdin' up?"

Ooh, can I please hit him? It takes all my strength to stay calm. He's of course referring to my former situation with Postcards, with Ethan. Must . . . resist . . .

"Peachy," I say briskly. "Listen, I've got a band for your party."

"Ah, interesting." Ari pulls his drumsticks back out of his crotch and starts tapping on his legs. "I know *someone* who'll be glad to hear about this."

I ignore this comment as hard as I can. "Knock it off. Also, your rudiments stink."

Ari's sticks freeze. "Like you'd know."

"Actually I do. Your paradiddles are sloppy because your right hand is botching the double beats. You need to work on your fundamentals."

Ari rolls his eyes, but he puts his sticks down again, this time laying them flat on his legs. "Obviously you've had a lot of time on your hands to study up on what real musicians do."

Oh, Ari. His outsides may look like potato, but inside he's pure turd. Invoking one of the classic barbs between clans of the PopArts tribe . . . God, I hate this. It's one of my least favorite positions in all of life. When you need something from someone, they have power.

"Who's the band?" Ari asks.

"Dangerheart," I say. "They're really, seriously good. And you know I know good."

"Members?"

"The drummer is Matt Prader, freshman but seriously gifted, Jon Lim is on guitar, he's that transfer, and then the singer is Caleb—"

"Hold on. Caleb Daniels? You want me to invite Mr. I-Just-Ruined-the-Best-Band-in-School?" He scratches his chin dramatically. "You know Android is going to be there, right? They'll be majorly pissed if I give Caleb a slot. . . . Of course that does sound kinda fun. Band fights are always good for party legends, but . . . it's gonna cost ya."

"What."

Ari's smile returns, this time shading toward mischievous. "Be my date to the party."

"Ha! No. Besides, I'll be working with my band that night."

Ari shrugs, letting his gaze drop to my chest again. He elbows his closest buddy to get his attention, then turns back to me and says, "Let me feel you up?"

Ari's friends crack up, but it might just be over the terrible shrieking of some poor token female in their game.

"Did you actually just say that?"

"I did." He grins moistly. I have actually heard females describe his lips as "yummy." "Thirty seconds. It doesn't have to be here. We can go to the janitor closet if you want. I'm good. Vanessa Quinn said I had the best hands in school."

"She would be an expert," I reply, again almost amazed

63

by his bravado. It would be so sad not to be immune to it. "Can you please stop being so gross?"

Ari just shrugs. "Twenty seconds?"

I huff check my phone. "I'm late. And I'm right about this band. You want them there. You already know you can't wait to see what Caleb does next, and your vile attempts at bargaining are going nowhere."

Ari finally groans. "Okay, last offer: you do a Hakalaka Eruption with me at the party."

"What's that, aside from probably vulgar and most likely culturally inappropriate?"

"It's a drink. Just have a drink with me at the party."

I realize that I need to give him something, so he can save face. "There will be no touching."

"I've still got time to change your mind," Ari says.

"Believe what you want, but okay, we have a deal." I allow a handshake.

Ari pulls out his phone and taps. "Just sent the invite to your school email."

My phone buzzes, and I click to the invitation. Not surprisingly, it's a photo of a woman's midriff, with a coconut bra. "Where's the info?" I ask.

"Under the coconuts." Ari grins. I tap the photo and sure enough, the coconut coverings pop off and the set times and load-in instructions are written in curves around the flesh beneath. "Very classy," I say, turning to go.

"I'll tell Jason you're coming," Ari calls behind me. His

friends hiss in appreciation of this comment. I pause, consider a comeback, but I knew that was coming, didn't I? Jason . . . just the sound of the name makes my skin crawl. *Remember, this is business*. After all, he would. I keep walking.

I find Caleb in the Green Room after lunch. He and Matt and Jon are at a table by the espresso machine. As I approach them, I feel a little swell of pride, or relief, or both. There's something about a band that immediately conveys strength. Dangerheart has had only two practices and they still have no bassist and yet just the presence of the three of them together suggests *potential*. They're like a secret society, and you can't help but be curious what they're talking about. Which is funny, because it's no big secret what bands talk about when they are clustered together: 30 percent is *have-you-heard-this-band*, 30 percent concerns the deeply technical features of music gear, and the other 40 percent is girls.

The room is full of other band clusters. Guitars in laps, drumsticks out. Two kids are playing around with a theremin, making wacky frequency sounds.

As I weave toward my band, I notice the two girls getting coffees eyeing Caleb. I don't know them, and I can't tell if they're gazing with interest or disdain. Some of both? It occurs to me that there's an upside to Caleb's summer meltdown. It makes him seem unpredictable. Passionate. These are good lead-singer qualities, as long as he can exude that without looking like he knows he's exuding it. Then it's just posturing and that's the worst. Luckily, at the moment he's hunched over his journal, deep into some lyric writing. Perfect.

"Hey," I say as I reach them.

"Hey," Caleb grunts. He doesn't look up. When I don't get the dark glimmer of his eyes, that three-quarter smile, I have to swallow my disappointment.

I sit down across from him. "Did you complete the operation, private?"

He just shakes his head tersely and suddenly I feel lame for continuing our joke. But maybe he's just nervous. I would not want to be in the position of trying to apologize to one person I dumped, never mind three. And I've learned that Caleb takes almost everything as seriously as it's possible to take it.

"No sign of them yet, commander," says Jon. He's got his black Ibanez in his lap, his fingers dancing in a near blur over the strings, making a tinny flurry of notes. He winks at me. Jon is like Caleb tonic. He keeps everything light. He's wiry and wearing skinny black jeans and a black T-shirt with an oil-painting image of John Denver and Miss Piggy that I've seen down at IronicTee. His teal sneakers match his spiky teal hair. His parents are from Thailand. He was on the waiting list to get into Mount Hope High for two years, after being at the ESL high school over in the Valley, so just being here still seems like a huge thrill.

"Hey, Summer, how'd it go?" Matt is on the other side of Caleb, a tablet in his lap. He's a cute kid. So young!

Freshmen are adorable. But he's also pretty awesome. Optimistic, and fiery, and a sick drummer, with a real edge when he plays. He's got dirty-blond hair and easy features, a little boy-band, and for a musician, he dresses kinda skater, with plaid sneakers, a gray hoodie, and purple jeans.

"What are you watching?" I ask him.

"John Bonham drum fills. He rules. Wanna see?"

Matt smiles hopefully. He's kind of infatuated with me. Obviously he knows I'm with Caleb, but he can't help it. I don't mean that to sound cocky, it's just that he wears it right on his face and it's cute. I can't help but smile at him. I already feel like he's my younger brother.

"Maybe later," I say, smiling back. I don't want to hurt his feelings. "But at the moment . . ." I fish into my bag. "Success!" I slide my phone over.

"Sweet!" Jon grabs it and immediately taps the coconuts. "Awesome."

"Great work!" Matt holds up his hand for a high five, looking terrified, like he'll mess it up and lose his chance with me. No worries, little brother, we can high-five.

No response from Caleb.

"Yep, it was no problem," I say. "I just had to make out with Ari for a few minutes."

Still nothing . . .

"Let him feel me up . . ."

Stiiill nothing . . .

"Caleb."

Finally his eyes pop up. "What?" He's got condition-critical Fret Face, with the bonus Knotted Brow of Doom.

I try not to sound annoyed. "Did you hear me?"

"Summer got us the Trial," says Jon.

It takes a second for Caleb to react, as if this is the furthest thing from his mind. "Oh, cool." He looks past me, out into the room.

"Yep, you're welcome," I say. "I take it you haven't talked to Android yet?"

"Here they come," he mutters.

I turn and see Trevor and Cybil emerging from the practice hall, along with another guy. Trevor is all angles and zits, wearing a plaid hat atop his long, greasy hair. Cybil wears a peach-colored thrift-store dress that labors around her square frame. Her orange hair is pinned back with thick barrettes.

They have joined the short line for espressos when Trevor notices Caleb. He stiffens and says something softly to Cybil, who doesn't look over.

Caleb stands up. "Hey, guys." They don't react until he steps over to them. I join him.

Trevor eyes Caleb. "What."

"How's it going?" Caleb asks. He shoves his hands in his pockets. I wish I could reach over and take one, but I don't think it would help.

"Pretty excellently," says Trevor. Man, is he still wounded.

"This is Alejandro," says Cybil, indicating the boy beside them. He's taller than us all and built like a truck, wearing a tank top, his arms wrapped in spiraling tattoos. "He's our new singer."

"Peace," says Alejandro in a frighteningly deep voice. He could be our age, he could be twenty-five. It's impossible to tell.

"We changed the band name to Freak Show," says Trevor.

Come on, Caleb, I think, *just apologize quick and end this torture.*

"Well, awesome," says Caleb, tactfully. "I can't wait to hear the new thing. Maybe at the Trial."

"You're going to be at the Trial?" Trevor shares an icy glance with Cybil. "How did you get that?"

"She probably did it," says Cybil, not looking at me.

I'm surprised by the venom in my direction. Cybil makes me sound like some kind of shark.

"We asked," I offer, hoping it helps.

Trevor stares at the ground. "That's bullshit. The Trial is for *established* bands. You have to earn it."

Apologize, Caleb, get it over with—

Except Trevor's not done. "Why should *you* just get to waltz back into the scene without any damage when—"

Caleb's hands shoot out, slamming Trevor in his concave chest. "What do you know about damage, Trevor?"

The whole room stops moving.

"Whoa." Alejandro steps in, looming over us.

"I think I know," says Trevor, regaining his balance, "that you're an arrogant asshole—"

"You have no idea what I'm going through!" Caleb's voice is full of wrath. Everyone in the room is staring and they both sound like children.

I grab his arm and pull. "Come on."

Caleb turns away. Behind us, Jon and Matt are on their feet.

"You're such an asshole, Caleb," hisses Cybil.

"Settle down, pard'ner," Jon says, invoking a cowboy drawl. Hang with him long enough, and you'll hear every movie accent there is.

"Okay, who needs some fresh air?" I say, leading the way to the door.

Once we're out in the hall, I turn to Caleb. "That wasn't the plan."

"Honestly, who fucking cares?" He throws up his hands, his gaze still not meeting mine. "I'm not sorry. I don't care. And Trevor was being a dick. He has no idea what it's like."

"Well, you also never told him."

"Because he's an ass. So they hate me, so what?"

"Caleb! So *what* is if the other bands hate you, then all their fans are going to hate you, and that bad vibe is going to spread like a virus! All you needed to do was say you were sorry."

"Yeah, well, I didn't! Now stop trying to *manage* me and listen to what I'm saying." And just like that, he stalks off.

"Wow," says Jon. "That all went well."

"Is he like that often?" Matt wonders, sounding worried.

"I guess I don't really know," I say.

Jon summons a British accent. "He has been a bit ornery today."

I watch him go, equal parts furious, wounded, wanting to scream and fighting the urge to run after him, something I am *not* going to do. "I'll see you guys later."

I try not to storm into calc, try not to think too much about Caleb, but that just makes the whole afternoon feel even longer. What was with him? And why couldn't he tell me? I want to ask him, but he's the one who left, so I resist the urge to message him.

Finally, in study hall last period, I feel my phone buzz against my leg. I slip it out under the table.

Caleb: Really sorry. More drama last night. Couldn't share with the others around. Should have told you this morning. Can we talk after practice?

I debate my reply.

Summer: I said I'd be home around 8, so I'll have to clear it with the powers. Since you never ask me out PROPERLY.

Caleb: I am a ruffian and a scoundrel.

Summer: Yes.

I let a few seconds go by.

71

Summer: But I want to know what's up.

Caleb: How about Tina's after practice?

Tina's frozen yogurt. A suitable apology.

Summer: Sure. And you better give me the SCOOP on your mood.

Caleb: It's fro yo, more like the DISH.

Finally, I smile a little.

Summer: :) See you then.

6

MoonflowerAM **@catherinefornevr 2h**
Summer's not here right now. She's eating frozen yogurt in the future.
#whereismyTARDIS

I clear the evening with my parents. They're usually fine
with this kind of thing. They know the grades are off to a
good start, and Dad keeps bringing up schools with good
law programs. I strategically humored him one night and
looked over his search results, even though the idea of college makes me ill. I mean, it's always been assumed that I'll
go. I'm just worried it will change me.

That's what happened to my older brother, Bradley.
We're not that close, but when he was in high school, playing sax and piano and operating as a mid-level rebel, I
looked up to him. Now he's a senior at Pomona and applying to med schools and he spends his breaks at home talking

about residencies and the changing face of health care. These days, he feels more like a junior partner in Carlson Squared.

I get my homework done at a coffee shop, then grab a bus across town, anxious to talk to Caleb, frustrated that it's three transfers to get to the Hive. My parents have offered to get me a car, but I don't want one. I can use one of theirs when I need it. I like the bus. And a car feels like a contract, like: here is this BIG THING that now means we have more say over you because we OWN the big thing and we can take it away. Not that they'd necessarily pull that kind of crap. But the bus keeps it from ever being an option.

The Hive is a concrete block of converted factory. The white facade has giant windows that make you think there'd be a cavernous space waiting inside, but instead, the windows look in on walls, and the whole thing has been cubed up into hall after hall of tiny practice spaces.

The entrance is flanked by clusters of musicians shrouded in cigarette smoke. There's every breed of band: hipsters in clutching T-shirts, pencil-thin jeans, and brightly colored sneakers; straight-up rockers, jeans torn and flannels ratty; metal bands, so many metal bands, with chains and hair and acne and sneers; a lost-looking trio of quirky kids who probably jam too much, clad in fez and tweed and thinking that anyone who plays a song shorter than five minutes is a slave to the corporate overlord. Everywhere, skin is tattooed and chins are rough with all manner of facial hair, most not quite successful. Passing among them is to suffer an onslaught of sweat and hair product and secondhand smoke.

I keep my eyes straight ahead. Musicians aren't like jocks; they don't catcall, they're all too cool for that. But when it comes to ogling, I almost prefer jocks: they just dumbly assess your dimensions on some primal mating level, like we live on a savannah. You feel like they can't even help themselves. Musicians, though, they judge you silently. Your coat. Your expression. The brand on your guitar case. Anything they can. Are you cooler than they are? Do you think you are? Are you the real thing? But you can't be. There must be flaws. Let's find them.

Inside, the claustrophobia increases. The air is stuffy, sour with pot and rank with body odor. As I move down the hall, there's an acidic twinge of vomit and urine. Dangerheart's room is on the fourth floor, up concrete stairs made uneven by years of gum deposits. The air is sticky with humanity, and everywhere there is the throbbing muffled pulse of bands, each room a cell in this musical organism, one riff bleeding into another as you pass each door.

I have to use the bathroom, but when I step inside, past the wild splatters of vomit and God-knows-what-else, and push open the only working stall door, I jump back at the sight of a girl making out with a guy.

She looks over her shoulder. "You need to go?" she asks mildly, her lips and eyes painted black.

"No, thanks. I'll hold it."

I hurry down the hall and pause outside door 418. I always arrive about halfway through practice, to give the guys time to bond, to get into it and let their guards down, to make their silly boy jokes. I feel like this is especially important since Caleb and I are dating. Arriving with him would be the girlfriend move. The manager isn't arm candy. The manager checks in and evaluates. Though I do love hearing them play, and watching Caleb sing, I try not to show how much.

I press my ear to the door. It vibrates with each kick-drum beat. They're crashing through a song called "Artificial Limb." It's frenetic and punkish, pretty fun but not quite there yet. I don't know that it should be part of the set long-term, but since they're just starting out, getting a full set of decent songs is all that matters right now, and "Limb" is definitely decent.

I knock when they're done and it's Caleb who lets me in. We lock eyes and I wonder if this will be weird or cool, given our fight before, and whatever was clearly bothering him all day, but he greets me with a relaxed smile, and I do the same. We're both in pro mode. We allow a brief hug, and I want more, but I hold it back. And yet just before the hug ends, he whispers in my ear: "Sorry about before."

"Me, too." His hand lingers on my wrist as he pulls away, and it's enough to get me through to Tina's.

I drop down on the couch against the far wall. The Hive

has a basement full of discarded furniture and busted amp cabinets, a sort of perpetual recycling system. When it comes to the couches, it's take at your own risk. This one was once a bright-green-and-purple paisley, but it's mostly a sort of moss color now, blotchy with stains, cigarette burns, and areas where the velour covering is almost completely worn away. I don't even want to know what rooms this couch has been in, what's happened on it, but we sprayed it with Lysol and Febreze and now it seems sanitary enough.

It's not like the practice space is glamorous anyway. Jon thoughtfully strung some cool little globe lights across the ceiling, but they barely hide the water stains and cracks in the wall, and even if it looked great, it's a windowless, vent-less room, and nothing can stop the general boy smell. Still, there's something special about it, because it's the incubator where the music comes to life.

"How's it going?" I ask.

"Pretty good," says Caleb. "Just ran through everything. About to go again."

"Cool." I open my notebook.

"Uh-oh," says Jon, "she's getting out the ledger."

"Come on," I say with a smile, "this is what you pay me for." I flip to my page of notes from last practice. In between scrawling doodles (not because I'm bored: I like to draw to the music, it helps me think), I have a short list of things to point out. I always like to let a practice go by before mentioning any critique to the band, as some things are just one-time issues, and work themselves out on their own.

They start with "Exit Strategy," which is upbeat and hyper. It's a little raw but sounds great.

Next is "Knew You Before." This is my favorite song so far, and I think it could be a big hit. But as they play it, I hear the main issue that I wrote down last practice. Jon has this pedal board that Caleb nicknamed Mission Control. There are anywhere from five to ten multicolored pedals attached to it at a given practice, cables snaking between them, and he is constantly fidgeting with knobs and buttons. During "Knew You," he keeps messing with a teal-blue pedal, and his guitar seems to waffle in and out of this time space.

I wait a moment after the song ends, and then say, "So, Jon, what are you going for with that spacey sound?" I've learned that Jon is the kind of person who responds to questions. He's self-critical and will usually intuit what you're getting at.

"You know," says Jon with a shrug, already tweaking another dial, "a kind of ethereal wash. Like your arms are out and you're spinning."

"Ah."

He looks up at me. "Was it too much?"

I shrug. "Maybe?" This is a good time to look to Caleb. I don't mention my critiques to him before I say them, because then it would be like we were ganging up. Also, I try to notice if I'm suggesting something that the band totally doesn't agree with, because if I am, it's best to back off and take a different approach.

"It could maybe be a little more direct," says Caleb.

"I liked when you had more fuzz on the riff in the verse," Matt adds.

Jon sighs, but it's not annoyed, rather a scientist hard at work. "Okay, I'll dial back the tremolo, kick up the overdrive, see if I can make it a little more urgent."

"Urgent is the perfect word," I say.

They go through it again and it's better, but I make sure to ask Jon, "What did you think of it like that?"

"Sure," he says, "that could work." Which is close enough to a yes from someone like Jon.

Next, they play "Chem Lab," which is poppy and about crushing on your lab partner. Caleb's lyrics are clever and fun: pipettes and titrates and love. But Matt has given it this really complicated beat: busy with lots of accents, when the song feels like it should just flow.

"Matt," I say when it's done, "that's a really cool beat, but it kinda loses me."

Matt's eyes always light up when I say his name, except then he immediately looks away, down into the space between his floor tom and bass drum. "It's just supposed to feel like a loop," he says, disappointed.

Matt is tougher than Jon. He takes criticism personally, and he's really proud of his beats. Drummers can get really focused on the sixteenth notes of a song, rather than the song as a whole. But I've figured out something that usually works with Matt.

"No, it's really cool, I just wonder if it's too syncopated. Probably seems obvious to a drummer. But the other day I heard that song 'Freeze Dried' by the Bulbs. Do you know that song?"

"Oh, yeah." There's at least a spark of interest in his eyes now.

I know that Matt thinks the Bulbs drummer is great. "Well, that song is sorta like this one, style-wise. He's doing some pretty cool stuff. It seems kinda laid-back. I don't know . . . might be worth checking it out." I actually know exactly which part of that tune I'm hoping he picks up on, but I figure that's about all that Matt can take for the moment.

"Sure, okay." He's still looking down at the floor, but he's nodding. "I'll check it out." This probably means he will.

"It's a cool beat you're doing, though," Caleb adds.

"Thanks," Matt says quietly.

I sit back and my heartbeat calms. It's always a little nerve-racking to try to give feedback, and I'm always glad when it's over. I listen to the rest of the set, doodling, catching nuances, writing down a note or two for next time but definitely not speaking it, and trying not to watch Caleb too much.

I do have one thing on my list for him, but I'll wait until

after practice to bring it up.

"Why haven't you showed them 'On My Sleeve'?" I ask as we walk from his car to Tina's, each with an arm around the other. We just finished a kiss that caused us to nearly walk into a fire hydrant.

Caleb has been smiling, and as loose as I've seen him all day, but mentioning the song suddenly makes him stiffen. "Ah," he says, "I don't know if it's right."

"Why?" I say. "Because it's too perfect?" I reach around and squeeze his ribs, but he just flinches a little. He's got a bag for some reason, this old leather thing that he used for his pedals and cables tonight. I haven't seen it before.

"It's not perfect," he says. He smiles at me, but it's a lame one, Fret Face in firm control. "I just feel like it's too personal. I mean, too honest. What fun is that?"

"Um, how about the fact that people are going to totally connect to it? Feel inspired by it?"

"Or laugh at how"—he makes air quotes—"*sensitive* it is."

"Oh, please."

He shakes his head. "It definitely does not seem like a Trial by Fire song."

"Well, I disagree, and I'm going to keep disagreeing until you change your mind." I let it go for now though.

I wait until we have bowls of frozen yogurt piled with toppings (peanut-butter cups, gummy bears, chocolate sauce, and whipped cream for me; Caleb is chocolate sprinkles only), and are seated at a table outside to ask: "So, now do I get the *dish*?"

But Caleb is a long way from his last smile. He's been tightening up by the second. Does he even remember the joke? Instead, he puts that old gig bag up on the table between us.

And as he opens it, he says, "I got a letter from my dad."

7

"You what?"

"My mom gave this to me on my birthday," says Caleb, pointing to the bag. "It was Eli's old gig bag. He left it in Randy's car the day he died."

"Your uncle Randy knew Eli?"

"Yeah. Randy and my d—Eli were in a band together earlier in high school. That's how my mom met Eli. Randy wasn't part of Allegiance, but they still hung out. My mom said that after I was born, Randy was key in getting Eli to pitch in."

None of this sounds like it makes Caleb very happy.

He continues: "They'd been hanging out in the

afternoon, and Eli forgot the bag in the car. Randy wanted me to have it."

"It's pretty cool," I say, running a finger over the cracked seams. "Looks like it's seen some real action." There are shreds of a sticker on the side, it maybe says Below Zero, but chunks are missing.

Caleb opens the bag. "It had his old pedals and cables in it. One really cool phaser pedal that I might use. But there's also a pocket in the lining on the side. I don't think Randy ever even noticed it." Caleb unzips it.

And pulls out a piece of paper with a ragged edge.

He places the page between us, turning it around so I can read the scratchy handwriting. "This was written by Eli," says Caleb. He points to the torn edge. "Looks like he ripped it out of a journal. Do you know about that book called *On the Tip of Your Tongue*? It's the collected journals of Allegiance to North. Mom has it at home. I checked this against Eli's handwriting. It looks exactly the same. But then the last entry in the book from Eli is dated July eleventh, 1998."

I look at the page. Top corner, a scrawled date: "July fourteenth."

"That was the night of the Hollywood Bowl show. On that last tour. The last show they ever played in LA." Caleb's face is white. "Read it."

I hunch over it. I'm wary of reading. My insides are spinning. I don't like this proximity to the words of a dead man.

To you who don't know me:

I guess it's fitting that now I wish I could talk to you, wish I could hold you, but of course I can't. And while I'm off making a mess of everything, you're somewhere learning your first words, your first steps.

I'd come see you, if I could. Duck out this greenroom door and grab a bus, use a fake name, never come back, but I can't. I should . . . but I just filled my vein and I don't want you to see your daddy like this.

Gotta do something though . . .

They're after me.

I'm not supposed to know but I do. Art becomes business becomes lies. The soul dies. We don't know it's dead until it's long since slipped from us, and we look back and see it waving sadly, as we move on, hollow inside.

I've become my faults, can't stay clean, destroy all the love that comes my way. I know these things. How did I get here? How now brown cow? Life is all just nursery rhymes. You already know everything you need. I'd love to say them with you.

I look up. "I'm not sure he was sober when he wrote this."

"I know." Caleb nods at the page and I keep reading.

I can't go on with the charades anymore. My costume is threadbare. And anything else my heart conceives is just going to be taken from me. They're going to take it all. Like any of it even matters.

And that's the cruelest joke: I know what's important, now, finally, and I can't have it.

But do you know what? The universe works in mysterious ways. Two years staring at the blank page and I finally had a breakthrough. I can finish the album. I have the final pieces and they're my best yet.

Exile. Anthem. Encore.

I finally know what to write about, thanks to you.

But first I have to get the house in order. These songs, these gifts are too precious to let the bastards steal.

I'm going to hide the tapes. And then I may have to do something drastic to clean up this mess. Or maybe I'll just mess it up more, so much mess that we just drown beneath it.

"Whoa. Drown?"

"I know," Caleb answers quietly.

It feels good to write to you. I can't trust anyone else.

Maybe with some luck, years from now, we'll go

together to see Vic, and get a Reuben with pickles. Then get a kiss from Daisy and search for a hidden yesterday.

For now, though, while I die in the spotlights tonight, at least I'll know that you're sleeping peacefully, unaware of me.

We are far comets, on impossible journeys. Maybe someday our paths will cross, and we'll find each other in all that dark.

—E

I sit back, heart racing. "Wow. Not all of that made sense to me, but . . ." I glance at Caleb, and can't resist looking around to see if anyone is close enough to hear. "This is obviously written to you."

"Yeah."

"Do you think this is a suicide note? That he—"

"Meant to drown?" Caleb shakes his head. "That didn't happen for another four months. But he thought something bad was going to happen to him."

"He says, *they're after me*. Who do you think he meant?"

"I don't know."

"Maybe it was no accident that this bag ended up in Randy's car. Do you think Eli hoped someday this would get to you?"

Caleb just nods, eyes on his yogurt.

"And then . . ." I look back at the letter. "Is he saying

what I think he's saying? About hidden things?"

"Have you ever seen the old tracklist," asks Caleb, "from *Into the Ever & After*, the album they were working on when Eli died?"

"I remember hearing about it. There were missing songs, right?"

Caleb taps the letter with his finger. "The three track titles were 'Exile,' 'Encore to an Empty Room,' and 'Finding Abbey Road.' He was working on them."

"But he wanted to hide them," I add. "He didn't trust . . . who? Band mates? Drug dealers?"

Caleb shrugs. "I think he wanted me to have them."

I look over the letter again. "What do you think he meant by *Vic* and *Reuben with pickles*? *Daisy* and all that?"

"I don't know. I did searches for those words, combined with Eli and Allegiance to North and everything, but there was nothing." Caleb suddenly slaps the table. "He was stoned when he wrote it. The whole thing might just be nonsense."

"But the songs might be real, Caleb. These tapes might be out there."

"Yeah," Caleb says quietly. "If they are, I have to find them."

I take his hand. I worry about getting his hopes up. Hidden tapes from his long-dead dad? How likely is it that they even exist? And if they do, how likely is it that they're even still out there? It's all hard to believe, especially considering this is the same guy who bailed on his band during the biggest tour of their lives, who literally went AWOL for two months. Who went swimming off the Santa Monica pier while high and wearing cowboy boots.

But seeing the look in Caleb's eyes, I decide to save all that worry. "Where do you want to start looking?"

Caleb shrugs. "I have no idea. I looked through this"—he reaches into the bag again and pulls out a paperback copy of *On the Tip of Your Tongue*—"but only a little. Maybe there are clues in earlier letters."

I look at the cover. There is Eli, along with Kellen, Parker, and Miles, and they're all glamming at the camera, tongues out, only instead of being decked out in leather and makeup like a metal band, they're wearing loose flannels and all have scruffy beards. They look like they're having a blast.

"Yeah, hard to believe they hated each other by the end," says Caleb.

The Eli on the cover looks so young, silly, and carefree. The one in the letter is so full of regret, so weary.

"Are we going to tell the rest of the band?" I ask.

"No. Definitely not."

"But wouldn't it be good to get their help? They all seem like good guys."

Caleb's face darkens. "We don't know if we can trust them yet."

I'm not sure I agree about that, but I'm fine keeping it

just between us for now. "Did you tell your mom?"

"No," says Caleb. "She made up her mind about Dad a long time ago. I think she'd definitely shoot this down."

As he stows the letter away again, I let my thoughts unspool. Something big has been on my mind since the moment I finished reading the letter. "If we found these songs, Caleb, I mean . . . we're talking about the lost songs of Eli White. It would be . . . huge. Can you imagine if we performed them—"

"No," Caleb snaps. "This isn't about profiting off my dead father's songs."

I recoil. It didn't seem like such a threatening idea when I was thinking it, but clearly Caleb is on edge. "Hey, come on. I wasn't talking about money. I just meant more like . . . You're his son, the perfect person to play them. And every band needs a break. This would be huge exposure for—"

"Summer, I said NO." Caleb lurches to his feet. He grabs his bag, knocking his empty dish to the ground in the process. "I shouldn't have told you."

"Caleb, stop."

"You're managing me again and that is exactly *not* what I need. I just needed you to listen."

I stand up, too, and try to brush off the sting of his words. "Caleb, I did listen, I'm just trying to help."

Caleb is silent, staring out toward the street. "Can we walk?" he finally says.

We throw out our bowls and walk up the sidewalk,

not touching. I want to reach for his hand, but suddenly I don't feel sure. This is the second time today that Caleb has accused me of managing him when I thought I was trying to help.

Was I wrong to jump right to the idea of what to do with the songs? Or was that a completely normal thing to think about? I know this must be hard for him; even the idea that he has a dad is a new one. But if we actually found those songs, how could we not release them to the world? Isn't hiding them away just as selfish as profiting from them? There's no doubt that people would want to hear them.

And . . . with the lost songs by Allegiance to North, you could write your own ticket. Any band would kill for that kind of break. You wouldn't need some heartless record label like Candy Shell to come along and sweet-talk you.

But maybe that's more about me than about Caleb. Because the manager of the band with Allegiance's songs wouldn't also need to fake an interest in law school.

Hello, complicated.

We eventually settle into trivial stories about relationship drama involving a few bands at school. When we say good night, he kisses me: same lips, same tongues, but somehow now there is distance. I refuse Caleb's offer of a ride and as he leaves me at the bus stop, I hate this new feeling that I have. Now that these songs exist, I worry that nothing in our relationship can be just us anymore.

8

I am halfway to practice when I get a text.

> Caleb: I think we have our bassist.

I respond immediately.

> Summer: No way! Who?

But then nothing.

I didn't even realize that we had any bass tryouts today.
Someone must have been referred to the band directly. At
this point, with only four days until the Trial, we'd come
to terms with the fact that Dangerheart would be playing
its first gig bass-less, with Jon using an octave pedal to fill
in the sonic hole. We did try out one person on Saturday,
but he turned out to be a forty-year-old guy named Rod

who wore leather pants and claimed he could still "rock it on to the break of dawn." Next.

The band has been sounding good, regardless. And Caleb and I are past the awkwardness of the other night. Sunday evening, we met up at Sacred Cow, an Indian place in the center of town, and read through *On the Tip of Your Tongue*, looking for any clues about those strange references in Eli's letter. We found nothing, but we did find two amazing quotes:

> *I guess that's why you should never eat sushi on a trapeze.*
> —PARKER, ON HURLING ONSTAGE AFTER A VIDEO SHOOT FOR THE SINGLE "SUBSURFACE REFLECTIONS"

And:

> *That album caught on so fast. It was like ear lube.*
> —ELI, ON THE RELEASE OF *THE BREAKS*

"Ear lube" made us laugh. A lot.

We also read a lot of darker stuff about Eli's stints in and out of rehab, and a time he got arrested for disorderly conduct on Sunset Boulevard. This was less funny. He ran out of a bar bathroom and down a street convinced he was being chased by the ghost of Jerry Lee Lewis, and he was screaming the lyrics to "Great Balls of Fire" at the top of his lungs. And his pants were apparently still in the bathroom.

The book made Caleb quiet. And the strange stories and lack of clues made the idea of hidden songs seem barely possible. But I can't get the possibility of them out of my mind, and I think Caleb feels the same way.

I hurry from the bus to the Hive, through the gauntlet of smoke and postures, up to the door, where I pause because the band is in mid-song. I can already tell by the humming of the walls that there's bass in the room. Its deep presence obscures everything. I can't even tell what song this is, yet.

Caleb starts to sing—

But wait. That's not Caleb.

It sounds like a girl. Yes, it's definitely either a girl, or maybe that's what Jon sounds like when he sings? But he never sings—

A shrieking whine of feedback suddenly grinds the band to a halt.

"Aww, man!" I hear Matt groan.

"Sorry," says Jon.

I knock. The door opens. It's Caleb. The usual dank smell of guy wafts out, only now it's tinged with something sweet. Strawberry gum?

"Hi." I lead with a smile, trying to hide my confusion.

"Hey, Summer!" Matt calls eagerly from across the room.

Caleb makes eye contact. There's Fret Face, but a slightly different variation. Eyes wider. "Hey." His eyes flash over his shoulder. "So . . ."

But I'm already there.

94

She's over by the drums, in front of a mic, a burgundy P-bass slung low. It seems nearly as tall as she is. Bleached blond hair, with dark eye shadow, or really dark circles, it's hard to tell. A simple green T-shirt that says "Product of Capitalism," black jeans and yellow sneakers, and yellow-white-and-red sweatbands on her wrists.

She levels a flat gaze at me, her mouth working on the source of the strawberry smell. I'm immediately on my guard and I want to ask *Who's this?* but instead some polite gene kicks in and I just say, "Hi."

The girl eyes me. "Who's this?"

Caleb's hand falls on my shoulder. "This is Val," he says to me. "Val, this is Summer, our manager."

"Val rocks," adds Jon.

"You're Moonflower Productions?" Val asks. She doesn't sound impressed. "So, you, what, mastertweet about the band, hang posters, fetch sodas?"

I meet her gaze. Really? This is how we're going to start? I feel a surge of adrenaline as I search for the right response, but all I come up with is, "It's more than that." Then, to Caleb: "I don't remember any replies to our ads from a Val."

"I didn't," she says.

"She was just here," adds Matt.

"What, you just magically appeared?" I head for the couch. "I've never seen you at Mount Hope."

"I go to Mission Viejo," she says. "I saw Caleb with

Android Necktie back in June, at the Irvine Street Fair. It was right after I moved out here. Been keeping tabs on him ever since."

So, you're basically a groupie? I think to ask, but instead the professional instinct wins again and I settle for, "Do you have band experience?"

Val scowls. "Of course. I fronted my own band back when I lived in New York. Kitty Klaws. You can YouTube us."

"We watched some," says Jon. "They were great."

I look at Caleb. "Was she singing?"

"Yeah . . ." Caleb's eyes shift. "We watched the videos and, I don't know, I just thought it might be cool if we tried the duo thing. Some of Val's songs, some of mine. But it's not a definite."

"Is she your mom?" Val asks.

Caleb nervous-laughs, and what bothers me right now is how this Val girl is making *him* flustered. Does that mean he thinks she's cooler, more intimidating than me? *You're being silly.* But I wonder if I am. Val is cute. Val can sing. She's a girl with a bass. Songs have been sung about such girls. And none, as far as I'm aware, about band managers.

Except, when I'm not feeling jealous—and I'm totally feeling jealous—I have to admit that Caleb has done something kind of brilliant. Having a second singing, song-writing member is a real strength. Granted, bands like the Beatles eventually blow apart fantastically—and maybe in

Val's case I wouldn't mind that, eventually—but still, this really increases the intrigue and cool of the band, if she's any good.

I also realize that acting skeptical/territorial/jealous is the stereotypical move right now, so even though that's exactly what I'm feeling, the least I can do is hide it. "Cool," I say, "can I hear your tune?"

Val looks down at her strings as she replies, revealing a hint of nerves. "Sure. Same one?"

"Yeah," says Caleb.

"Okay." Val leans up to the mic. "This is—" She pauses to cough. It sounds like she smokes. "This is 'Catch Me.'"

The band blasts into a high-speed tune with a rapid-fire beat and eighth notes on the bass.

Val starts to sing the first verse. I've seen Caleb sing a few times now. He balances a sense of vulnerability with emotional power, alternating between glancing at the crowd and closing his eyes, in and out of himself like he and the audience are searching for the story of the song together.

Val is totally different. Darker. Harder, but also more fragile. Her eyes are open and glaring. Daggers made of glass. She locks on things, occasionally even me, and it's an angry, accusatory gaze, the purse to her lips. It's like there's a bulletproof panel between you and her, and yet, you feel like that glass is there for a reason, like behind it there is a deep well of sadness. Even in spite of our rough beginning, this sense of her stirs a feeling of empathy in me.

The music switches, and Val nods to Caleb, who quick nods back, musician-speak, and when Val hits the high long notes of her chorus:

I dare . . . you . . . to . . .
Catch me . . .

Caleb layers his voice right on top and it's . . . well, I have to be honest: it's fantastic.

I get out my notebook and write down the word "romantic." I don't mean cheesy, and I don't mean like romantic between the two of them. It's what a listener will feel (and then they'll assume the romance). I wonder what it must feel like to sing in harmony—I mean, that's got to be intimate, right? Damn, I want to know. And I feel the jealous tremor crawl deeper, thinking that I'm so right for Caleb, in so many ways, and yet Val has waltzed in here and shared that connection with him in just a few minutes. How can I compete with that?

Keep it together! I shout at myself. Gotta stay professional. And professional me knows that these two sound amazing together and the future of this band just changed radically for the better.

So I get my phone and post:

MoonflowerAM @catherinefornevr 3s
WHOA. Caleb and Val: Mount Hope's Lennon and McCartney?
#dangerheart #swoonalert #canthearoverthescreamingfans

They transition into what seems to be a bridge, but a wicked scream of feedback explodes from Jon's amp. Everything crashes to a halt.

"Shit, sorry." Jon bends over his pedal board. "I just gotta rearrange the chain."

Val shakes her head. "You don't need pedals to rock," she says.

Jon looks up and replies in a surly, Liam Neeson–style Irish accent: "I'll not have yer insolence, Miss Valerie."

Val smiles, sort of. I begrudgingly take note of this, too. Val is going to be an ally in keeping Jon's sci-fi-sound tendencies in check.

"How was that harmony?" Caleb asks Val. He sounds uncertain, like he wants to be sure she liked it.

"Pretty close," she says. "Maybe a little too parallel in spots."

"Ah," says Caleb, apparently understanding what she means. "So a little more counter movement."

"I think so? Tone was good, though."

"The sort of distant thing?"

"Exactly. I'm the soft. You bring the edge."

"Cool. Got it."

I listen to this, an instant shorthand between them, and it makes me burn.

"So, what did you think?" I find Caleb looking at me. I frown, trying to say to him, *that's a question for private,* and the fact that he's asked in public means there's only one answer he wants from me.

I could be mad about this, I could tuck it away to talk about with him later, but, really, I know that what's happening here is serendipitous and perfect. "It's totally going to work."

Val picks up the tunes fast and adds another of hers to the mix, and practice is pretty great. I sit on the couch soaking it in, and whenever I need to take my mind off Val I attend to band business: posting candids to Pinboard; updating the BandSpace forum, which right now only has three fans but should grow; sending the band's updated set list to my blogger friend *Bronyfriendkillkill*, who's making photo collages inspired by the song titles. I also email Blaire Nolan, a talented filmmaker in the junior class, about shooting a video, which reminds me that we need to talk about that as a band.

At the next song break, I bring it up. "Caleb, did you guys think any more about a single for the video?"

"Oh," he says, "yeah, well"—he glances at Val even though I feel like she shouldn't get a say, but then I remind myself that if she's going to be in this, she should—"we were thinking that 'Knew You Before' would be good."

Val thinks. Nods. "That's a good one."

"Did you show them the *other* one?" I ask Caleb.

"Oh, er, no." Of course he knows what song I mean.

"What other one?" asks Matt.

"Just this song . . . ," says Caleb.

"It's called 'On My Sleeve,'" I say. "It's the first song I heard Caleb play."

I can see Caleb's nerves tightening up. It still surprises me that he gets shy. "It's not ready," he says.

"Liar. It's more than ready."

"Don't get shy now, C.D.," says Val. Really? She's shortening his name after an hour? "I didn't drive through the traffic vortex of hell to have you wuss out on your secret hit."

"It's not a se—"

"PLAY IT," we all say.

"Okay, fine." Caleb sighs but it's just theatrics. He moves the capo up the neck of his acoustic, and I see his fingers fidgeting in a way that they haven't up until now. He sits down on his amp and takes a minute to adjust the mic. Everything about how he's moving says he's nervous.

"Ready?" He seems to be asking himself, and then he takes a deep breath and starts to strum slow chords, his acoustic ringing. Despite the thump of drums invading through all the walls, the acoustic seems to create a delicate balloon of space, almost more captivating in its simple metallic jangle than when the whole band is in.

He glances up. "It's called 'On My Sleeve.'"

He sings:

You never knew what you left behind
Never cared to come back

No matter how much light shined on you
You took it with you into the black

He's far off inside when he sings this, eyes closed or checking the chords. Every once in a while he looks up, and it almost looks like he's making sure of where he is. And then once he's sure of time and space, he's gone again.

Did you know what you were missing?
Did you know I never knew?
Sunday afternoons, fights we could have had
Could I have saved you?

Would you be here . . .

But now I wear you on my sleeve
Always waking from a silly dream
Where I find you, alive and well
And your smile erases all the hell
I never knew was . . . missing

As the chords come back around, Jon begins to spin a spiderweb of silken guitar notes that feel like breeze blown. Matt makes the kick drum pulse on each quarter note and starts a chimey pattern on the open hi-hat and cymbal. Val makes the bass roll like thick fluid. They are all eyes closed, heads down, feet tapping, searching, finding . . .

As Caleb hits the chorus again, I feel like I unstick, gravity suspended.

MoonflowerAM @catherinefornevr 1s
Can't . . . breathe . . . #dangerheart #O #M #G

Matt moves to the toms, adds the snare. Jon's notes make a whirlwind around us. Val's bass starts to sprint. Caleb, head up but with eyes still closed, starts to sing high *oooh*s, fragile and chipped, like leaves somersaulting over frosted grass. This song is an autumn dawn, the air crisp and scented with decay, the light angled and faint.

They create this huge sound, we are all in it, and finally Caleb's eyes open; he checks with everyone, and they end on a huge unison ringing chord. As it fades away, they trade glances. Everyone knows.

"Dude . . . ," breathes Jon. "I can't *wait* to see those BandSpace girls freak out about that."

"It's good," says Val. "Really, annoyingly good."

"Thanks," says Caleb.

"That's the single," I say. "I mean, right?"

Caleb eyes me seriously. "I still have a hard time imagining playing that in front of a bunch of our drunk classmates."

"Can you imagine playing it in front of ten thousand screaming fans?" asks Jon.

Caleb chuckles. "Yeah. That's easy."

I hear Val sigh. "'On My Sleeve' it is. Are we done?"
She drops to her knees to put her bass in its case. "I gotta go.
It's a long way back down south for me."

"Sure," says Caleb. "So, you're in the band, right?"

Val glances up at him. "When's the next practice?"

Afterward, Caleb and I head to Tina's again. It's Caleb's
idea, and I am glad for how refreshingly not Ethan this
choice is. All his choices really. Ethan only ever wanted to
go to Whimsy Cafe, the kind of place where you felt like
you had to order a painstakingly prepared espresso bever-
age, and the person who made it for you would perpetually
sneer around a lock of maroon hair, likely because of how
uncomfortable their pencil jeans were. The kind of barista
who would literally die if she saw you ladle an extra scoop
of peanut-butter cups onto tropical bubblegum fro-yo like
I did just now.

"So, tell me I was right about 'On My Sleeve,'" I say
once we're sitting with our bowls. Both of us went with the
large size and added extra toppings. I was just feeling hungry, but it's probably also stress eating because of proximity
to a show.

"You were right," says Caleb, smiling.

"Val is good, too," I say after a bite. I feel a spike of
nerves saying this. She's obviously what I wanted to talk
about most. But I don't want it to seem like jealousy. "Is it
weird, though? This girl just showing up, a fan of yours?"

Caleb shrugs. "She doesn't act like a fan. And she can totally play. I just feel like we got lucky. We need someone like her, who's . . ."

"Please don't say hot."

Caleb reaches over and rubs my arm. "I don't think she's hot."

"Not even the singing part?" I say.

"Okay, that's a little hot. Our voices sound good together."

I nod. "Like—"

"Ear lube," we say together, and somehow this is the key. For the rest of the yogurt time, and then for a significant period of time sitting in the car before driving home (I take a ride this time), it's just us.

9

The next Friday night, I find myself watching a boy with
a whipped-cream smiley face painted on his bare chest try
to walk across a rope, an inflatable doll hanging on to his
shoulders.

Below stretches a trench of molten fire, bubbling.

Surrounding: a horde of wet, sandy, flower-adorned,
similarly creamed onlookers.

They chant: "Ha-ka-la-ka! Ha-ka-la-ka!"

The voices swell as the boy makes his way across the
undulating wire. Legs wobble. Lava boils.

"HA-KA-LA-KA—"

He lurches, the doll slips free. The boy lunges to grab

it and plunges to his doom.

The crowd explodes.

He emerges from the red-lit trough soaked and slicked. The "lava" smells like vegetable oil and cherries and, at this point, who-knows-what-else.

"BadASS!" Ari Fletcher shouts through a megaphone. His nose is zinced white and he's wearing a straw hat and Hawaiian shirt. He's standing on a stepladder, made sinister by plumes from the nearby bonfire. "Next up we have Vivien!"

"These are not my people," Val says under her breath. She's almost always scowling, but this look is nearly fearful. "Why do I feel like if they turn and see us, they're going to eat us?"

"If we pour punch all over ourselves," I say, "it may hide our scent." Val and I share a glance, our first moment of actual bonding.

I put down the two drum cases I've just carried down a winding sand path and catch my breath. Here we are: the wide beach, the raging bonfire, the glimpse of surf, the Fletchers' glittering house above and behind us. And again I have that feeling of going in circles, and wonder if I'm the stupid mouse that walks right back into the same trap. By bringing Dangerheart here, I have opened myself to the possibility of losing my band again. I gaze warily around the crowd, wondering if the sharks are already here. One shark in particular . . .

The next couple hours will be no picnic. I've dressed up a little for the occasion, as much as I could stand. Wrap skirt I got in Hawaii and a flower-print T-shirt. Looking around, I see that to really fit in I should be wearing a bikini top, despite the chilly evening breeze.

The band is lucky; they get to be on the stage. And they don't have to worry about costumes. Val is in her usual T-shirt, slouchy jeans, and sweatbands, though she's done up her hair with fresh green stripes. The rest of the band just looks like themselves.

Caleb arrives beside me. "Yikes," he says. The bonfire light flickers in his eyes and he grins. "This is insane." It's not a full grin though. Fret Face is tugging at the corners.

I rub his arm. "You're nervous."

"I'm okay."

"Liar."

Caleb's been tense. The week has been totally focused on getting gig-ready. We've barely spoken about the letter, only to report to each other that, after searching interviews and articles online, we've both come up empty on any more clues as to what Eli might have been up to. The show has been a welcome distraction, but it's still pressure: first gig with a new band, it doesn't matter how talented you are. And Caleb wants it, bad.

And he also doesn't want to talk about how badly he wants it, so I move on. "Some scene, huh?"

There are at least a hundred kids congregating around

the lava pit, where the next sacrificial soul is hoisting herself up onto the rope, this time holding a boy inflatable doll. Others swarm around the grass hut where drinks are being served, or near the giant bonfire. Everyone's dressed for the tiki theme, from grass skirts and surf shorts all the way to very unfortunate "native" attire. Many are already stumbling. A few of the drinks that are leaving the bar are in coconuts and aflame.

"Wow. *Lord of the Flies* meets Abercrombie and Fitch," says Jon, arriving beside us. He scans the crowd. "Yep, none of these girls are going to be into me."

"What are you talking about?" I ask. "You're the lead guitarist in this crowd's favorite band."

"Nobody's even heard us," says Jon.

"Not yet."

"Watch out!"

We all look up to the sound of dull thudding, and see Matt's bass drum case thundering down the path like a runaway boulder, Matt chasing it. We scatter as it thumps to a stop. A nearby herd of girls sees this and giggles in eerie unison.

"Sorry," Matt says breathlessly, frowning as he notices the laughter.

"I guess that's why you should never eat sushi on a trapeze," I say, and we all laugh. Matt manages to smile, and gives me puppy-dog eyes of gratitude.

"Smooth move, Matty," says Jon, throwing an arm

around him. "Looks like I'll have you to huddle bitterly with after the show."

"Now now," I say, "you boys are getting phone numbers tonight. I guarantee it." I actually already have an idea for Matt, although I'm not sure how it will go over.

"Are you *serious*?" The last member of our group to arrive is Randy, Caleb's uncle and our official roadie for the evening. He has a van for his house-painting business that we could all ride over in. It would be a cooler ride if the back wasn't a windowless metal cargo space lined with shelves of paint.

"This looks just like it did twenty years ago!" he says with a smile. Randy's a round guy, barrel-chested, his face overrun by a farm of reddish hair. "Trial by Fire!" he announces to the world. "Same as it ever was." He holds his hand to his face, dips his sunglasses, and says, "Look where my hand was."

"Nobody gets your Talking Heads references," says Caleb.

Val punches Caleb in the shoulder and actually smiles. "Shut up. I do."

I notice that. The punching.

"Thank you, Valerie," says Randy. "At least someone has some respect for rock and roll legacy. Man . . ." He gazes at the scene. "I remember back—"

"If you say 'back in my day,'" says Caleb, "you have to leave."

110

Randy pauses, flustered, then continues. "Back . . . when we played this party, which was, in fact, *in my day*, there was no stage."

"What was your band called again?" Val asks.

"Savage Halos."

"That is my favorite band name ever," she says.

"Get a room," says Caleb. "Except don't because that would be super creepy."

"That would bother you?" Val asks him.

"Um, just a bit." Caleb kind of smiles.

Something flashes between their gaze. Maybe I'm just making it up. My sensors are clearly on maximum sensitivity, but still, I wish they didn't have to be so chummy; then again, professional me knows that of course they're in a band and there needs to be camaraderie. But still . . .

"So you were here, at the first Trial?" Jon asks.

"I was here, and Savage Halos opened for this other band, a bunch of plucky kids who called themselves Allegiance to North. I watched them turn this crowd into a supernova. That night was the beginning of the rest of our lives." As Randy says this, he looks wistfully toward the ocean.

I glance at Caleb, hoping he's not reading into it, knowing that, in a way, his life began right here that night, too.

"Can we just go?" Caleb says darkly. I guess he did. Fret Face is in full control.

"To the battlements!" Jon shouts, a knight leading an army.

We trudge through the sand to the side of the stage.

Soundmen are checking the mics. Dangerheart is slated to go second, after Freak Show. We pass Trevor, Cybil, Alejandro, and their new drummer, Lane, in the roped-off area beside the stage. Only Alejandro says hello.

Dangerheart sets up and does a quick sound check. They play a minute of music and it sounds great, but Caleb's eyes are down, either on his guitar or the stage floor. I find myself urging him to look up, to engage.

After, Caleb and I head to the grass-roofed drink hut. As we weave our way through the crowd, I catch glances at us, and the sense of repetition grows. Summer with another band boy. I stuff my hands in my pockets, just in case Caleb gets any hand holding ideas, but he's looking dark and distant. And then I kind of hate myself for caring what anyone might think.

The hut is rickety and cockeyed, built by Ari and his friends, who probably learned about woodworking from YouTube videos. There's a line of kegs and multiple margarita machines on tables inside. On the corner of the warped bar, they've built a small mountain out of ice. As we stand there, a line of people step up one by one and a shirtless beefy kid slides electric-orange Jell-O shots down into their mouths. My old friends Callie and Jenna are in line, wearing extremely revealing bikini tops and cutoff shorts. I want to give them my sweatshirt. Jenna is even wearing a cowboy hat. Yee haw.

"Hey, Caleb," says a girl behind the bar. Missy Prescott. We don't know each other, except of course that she knew Ethan Myers intimately last spring. She's wearing the world's smallest bikini. I wonder if it requires adhesive. She's also smiling at Caleb like I'm not even there. "Are you playin' tonight?"

Really, a fake Southern accent? I huff and tap the bar, but I don't say anything, curious to see how Caleb handles it.

"New year, new band," he says with a smile. "How was your summer?" As he's making small talk, he reaches beneath the bar top and squeezes my hand. He's good at being social, and I need to remember that's a good thing for a lead singer.

"Do you know Summer?" he says.

Missy glances at me, her smile store-bought. "Hi." Right back to Caleb. "What can I get you guys?"

I wonder what Caleb will order, and I feel my usual hesitation about whether or not to drink. I'm okay with it, and will on occasion, but the thing that will kill it for me is the feeling that there's pressure. Plus, this is a work night.

"Just Cokes," says Caleb. He turns to me. "If that's cool? I don't drink when I play. I don't like to lose control."

"That's fine," I say, relieved to hear this.

We get our drinks and move away from the bar to a spot where we watch the contestants trying to cross the rope over the lava pit. The rope is so wobbly that no one makes it

113

further than halfway, and no one seems to mind.

"I'm wondering if you were too good at that," I say to him.

"What?"

"Miss Missy back there."

"Come on, she's cute, but only in a manufactured kind of way. Not a real bone in her body, I don't think."

"Well played." I have an urge to rub his arm, but I hesitate. The surroundings are still spooking me.

Caleb takes out his copy of the set list and looks it over.

"It's a good set," I say.

Fret Face. "I'm not sure about 'On My Sleeve.'"

"Come on. I can't believe you're second-guessing that song again."

"No, just . . ." He looks around. "Everyone's here to have fun, not to hear some downer ballad."

"It's not a downer. And nobody will have any idea *who* you're singing about. People adapt songs to be about themselves."

"Yeah."

"You're nervous."

Caleb kinda gulps. "I want it to be good. I always get amped up before shows. It'll be okay once we're playing."

"Is it being here, too?"

Caleb focuses on folding his set list. "What do you mean?"

"Randy was talking about Eli being here, now you're

here. I mean, it's understandable if that's on your mind. You know, like life repeating itself."

"That's not how it's going to be." Caleb abruptly steps away. "I should go tune. See you after the set?"

"Right." I try to offer him a smile. He's half turned to go, but then he turns back and steps close. He leans in for a kiss.

Except I glance around, wary, and *no!* Why did I do that? And it immediately breaks the spell. Caleb pulls back. "Okay, sorry." He walks off.

As he leaves, I swear to myself. We've lost our groove. He's nervous, but it's my fault. I shouldn't have mentioned Eli and why do I even care what everyone thinks? But I'll let him go. Things will be better after the set.

To be sure, though, I send him a quick text.

Summer: Sorry about the weird. Break a leg! But not really.

I pause for a moment thinking of ending with *love you*—it would be the first time either of us said it. Almost a month, it's time, isn't it? But would that be weird right after having a moment of awkwardness? I end it with *xo* instead and hope the love is implied.

I distract myself by moving around the party and finding moments to post about.

MoonflowerAM @catherinefornevr 8:45pm
Does Dangerheart sound better when you're covered in lava?
#Dangerheart #trialbyfire

115

I make a quick movie of a boy trying to cross the lava pit and falling in, and post it to BandSpace.

"SUMMER!" Ari emerges from the crowd, strutting toward me, megaphone to his mouth. "SWEET PARTY HUH—"

I wince and slap the megaphone down. "You were saying?"

"Sweet party, right?" he says breathlessly. His face is beet red. He smells like sugar and booze. "You ready for that Eruption?"

"After the set," I say, offering him a professional smile. "Thanks for inviting us."

Ari nods. Sways. His eyes swim down me but then his gaze shoots to our left. He raises the megaphone. "KYLIE!" He careens off.

"Hey, Summer!" I turn to find Maya hurrying over. "So excited to see the new band!"

"Hey, thanks! Me, too." I take her arm. "Stay with me, I have someone for you to meet." I send a quick text.

"Ooh, so secretive!"

A minute later, Matt shows up, breathless. He literally ran in response to my text. "What's up?" he asks, eyes hopeful.

"Matt, I wanted you to meet Maya. Maya, Matt, reverse, there you go. You two should get to know each other. Maya is an awesome band manager. And Matt rocks, he's a great drummer and he's"—I'm already saying what I planned to say when I realize how he's going to take it—"like the little brother I never had."

Maya flashes a smile at me. Matt on the other hand, is beet red and not smiling. "Hey," he manages politely.

Ah, crap. It's a look that makes me feel bad about the brother comment. But maybe it's necessary to train his puppy-dog love on someone else.

I help the two start up a conversation, and it's just starting to go somewhere, but then there's a whine of feedback from the stage.

"What up what up," Alejandro intones into the mic. "We are the Freak Show, Freak Show . . ." He looms over the edge of the stage, his voice deep and sinister. All around us, people's heads turn.

The band has been reinvented in black outfits. Lane starts thumping quarter notes on the kick drum, in a loping, heavy rhythm, like the perfect tempo to sway hips. All at once Alejandro, Trevor, and Cybil jump up in the air, landing in unison and crushing the first chord of their song.

The entire party begins to stir. Beside the stage I see Val, Jon, and Caleb snap to attention.

Freak Show bobs, their heads lunging up and down. They play a unison riff, fibrous with guitar crunch and drum throb and bass punch. It lumbers along like some kind of dragon on thick reptilian legs, undulating, wrapping everyone in its grip.

Fear what you won't understand
Fall under Freak Show's command

Alejandro's delivery is part singing, part spoken word, and completely commanding. The groove is undeniably infectious. It strikes me as a little too harsh, but it's doing a number on the party. Kids are rushing up to the front of the stage, to listen, to dance, but also to thrash. Their fast-forming crowd seethes, and once the space becomes tight they start to throw themselves around. There is a free, fluid movement around the edges, but in the middle, delirious bodies slam into one another.

The songs ends and there is a huge cheer. Their second song begins like a sprint, upping the ante, the pulse and danger. It races like a car out of control on a cliff-side highway. The crowd grows bigger.

This is when you understand
We've got the power in our hands

Alejandro starts rhythmically jumping. The crowd joins him. Even in the soft sand you can feel the thumping of all the feet joining in.

By the third song, it has become clear that Freak Show is for real. And I can see Caleb watching them from beside the stage, knowing it, too. Not like this is a competition, except that between bands and egos, it always is. I hope he doesn't let it rattle his nerves further.

Freak Show goes and goes, and their last song runs long. I keep checking my watch, and I can see Jon doing the same beside the stage, but there's nothing to be done. They've created a frenzy out front, and everybody wants them to keep going. They pound on, looping their final dramatic groove over and over. The center of the crowd is a violent frenzy. A kid walks by me with blood dripping from his zinc-coated nose, eyes glazed, his girlfriend guiding him out of the fray.

Freak Show out.

Alejandro slams the mic down on the stage and the band abruptly but expertly halts and then walks right off. The crowd explodes, cheering on and on.

"Well," says Matt, sounding queasy, "time to go set up." I watch him slink up to the stage and start moving his drums into place.

Amidst the continued shouting, Alejandro returns to the mic and says, "Thank you. I don't know about you, but I'm gonna go try that lava pit, if anyone wants to join me."

Some of the crowd was already scattering anyway in the aftershock of that set, but now there is a huge movement of kids toward the lava and I can't help but wonder if that was an intentional move by Freak Show, to sabotage Dangerheart's set. Either way: not cool.

By the time Dangerheart has set up, the area in front of the stage is only sparsely populated. I see Caleb seeing this as he's tuning. I hope it's not getting to him. Then he moves over to Val and talks into her ear. She cocks her head, looking angry, though with Val it's hard to tell. Caleb goes on to Jon and then Matt, telling them something, then he returns to the mic.

"Hi, we're Dangerheart," he says to scattered applause. I can hear the sudden lack of confidence in his voice. I know he's reading the vibe right now. Having to perform in the aftermath isn't easy. And he was already off from the ghosts in this place, and from me. *Come on, Caleb, just do your thing.* The move here is to not care. To just do your thing and eventually the crowd will come around. . . . "This first song is called 'Exit Strategy.'"

Wait . . . I check the set list on my phone. The first song was supposed to be "Knew You Before," but instead Caleb has called the band's fastest, most rocking song to be first. He's feeling pressure to match Freak Show's energy level. But that's not going to be possible. Not in the same way, anyway.

Still, this song is a good one. Matt's beat bounds along and Jon plays a high slide guitar part over Val's speedy bass line. When Caleb sings, it's on the edgier side of his range.

Do you see me wondering
Where you went, and what I'm gonna do

120

And I can't take it anymore
Chasing ghosts, just trying to find you

He doesn't sound warmed up; this is a tough song to do cold, and yet, I look around and see that some heads are turning. This could still work. But I can also tell that Caleb is pushing, singing with extra grit, chunking on his guitar like he's trying to break it. It makes him sloppy, and I see Val glancing over at him. She can tell, too.

The song ends and there is scattered applause.

"More Freak Show!" someone shouts, drunk. And why is it like a universal constant that there must be at least one stupid heckler in every crowd? His comment causes a ripple of snickers.

Shake it off, I think, watching Caleb. He's tuning again, head down. I want him to smile, to make a joke with the crowd, to be the easy version of himself that I've glimpsed now and then, but he just looks to Val who nods and they start the second song. It's "Knew You Before," back to the plan . . .

Caleb is still pressing, and Matt is playing harder than normal, too. At one point he drops a stick and fumbles for another. Caleb shoots him a glare. That's not good either. Never acknowledge the mistakes. The audience barely ever notices the mistakes, unless the band calls attention to them, but they can always sense when a band is frustrated with one another, and it can be poisonous.

But all that said, they nail the song. And the crowd notices. Next they go into "Chem Lab," and finally, now they are sounding like the band I love. Sharp, upbeat, the song really turns heads. Some bodies start to dance. They end to real applause. More people return to the stage.

They start "Catch Me," and Val brings it. I'm glad for her right now. She's not pressing or changing her approach; pissed and on a mission is her default setting. By the time the three songs are done, that one drunk heckler (who still won't leave), has been nearly drowned out. It's going over well. Caleb must see that—

Except then I see him going over to Val again. I check the set list. "On My Sleeve" is supposed to be next. Uh-oh. Val starts shaking her head emphatically, Matt is shrugging . . .

Caleb returns to the mic. He glances over at Val. I hear him say, just picked up by the mic, "Come on, let's just do it?"

She shakes her head. Oh, Caleb, breaking so many rules of the stage right now. Because if I can feel the indecision, the crowd can, too.

Caleb turns back to the mic and says, "This song is called 'Soundtrack to a Breakdown.'"

Wait, what? They've only rehearsed this song maybe twice with Val. It wasn't even supposed to be in the set, but Caleb starts to play it. The first verse is just him, fast acoustic strumming with low, seething vocals that sound right on

122

the edge of losing your mind. I see the band looking around at one another, Val to Jon to Matt, and their gazes are easy to read: Caleb has clearly started without their agreement. But if they don't join in, they'll leave him out to dry and the set with be ruined. Dammit, Caleb!

I did not expect this from him. And I can see the rest of the band trying to decide. To go with Caleb is to let him get away with a power trip, or a freak out, whatever this is. But to not go with him is to sink the gig. I flash all the way back to the first day of school, when I wondered if he was a head case or just going through a tough time.

Maybe I was wrong.

Just as Caleb gets to the end of the verse, Matt clicks his sticks and the rest of the band jumps in for the chorus.

This is all moving around me
This is all second nature to you
I hang on tight against the wind
I count on you to pull me through

Man, I wish they were playing "On My Sleeve" right now. This isn't bad, though. Unpolished, but raw can be good.

Except after another verse and chorus, the song hits a solo section, and while Jon begins to climb high in the atmosphere, Caleb starts jumping up and down, emphasizing the beats of his rhythm line. Too much though: his shoulder slams into his mic stand. There is a moment of slow time as the stand teeters, and then it crashes over, causing a huge booming pop as the mic hits the stage. Everyone is thrown off.

Caleb spins to stare at it, and just at that point, the band returns to the chorus, but Caleb is a step late. His hands clamp down and he hits a chord and it's just so totally wrong, like cats fighting in the dark. Caleb yanks his hands away from the fret board, staring at the guitar like it's betrayed him. His hands return, his fingers dancing in the air over the frets, trying to remember where to go. Val is shouting at him, I can hear a faint sound of it even from out here.

Caleb turns to her. He nods, bending to pick up his mic. At least if he sings, it will be fine—

But as he's bent over, his guitar strap comes undone, and his guitar topples to the stage in a terrible crash of string noise.

Matt and Jon are looking to one another, panicked, and then Matt does a big fill down the toms while nodding his head, and when they hit the end of the bar they slam to a halt. It's an impressively timed ending that almost sounds planned, and *almost* saves the song.

There are a few faint claps. Caleb, scrambling to pick up his guitar, grabs the mic with the other hand and speaks into it sideways. "Sorry about that."

Someone boos. Drunk guy yells: "You suck!" A girl snickers.

Caleb stands and fumbles to reattach his strap. Val

stalks over to him and talks into his ear. I can't hear it, but her look is lethal.

People start to walk away, here and there. Caleb looks out at the crowd. The rest of the band is looking at him. He seems frozen . . . and then he leans into the mic and says, "Thank you very much. Good night." And walks off.

No, Caleb. No.

Matt and Jon share a perplexed glance. Val is already storming offstage.

I'm frozen, staring, hoping they'll come back on. But after an awkward few seconds of silence, music kicks in on the PA speakers, and a soundman comes up and starts pulling mics off the drums.

I keep standing there, wondering what to do now.

This couldn't have gone worse.

"Hello, Summer Carlson."

Or maybe it could.

My gut clenches.

What lurks in these shark-infested waters . . .

I don't turn around.

He steps up beside me, watching the stage. "It's so nice to have you back." Jason Fletcher. Ari's older brother. He's a scout for Candy Shell Records, aka, the one who took Postcards from me.

He smiles. "And look, you brought me a new band."

MoonflowerAM @catherinefornevr 1m
Or maybe, I really am that foolish version of me. #lifefail #perfectcircle

I'm frozen between urges. To walk away wordlessly? Explain to him what a giant ass he is? To toss this Coke in his face? His wide grin tells me that none of these options would work. Well, maybe the Coke. "What are you doing here?" I ask, looking past him, as if being seen with him is kind of embarrassing.

"Just keeping one eye on little bro," Jason says, "and as always, the other out for new talent. So, that was your new band. Hmm . . . All the parts are there. They've got real potential. Kind of a train wreck just now, but in the right hands . . ."

I glare sideways at him but Jason's grin just grows. He's had his teeth professionally whitened to a sharklike shine.

He's wearing an olive-colored suit jacket over a wife beater, which means we're getting far too much of his hairy chest, and I want to tell him: nobody except cougars like that look, Jason. He's also sporting a hipster hat that might have worked five years ago *if* he was Justin Timberlake, which he is so not. He's a day unshaven in that professional way. Ugh.

But I am not caught totally unprepared. I brought some ammo in case this happened. "I'm surprised you're here," I say. "I saw that Postcards is having trouble selling tickets on their Southeast tour leg."

Jason's smile fades a touch. "Says who?" This sounds like news to him.

"Says the Twitterverse. There's a way that bands push when they need to fill seats. It's pretty easy to spot. You probably wouldn't know."

Jason almost seems like he's considering this, but quickly shrugs. "That's publicity's problem. My job is to find the talent, not change its diapers."

SO MUCH the urge to crush him or throw sand at him or something, anything. Postcards may not be my favorite band right now, but they don't deserve to get hung out to dry. "And so," I say, "if they don't make this tour a success, then what? Wait, I know this story: Less funding for the second record, and soon after that you drop them and send the next fresh batch of faces out."

"Aw, you make me sound so heartless," says Jason.

"I hope so."

Jason keeps smiling, and holds a business card out to me. "I want to talk about this new band of yours. And about you."

"You've got to be kidding me. Why aren't you going after Freak Show? They just killed it."

Jason shrugs. "They did, but they're not really my thing. Don't get me wrong, I'm going to drop them a line. There's a place for them in the game, for sure, but . . . there's no accounting for taste, I guess. Luckily, I'm a tastemaker. And, surprise surprise, you and I like the same things."

"You really know how to make a girl want to barf."

"Please. We might be more alike than you think. I'll admit, I didn't think about you for more than two seconds when I signed Postcards, but . . . here you are again. I'm wondering if I underestimated you. You've definitely got an eye for talent. Maybe we should be working together."

"Um, no."

"Come on," says Jason. "I'd give you an internship, an office, access to all of Candy Shell's media contacts . . . I could have a scout in the minor leagues, and you could take your thing to the next level."

"I already said no." And yet I don't mind being told I was underestimated, and I hate how appealing most of his offer sounds. Everything except working for Jason. If he's what you need to be at the next level, then I have to wonder if I've got what it takes. But there's got to be another way to get there.

Jason pulls his card back. "Well, I'm going to let you think about it. In the meantime, tell your band I thought they were great for a couple songs there. I think they need a little more time to simmer . . ."

"I believe in them," I say.

"Hang on, I wasn't finished," he says. "I am also looking for an opening act for a West Coast tour with Sundays on Mars. Four dates in October. Your band here *might* be just the right fit, if they get their act together."

I try not to give Jason the reaction he wants, which is, *Whoa, REALLY?* Sundays on Mars is a big deal. An opening slot for them would be a huge break. But it's Jason. Once a shark, always a shark . . . right?

"You'll tell them that, won't you?" he prods. "Unless you want me to . . ."

"Okay, fine. Good-bye."

Jason keeps grinning but doesn't move, so I stalk off.

"See you around, partner," he calls after me.

I keep my head down as I head for the stage. On the way, I check my feed, looking for a distraction that will erase Jason from the last two minutes of my life.

The reviews of Dangerheart's all-too-brief set are mixed.

From:

Marissa @fluttershy1346 13m
This is the new band that matters. They are raw and for real.
Enigmatic singer is H-O-T. #Dangerheart

to:

When I get to the side of the stage, Caleb is gone. I don't see Val either. Jon and Matt are packing up their gear while the next band, Thesis in Blood, a college swoon-metal band from Loyola, sets up.

"What happened?" I ask them.

Matt and Jon are both head-down. "Caleb lost it," says Matt.

"Couldn't you tell?" says Jon while disassembling Mission Control.

"Yeah. Where is he?"

Matt just shrugs. Jon waves a hand toward the party. "He took off that way."

As I text Caleb, they start hoisting their gear.

"Where are you guys going?"

"Home," says Jon. "My friend Abe is giving us a ride."

"Can you stick around?" I ask. "I'll find Caleb, and we can have a quick band decompress and—"

"What band?" says Jon. "If this is how it's gonna be, I'm finding another band."

"Come on," I say. "How about we meet up at the Hive tomorrow. Caleb needs a chance to explain."

Matt huffs. "Why?"

"Just . . . please?"

Jon looks to Matt. Matt looks at me.

"Hey, guys!" Maya appears beside me. I want to shoo her away. "Short set, but cool!" She is gazing supportively at Matt. "Your drums sounded great."

"Thanks." Matt flashes a glance at her and then back at me. "Are you coming with us?"

"Come on," I say, but it's halfhearted. Can I really blame them? "Nah. I gotta find Caleb."

Matt's gaze stays on me. Then finally he looks at Maya. "We're going to Mike's Burgers. You wanna go?"

"Oh, well, sure!" Maya hurries over and grabs a drum case.

"I'll be in touch," I say.

Matt has already turned. Jon shrugs. "Kick Caleb in the balls for me, please?"

"Right."

I head back toward the drink hut, but I don't see him. No reply to my text either. I try again.

Summer: Hey, it's just me. Where are you?

I find Missy leaning over the counter whispering into a lava-soaked dude's ear.

"Is Caleb around?" I ask. When I repeat it, she finally glances over.

"He was here. Got a Jell-O shot and a beer and went that way." She points away from the party, up the beach, then adds, with obvious delight, "He was with some girl." I try to hide any and all reaction to that, but I must have one,

131

because Missy adds with a smile, "She was all over him."

"Great. Thanks." I head past the bonfire, where I get side-slammed by a beefy guy in a white baseball cap and a girl in swim goggles who proceed to fall in a giggly tangle. Their friends are laughing like it's *hilarious*. I hate people.

Suddenly Ari appears in front of me, megaphone to his lips. "SUMMER," he says, the electrified voice feeding back. "IS NOW THE TIME FOR THAT F—"

I snatch the megaphone, turn it so the wide mouth faces the sky, grab the coconut cup from the girl to my left, and dump the lightly flaming contents into the megaphone. It shrieks like a wounded duck and sparks jump from it.

"Dude . . . ," says Ari sadly.

I keep walking. Ari probably didn't deserve that. Whatever.

I trudge through the sand, wound so tight I'm barely breathing. I want to find him, but I don't. What girl? What the hell happened to the Caleb I knew? Is this just because I didn't kiss him before the set? Probably not, though that likely didn't help. The last thing he needed was more uncertainty, with all the ghosts around him already. And yet . . . *he was with some girl* . . . suddenly I'm just feeling hamster-to-wheel again, Ethan to Caleb. But no. I know he's not like that. Don't I?

I reach the perimeter of the party, where the sound of the surf can actually compete with the music and voices.

Couples have stumbled away to lie around pawing at each other. Some are splashing each other in the surf like eight-year-olds. Or maybe it's romantic. But maneuvering around the spray of their fun is unbearably annoying. Further up the dark beach, a drum circle drones. The sea breeze carries the echoes of their bong.

I get past the last party satellites, to complete darkness and sea. Stars and cliff-side homes glitter. Part of me wants to just keep on going, on through the night, to whatever new world seems certain to lie at the far end of the coast. Instead, I take a deep breath of the sour air and turn back, walking the tideline toward the firelight. I study the small groups and couples and pass the occasional loner gazing into the dark. Some glance up, hoping I'm the other lost soul they're destined to meet. Sorry.

Finally, I see a figure with the unmistakable outline of Caleb's hair and nose sitting in the sand.

But then the silhouette moves and— Oh, hell. He's not alone.

Someone leaning on his shoulder. Firelight catches blond hair, a petite frame . . .

I hear the murmur of their voices, and move as close as the rustle of waves will allow.

"It just didn't feel right," I hear Caleb saying. "I hate how it always has to feel right, like you have to be perfect."

"You don't. You can't expect that of yourself." Crap. Of

course I know that voice, despite how it's muffled by the contact between cheek and shoulder. Legs side by side . . .

"Jon and Matt are probably mad," Caleb says.

"Just apologize. I'll help. They don't have the burden you do, being lead singer."

Caleb shrugs. "Summer's going to be pissed."

"Obviously," I hear Val say. "But you can't expect her to get it. She's not like us."

Her head falls back to his shoulder, and her hand reaches out and rubs his knee.

"No," I mutter. "Apparently I'm not." Summer the bitch. But I don't even care.

Caleb spins around, flinching away from Val. She looks up at me and glares, as if I'm wrong to be disturbing them. As if she actually has a right to feel that way.

"Summer—" Caleb begins.

I hold his gaze just long enough for him to know, to feel whatever guilt he's capable of feeling, and then I storm off.

Back toward the stupid, stupid, party, back to last year, making the circle of failure complete.

11

I don't want Caleb to follow me, except when I hear his footsteps, hear him calling, I realize that if he hadn't, whatever shred of a chance of this *not* being over would have been lost.

"Summer."

I keep walking, trying to breathe, to fight the tears. I don't want him to see me like this. I don't want him to think I'm this breakable. He'll think it's all because of him and that will only give him more power. These tears aren't about him. They're about me being an idiot.

"Come on, please." He grabs my arm and I spin.

"Come on, what?" I'm nearly yelling. I can't help it. "Is this where you try to convince me that what I just saw was okay? That Val was just *being there* for you, that she understands you in a way that I couldn't possibly—"

"No—"

"—because the two of you are *burdened* with the great task of being lead singers? Spare me—"

"I was going to say I'm sorry! But also that . . . that wasn't my idea back there. I—I didn't even know what that was."

He's saying this with a serious face but he also smells like beer. Not helping. I almost point that out to him, but then I'll just sound like his mother.

"How could you not know what a girl leaning on your shoulder and stroking your knee was? Not to mention your ego."

"She wasn't *stroking*. She just sort of . . . patted me there."

I just look at him.

Caleb throws up his hands. "I'm serious! She followed me after the set. I just wanted to be alone, but she was making sense. Val's smart about stuff. I don't mean you're not, at all, just . . . I—"

"You guys speak the same language, yeah, I've noticed."

"Well, I don't know about that, but . . . whatever. We'd only been there for, like, a minute, when you showed up. I didn't expect her to lean on me like that."

"You didn't stop her."

Caleb glances at the sea, searching for words. "I was

still trying to figure out what to do about it."

"What was there to figure out? We're—or maybe we're not."

"Summer, we *are*, but she's in the band, and I didn't want to make her mad, especially after how I acted on stage. I still owe Matt and Jon an apology."

"They left. And said the band was over."

Caleb bites his lip. "Great."

"They're just mad. They'll probably come around. You were saying, about Val . . ."

"Just that I think she meant it as kind of a friend thing."

"God, Caleb. Girls never mean hands-on-knees as just a friend thing."

"Well, okay . . . but what was I supposed to do? We need Val. And I am not good at holding things together."

"I'm coming around to that idea."

"Besides, you were weird before. What was with you shrugging me off right before the set, when I tried to kiss you? Were you embarrassed? 'Cause I'm not."

"I—" I hate that he's brought this up. It doesn't feel fair, but maybe it is related to everything that's happened, like I feared. "That was me feeling the pressure. Of being here, again. Of being exposed. Having people see me as a serial band groupie who should know better."

"Which is ridiculous."

"Or."

He reaches for my shoulder. I don't react one way or

the other. "You have to believe me. I was just trying not to screw anything else up. I don't think Val was going to try anything. It didn't feel like that. And if she had, I swear I would have stopped her."

I shrug. Wipe at my stupid face. Look away, look back. "Tell me what happened onstage."

Caleb opens his mouth, but then looks out at the water and sighs. "I just lost it. Being here, thinking about Eli, having Freak Show be so good. I let it get to me."

"You should have trusted yourself. Trusted your songs."

"I don't know how to have that kind of faith sometimes. And I had this awful thought, too. I wasn't just freaking out, and then being mad about the fact that I was freaking out, I was also thinking that . . . maybe I *should* fail."

"Why the hell would you think that?"

"Because, I was thinking, *If this crowd likes you, loves you, then what if you're starting down the same path as Eli?* What if success leads me to make a mess of my life, too?"

"Caleb . . ." Hearing this is so tragic I almost well up. I'd never even considered this fear of his, but it makes perfect sense. Add that to everything else . . . I almost want to laugh. "Could this be a bigger mess?"

"I haven't drowned yet."

"Sorry," I say quickly. "Didn't mean it like that."

"I know." Caleb's gaze stays far out in the black sea.

I pull on his arm and we sit on the hard sand. But I do not put an arm around him or a head on his shoulder. Not yet. "I already told you, you're not him."

"Eli or Ethan?"

"Ha. Neither. You need to know that. And I guess so do I."

Caleb digs at the sand with his finger, drawing a ring. "I saw you talking to Ari's older brother, after our set. Isn't he from Candy Shell?"

"Yeah, and he's a jerk."

"Sure . . . I hate to ask, but did he say anything about the band?"

"Actually, he said he liked it. That you guys weren't bad . . ." I should tell him about the touring offer. Wouldn't a professional band manager inform her band about a huge opening gig? If she trusted the person offering. Which I don't. Except he also offered me the internship . . . but I remind myself that I can do it without him. "That was it."

We fall silent and I hate this. I'm still mad at Caleb and yet I'm keeping secrets. How is that any better? I don't understand how things went so far sideways in one night. "I want a do-over," I say.

"Me, too." Caleb reaches over and rubs the back of my hand. It feels so excellent. Still not moving any arms or leaning my head though. Not yet.

"There they are." We look up to find Randy. He drops down beside me. He's soaked in red goo.

"Tell me you didn't do that," Caleb says, sounding equal parts awed and mortified.

139

"Had to try the fire pit!" He slaps Caleb's shoulder. "Big old hairy guys are money for this crowd, especially when they fall in a sideways cannonball and soak half the audience."

"That was your real goal," Caleb guesses.

Randy salutes. "Just doing my duty to my stereotypes." He wipes more of the sweet-smelling slick from around his eyes. "So," he says, looking past me to Caleb, "got a case of the crazies up there, huh?"

"No, just messed up." I catch Caleb glaring at Randy.

"What?" I ask.

Randy raises his eyebrows at us. "Nothing, I guess." He starts running his fingers over his beard and flicking red goo off.

Caleb is back to digging in the sand.

"Caleb, what is it?"

"Nothing, it's nothing. I just freaked. I already told you."

Randy rolls his eyes. "Dude, stop being an idiot and tell her."

"Yeah." I turn his chin toward me. "You heard him."

Caleb shrugs. "It's no big deal!" He's practically whining.

"Clearly it is."

Caleb runs his hands slowly through his hair, then looks at me. "Fine. Randy is referring to my shrink-approved anxiety issues. Generalized anxiety disorder, technically. I have medication I can take when it gets too crazy, but that's not that often. And I don't like how it dulls me."

I feel my shields going down, and I rub between his shoulders. "Why didn't you tell me that?"

"I don't know," says Caleb. "I was hoping I could manage it and you wouldn't have to know. It's not a very cool thing for a potential lead-singer rock star to have. And I hate when people classify me."

"I wouldn't have classified you."

"Yeah, but . . . once people know you have a weakness, they assume it's always going to be an issue, which technically it is, but it can be an excuse. Not for me, for them. Like if the going got rough, you might decide to find a band whose singer didn't have a *condition*."

"Jesus, Caleb . . ." I'd tell him he's an idiot for even thinking such a thing, and yet, flash to earlier this week, when I imagined him dropping me because I couldn't be his sing-in-harmony girl (though there's still tonight's display, but I'm thinking more and more that Val was the main instigator there). "I like you, not some idealized version of you. The anxiety's part of what makes you, you."

"It was part of Eli, too," he says.

"You're not him."

Randy chimes in, "Listen to your manager. You are *so* not Eli. And I mean that in the best possible way."

Caleb shrugs, as if he's considering believing it, but that's all. "The point is, every show feels like a high wire.

Which can be great, until you fall off. With everything tonight . . . Sometimes it swallows me up. And the worst part is I get how important a night like tonight is, like how the world is an enormous and constantly moving place, and I want to grab on to moments for all they're worth, except then I get so worked up that it backfires." He sighs. "It's a lonely feeling."

My heart is time traveling, applying this new information to everything from tonight. Not that tonight didn't happen, but there was more to it, and I get why he didn't tell me, and I just want it all to be over and for neither of us to feel lonely when we're right here together. "Far comets," I say quietly. I put my arm around him.

"It's okay, nephew," says Randy. "The great thing about rock 'n' roll is that there's always another gig."

"I guess," says Caleb. "Right now I'm just hungry."

"Burritos," says Randy, as if he's making a wish to the sea.

"Reuben with pickles," says Caleb absently.

"Ask for Vic," I add, and I put my head on his shoulder.

There's a moment of silence. I feel a strange sensation and turn to find Randy staring at us. His brow is furrowed like he's heard something blasphemous. "What did you just say?"

"It was in a letter I found," says Caleb, "inside Eli's old bag. I'm guessing you didn't know it was there."

His expression contorts more. Now it's like we're saying

142

something blasphemous in a foreign language. "What kind of letter?"

"To me. From a few months before he died."

Randy rubs his face slowly. "Holy crap, really? And it said something about Vic?"

"You know who that is?" I ask.

Randy nods slowly. "Vic is a legend." To himself: "I mean, that's gotta be who he's talking about, right?" To the ocean: "Obviously, who else would it be?"

"Earth to Randy," says Caleb. He's dead serious now.

"Vic is a waiter at Canter's Deli," says Randy. "On Fairfax. It's a classic joint. Allegiance used to go there after shows. You'd see famous bands, too, and TV stars. Eli loved going there."

"Is there a Daisy there?" I ask, remembering that other line in the letter. "Or did Eli know a Daisy?"

Randy scratches his sticky beard. "Not that I know of."

"Did you ever go to Canter's with him?" Caleb asks.

"Yeah," says Randy. "Early on, a bunch, but . . ." In his pause, I sense him skipping over something. Something big and subterranean. "Not in the later years."

"He wrote the letter right before the Hollywood Bowl show," Caleb adds.

"On the last tour? Jeez," says Randy. "Did it even make sense? Eli was off the deep end around that time. Heavy drug use, and really paranoid."

"About what?" I can feel Caleb wondering the same

143

thing I am. Does Randy know about Eli's lost songs? Does he know about "the tapes" that the letter refers to?

"Ah," says Randy. "It's complicated."

"Hello," I say, "we're eighteen. We get complicated."

"Sure, but this is boring complicated. I think Eli felt like the other guys were going to screw him out of his money. Eli and Kellen, the bass player, they *hated* each other by the end. Like, separate-cars-to-and-from-the-gig hated. After Eli bailed on the tour, they tried to sue him for lost royalties on the canceled shows and . . . man, it was as ugly as rock 'n' roll gets. They were even threatening to go after his family, since Eli had lost most of his money, but they dropped the lawsuit when he died."

I grip Caleb's shoulder. The letter's warning: doing something drastic to clean up the mess . . . I wonder if he'll bring it up. I hope my squeeze gives him the message to keep this between us, for now.

Caleb must feel the same. He digs intently at the sand, then adds, "I want to go there."

"Canter's?" Randy asks. "Sure, we could go sometime."

"How about now?" I suggest. "I think we've done about all there is to do here." As I say it, a guy comes staggering down the beach, reaches the surf, and barfs into the sea. "Well, except that."

Randy looks at Caleb with concern. "You sure?"

Caleb flashes a half smile at me, the first in what seems

like years. "Actually, yeah." He starts to get up. "That sounds great."

"Well, I could certainly use some matzo-ball soup," says Randy. He looks down at himself. "Maybe I'll say I'm an extra in a horror film."

As we walk back, I hope I was reading the moment right. Is Canter's too close to more ghosts? Caleb is Fret Face and quiet, but I need to wait until we've navigated this hideous party one last time before I can ask him.

We return to the stage for Caleb's gear. Val's stuff is already gone. Lucky break, though I was directing a short fantasy in my brain where I would march right up to her and ask her, you know, "What the hell?"

As we trudge up the dune, the echoing drums and drunken shouts fading behind us, I fall back beside Caleb. "I know going to another of Eli's haunts doesn't sound fun, but that stuff Randy said . . ."

Caleb nods. "The trouble Eli was in . . . if he was thinking of killing himself, then the stuff about Canter's might be a clue. If he knew he wouldn't be around to give us the tapes, then maybe . . ."

"Vic knows something," I finish.

"Exactly what I was thinking."

Despite all this possibility, not to mention all that's happened tonight, the pure gravity of what he's saying hits me again. I can't even imagine not having a father, never mind learning that he was a famous dead guy whose footsteps I'm

145

following in. I'm holding Caleb's guitar case while he lugs his amp against his chest, but I reach out with my free hand and touch his chin. I just want to be so careful with him; I need him to know it.

"You don't have to say 'us,'" I say. "You're going through so much. I just want to help. It doesn't have to be—"

"Summer."

My name in full. I'm there.

"I want it to be us." He glances back at the beach, almost like the ghosts of tonight's mess are wailing to him. "If that's okay."

"Yes, Caleb," I say. "It is more than okay." Finally there are smiles. He steps toward me and tries to lean in, but nearly falls over with the weight of his amp. I catch the bottom of it. "Crushing my toes would really ruin the mood."

"Sorry." We kiss, and as soon as our lips touch, it seems like the sound of the surf and the smell of salt increase and we could be anywhere, marooned, just us—

"Ugh. Come on already!" Randy calls from above.

But we're not. We're here. Tonight.

With business to do.

I pull away, rubbing Caleb's cheek. "Come on, let's go see Vic."

MoonflowerAM @catherinefornevr 2m
People have this idea about LA. I have that idea and I live here. But then
there is this other LA...

"*You* want to see Vic."

The young host sneers, eyes fixed just past us, his question delivered in a flatline tone. He's a few years older than us. Aside from his black apron, his fashionable square glasses and coiffed hair scream struggling actor.

"Yeah," says Caleb, trying to match the venom. "Does he still work here?"

The host gives us a theater-camp-quality eye roll, and continues delivering answers as questions and questions as answers. "Of course he does? You're sure it's Vic you're looking for."

"Do you need us to say it in Shakespearean, Kenneth

Branagh?" Randy snaps. He's been standing over by the door, checking out a line of signed rock-star photos on the wood-paneled wall, like Guns N' Roses and Van Halen. He squeezed out his shirt just before we came in, but he's still dripping red goo on the floor. Caleb nods to the puddle, and Randy rubs his foot over it, trying to look casual.

The host doesn't notice. He's busy rolling his eyes and running his hand through his hair. He counts out three menus like this is the most menial thing he's had to do all day. "Right this way?"

He leads us into the main dining room. It's full of every Hollywood type, from expensive and slick to blue collar and lumpy; hipsters, hags . . . it's the kind of place that should still have swirls of cigarette smoke mingling above every table. The booths are brown vinyl. There's a counter along one wall, the clatter of the kitchen beyond that, and the din of an unpolished rock band tumbles from the lounge down a short staircase.

But it's the ceiling that captivates me. It's a mosaic of backlit glass panels, depicting autumn foliage like I saw once on a family trip to Vermont. It covers almost the whole dining area in a serene glow of orange and yellow, with traces of robin's egg blue sky. Does it make any sense in Los Angeles? No! But there is something about it, something so perfect. It's one of those things that's just amazing, for no other reason than its amazingness. I don't want to know why they chose that ceiling. I just want it to be.

Struggling actor seats us in a booth in the center of the room. He's gone before the menus hit the table.

"Gotta get the matzo-ball soup," says Randy. "A Reuben for sure, order of pickles, potato knishes . . ."

"I'm not that hungry," I say, still gazing up at the leaves. Randy shrugs. "Get whatever you want. That's just for me."

"I don't see it." Caleb is running his finger down the list of sandwiches.

I open my menu and look, too. The menu is exhaustive. After a minute, I agree: "There's no Reuben version with pickles."

"That's because nobody eats them that way," says Randy. "Except Eli. Pickles on the side? Sure. But in the sandwich . . . I think he just did it to be different."

"What do you want."

A man has appeared at our table. It's like he just popped out of thin air, or more likely out of a time vortex. He's wiry, and wearing a black silken shirt that billows around his skinny frame and is tucked into dark jeans. A toothpick rolls around between his lips. There's a cigarette at-the-ready behind his left ear. His thin gray-black hair is slicked over his oval skull, and his face is all shadow and stubble.

"Vic," says Randy. "You remember me?"

Vic just looks at him.

"That's okay," says Randy, suddenly deferential, "I used to come here with the guys from Allegiance to North."

No reaction. Vic taps the pencil in his hand against a small black notebook.

Randy's eyes flash to Caleb. "This is Eli's son."

Vic looks down. His expression barely changes, but his voice does. "I liked that kid." Less like sandpaper now, more like shag carpet. And coming from Vic, the word "liked" sounds nearly like a profession of love. "Damn shame what happened to him." His eyes sharpen, like he's analyzing Caleb. "You couldn't have been very old when he died."

"No," says Caleb. "I never knew him."

Vic nods. He flips open his notebook. "What do you want." Apparently that's it.

Randy starts to list his order. "Matzo-ball soup, potato knish, order of blintzes, Reuben . . ." But Vic isn't writing. Instead, he looks back at Caleb, checks his watch, and looks over toward the door.

"What?" Caleb says quietly.

I wonder . . . so I say it for him. "We'll split a Reuben with pickles."

Vic's eyes finally flash to me. He's either studying me, or considering killing me. But he nods slightly. "And to drink?"

"Two Cokes."

He collects the menus. "Be right back."

"I—" Randy starts but seems to have the good sense to stop. "Well, he's as unfriendly as I remember. Do you think he heard my order?"

A server brings us water, and then suddenly Vic stalks past us in a major hurry. We all watch him as he proceeds to one of the semicircle booths along the wall. There are four scene-sters slouched there, fitting every cliché. Vic says something quietly. A shadow passes over the alpha guy's face.

"Excuse me?" he says.

Vic holds his hands up, as if to say "Settle down," then he leans close over the table. We can hear the faint murmur of his voice under the din.

"The FUCK—" one of the dudes starts to say.

And then who knows what Vic says, but suddenly they all look down into their laps, like they're being scolded by their mothers. And then, together, they stand up, pick up their plates, and slide out of the booth. Vic whistles and motions and a bus girl comes over and helps gather their cups and cutlery. Vic leads the group to a booth across the room. Then he strides back past us.

"Wonder what that was all about," says Caleb.

"Vic is connected," says Randy. "Let's just say, that guy could arrange for things to happen."

"This way." Vic is in front of us again. He collects our napkins and silverware and adds our menus to the one he already has under his arm.

We scoot out and follow him to the booth he just emp-tied. He motions us in. As we sit, I notice the displaced guys leering at us, but they keep quiet.

"Here you go," Vic says, businesslike, putting the new cutlery in front of us. "I'll leave a menu if you want anything else," he says, placing one on the table.

"This is weird," I say, glancing around the booth. "Is this the VIP seating or something?"

"Kind of," says Randy quietly. "This is the exact seat we sat in after the Hollywood Bowl show."

"Guys," says Caleb, "check out this menu."

The menu Vic left looks nothing like the ones we ordered from. It's folded and beat up, the laminate cloudy and chipped, the black edges frayed.

"That's the old-style menu," says Randy. "They replaced those years ago."

Caleb slowly opens the menu, and I think we all feel it. Something is going on here, as if we're barely in control anymore.

"Check it out," Caleb says quietly. He points to the top corner of the inside page. Someone has etched blue lettering into the plastic with a ballpoint pen.

AⲦN

No one comments; instead we just start scouring the menu from three angles, looking for clues.

When I see one, I can't help whispering: "There."

Halfway down the first page, under the egg dishes, the "I" in "Spanish Omelette" is colored over, a blue indent.

"Here's another one." Randy points to the opposite page. The "B" in "Blintzes."

"Here's a 'T,'" says Caleb.

"Do you think it's a message?" says Randy.

Caleb and I don't answer. We already know it is. Under the table, he squeezes my leg. There is so much energy vibrating around us right now, excitement, fear, potential, the protective cloak of a secret, all of that and then some.

We lean close, combing the menu. I get my phone out of my bag and open a notepad. We start from the "I" and call out letters, our fingers running over the plastic, feeling for indents like ancient runes.

"T."

"S."

"It's . . . ?" I say.

More letters.

"A-l-l . . ."

"About . . ."

"The . . ."

"Vinyl."

"Of course it is," says Randy. To the air beside him: "Vinyl always sounds way better than CDs." To the ceiling: "Not to mention freakin' mp3s. Might as well flush your—"

"That can't be it," says Caleb. "It has to mean more."

I hear the disappointment in his voice, and feel it, too, like an adrenaline wave just broke inside me, and now there's a mess of foam running this way and that. "Yeah. He wouldn't send us here, to Vic, to this menu, just to make a vague reference, would he?"

"Unless he was high when he did it," says Caleb.

That crossed my mind, too, but I'm not giving up hope yet. "No, it's got to be more specific."

"I don't get it. What were you guys expecting?" Randy asks.

"I don't even know." Caleb leans back and lets his head fall against the back of the booth.

"Eli was into collecting vinyl," Randy muses. "Maybe he left his records for you? I don't know what would have happened to them, though."

I keep scouring the menu, but there's nothing else there.

"Maybe we've been making this whole thing up," says Caleb.

Vic returns with a large tray by his shoulder and starts laying out our food. He's mostly just doing his work like normal, but at one point, he looks at Caleb, then over to me.

Something about his expression . . . and I find myself asking: "Is there anything else?" Maybe he knows what this is, what we're missing.

He glances away from me for a second, almost like he's looking at something behind me. Then back to the table. "Do you need a refill on the waters?" He asks like he has no idea.

"No."

As he leaves, I glance over my shoulder but there's nothing there except the blank tan wall and a black-and-white picture of an old actress.

Randy starts digging in. I lean back and join Caleb, shoulders touching, gazing up into the brilliant autumn leaves.

"This was dumb," Caleb says quietly. "I didn't even want him in my life in the first place." He sounds so defeated.

"I'm sorry." I'm not sure what else to say. I feel bad for suggesting we come here, for getting our hopes up. Exhaustion weighs me down. My legs are sore from all that trudging through sand, and my whole body feels sticky from the salty beach air. As I turn my head to look at Caleb, my neck sticks to the brown vinyl of the booth.

Vinyl.

I sit up. Start running my hands over the seat around me.

"What are you doing?"

"The booth." I say. "Vinyl." It doesn't seem likely. . . . Thousands of people have sat here in the years since Eli was here, but . . . I examine it anyway. Caleb starts to do the same. Running our hands over the contours of the seat, then spaces between cushions, the underside where the seat meets wood. Then I remember Vic's gaze. I feel behind the curved top of the booth, in the crevice where the vinyl meets the back wall.

My fingers find a sharp edge, a tear in a seam, and a

sliver of exposed padding. I press around it . . . and find something hard. I pinch and pull. . . .

And remove an object.

"I found something." I spin around.

It's a small rectangular case made of opaque plastic, about the length of a credit card, and a half-inch thick.

"That's an old videotape, right?" says Caleb.

"DV tape," says Randy. "Late nineties, I'd guess. Wait . . ." He looks at us, understanding making him pale even with the red residue. "Is that from . . . Eli?"

"We think so." Caleb takes it from my hand. Turns it over.

"What the hell is on it?"

Caleb looks at me. *Should we tell him?* I nod.

"I think it's 'Exile,'" says Caleb.

"EX—" Randy nearly shouts, simultaneously hopping in his seat. He contains himself and leans close. "Exile? You mean the *song* 'Exile'? The—"

"Yes, that one. And maybe the other ones, too. 'Encore,' 'Abbey Road.'"

Randy gazes at the tape again like it's a sacred artifact.

A message from a dead man.

Vic doesn't return. We nibble at our food, barely. Caleb holds the tape in a tight fist on the seat between us.

After a few minutes of stunned silence and glances in all directions, wary of our secret being known, we make plans: Randy will search out a DV camcorder in the morning, as soon as vintage stores are open. Caleb and I will meet at his house.

"What about the rest of the band?" I ask him.

"Can you trust the others?" Randy asks. "How long have you known them?"

This is what I am thinking, too, even when I can remove my obvious desire for Val not to be there.

But Caleb shakes his head. "I already blew up one band because of this." He taps the case. "They probably think tonight was just me being some lead-singer diva. They all should've walked offstage when I started that other song, but they stuck it out. They had my back."

Caleb's right. "It will be hard to keep this from them," I say. "It will probably just mess things up further." When my Val-mistrusting side can keep quiet, it feels like the right move is to tell them. And I don't mention the other thought on my mind, because I know Caleb isn't sure what he would do with these lost songs, but I can almost guarantee that the rest of the band will immediately picture what I do: Dangerheart revealing them to the world by playing them live.

Caleb thinks for a second, then nods. "Let's tell them."

13

I wake up early Saturday, though it could never be early enough to beat Carlson Squared, professional go-getters. I hear them bustling downstairs, and decide to wait out the fray and check email in bed.

There's one reply I was hoping for, from Marni Rodgers. She's in charge of the Harvest Slaughter. People dress like slasher film characters, zombies, or any other ghouls, and the bands dress up, too. We even pick a costume winner, who has the honor of getting Carrie'd onstage (it's fake blood; one of the PTA dads works for Sony).

```
Thanks for writing, Summer. We do have
one more slot left for the event and we'd
```

be happy to have Dangerheart. They will
open for Freak Show. (Did you see them last
night?? OMG!) Cheersies! —MR

"Cheersies," I mutter. I wonder if Marni even saw Dangerheart. Maybe that was for the best. I write back and
accept. And then it occurs to me: what if we can also show
up there and reveal a lost Allegiance to North song to the
world? Can't jump that gun, though. But at least, in spite
of last night, we have a next gig. That is, if the band is still
together. I hope Caleb was able to get them to come over.

Mom is already out running errands when I get downstairs. Dad is watching a news talk show while reading from
his tablet. On the weekends, he gives himself permission to
dress down, but he's still wearing khakis and shoes and a
polo shirt tucked in.

"How was last night?" he asks as I get coffee and toast
a bagel.

"Not bad. Kind of a dumb party. Then we went for
food."

"'We' being . . . this new band you like?"

"New band I manage," I say.

"Ah. I thought you weren't into that anymore?"

"These guys are good," I say. Then, in case I sound like
I'm taking it too seriously for Dad's taste, I add, "I don't
know, it's fun." "Fun" makes it sound like a little hobby and
keeps him from inquiring further.

I sit down to eat. Dad joins me. Uh-oh.

"I've been thinking. . . . ," he says. He's using "Dad-Friend" tone. "How about we go to see a couple schools the weekend after next? You guys have that professional development day, so it's a long weekend."

"Oh. Um."

"I found a couple good pre-law programs and we can make a loop. Stanford Friday and UC Berkeley on Saturday. They offer tours. I may have even scheduled a couple, and mentioned your law interest."

I feel a surge of frustration, wishing once again that Dad might somehow see who I really want to be on his own, but I reply, "Sure." Except as I'm saying it I remember that the Harvest Slaughter is the same weekend. "Well, but, Stanford? Really? There's no way I'm getting in there."

"Cat, come on. You don't know that. And there's no harm in looking."

"Well, okay." Of course that wasn't going to work. "But can we be back by Saturday night? There's a dance."

"Oh, didn't realize that. You have a date?"

"Yeah." Technically, not a lie. I have a date with a band. "I'd really like to go. This year is my last chance for this kind of thing."

"Ah." Dad taps on his tablet. "Well, I think we can make it back by the evening. . . ." He doesn't sound thrilled.

"Are you sure that's okay?" I ask.

"Yeah, that will be fine." He sounds disappointed, but

160

I know that he's sensitive to the idea of me growing up and leaving, and he always wants me to embrace what he thinks of as the traditional high school things. A date to a dance fits his parameters. "That will be fine." He taps on his tablet. "And is your new band playing the dance?"

He's also smart enough to read between the lines. "Oh, yeah, I think they are."

Dad's brow furrows as he types. "Looks like there's a different tour time we can get." His gaze flashes to me. "I just . . . you were so upset a few weeks ago. I mean I know you love music. . . . These band types though . . ." I know what he'll say next. "I know what they're like." He's referring to how he used to play piano and was in a cover band for, like, three months in high school.

"Dad, it's no big deal," I say, a little frustration slipping into my voice. "They're nice guys. One's a girl."

"Okay, but . . ." I can hear Dad shuffling through what to say. "I just picture you with, you know, other kids more like you."

I shove bagel in and just sort of nod. Then I wait him out. It's not until Mom is back and I have the car and am driving through the exclusionary gate of the Fronds, our sterile lab of a housing community, that I slam the steering wheel and start swearing at everything from the pedestrians to the clouds in the sky. But mostly at my dad. *Kids more like you* . . . I know he means well, but for who? For Catherine. He doesn't even know Summer exists.

As I drive into town, I look around the sprawl of communities just like the Fronds, and more than ever, all I can think is *I* . . .

Don't.

Want.

This.

I feel like being here, behind these walls, how could the magic or chance opportunity of life ever find you? This place feels like a choice for safety over possibility, money over art, conformity over individuality. What are these people living for? From here you can't actually reach for your dreams. Instead, you just idolize those who do, but also celebrate when they fall, when they burn out and self-destruct from trying. That way we have our cautionary tales. They make us feel safe, remind us that we're not missing anything while we sit inside these prisons.

Or then again maybe I'm wrong. So many people choose this. Choose the Fronds. Choose Catherine. So many people want that for me. Smart, caring people. If I reject it, will I realize someday that I was a fool? Would it be better to be safe and unhappy than in peril and alive?

Poor car steering wheel, but by the time I get to Caleb's, I've cooled off. Their house is small but cute, a mission style with pretty flowers out front.

Caleb's mom lets me in. "Hi, I'm Charity," she says brightly.

"Hi," I say, "I'm—" I pause for a second, stuck between

162

saying Catherine or Summer. Charity is dressed for the office, a portfolio under her arm, and this trips my Carlson Squared circuits. But then I hate myself for even debating this, and now I'm standing there like an idiot—

"Summer," says Charity. "It's so nice to meet you." She sticks out her hand and we shake. "Caleb mentioned you the other day, and when I asked him about you he got all grumpy and said you were 'cool.' That's how I could tell he's really into you."

"Oh." I try not to blush, but there's no holding it back.

"I think it's so great that you manage the band," says Charity. She shifts the stack of papers to the other side, and I catch a faint smell of cigarettes. "I loved hanging out with bands when I was your age, but I never graduated from groupie status." She glances to the sky, like her past life is up there somewhere. Then she shrugs. "Well, except for two weeks as the drummer in an all-girl Zeppelin cover band."

"Wow," I say. "That sounds pretty awesome."

"Awesomely terrible."

"Well, my mom can't utter a single sentence that cool." I feel guilty immediately after saying this, even if it's true.

"Bah." Charity waves her hand, then checks her watch. "Gotta run. People to save, insurance companies to swear at. Here, I'll show you downstairs."

I find Caleb, Jon, and Matt sitting on the carpet around a coffee table.

"I'll see you around dinner, Caleb," says Charity.

163

"Okay, good luck," Caleb replies. There's something in their back-and-forth, so easy and understanding, more like they are partners than parent-kid, at least the version I know. Two people whose identities are not secrets from each other. I realize that while it sucks to have my parents want a different version of me, it's just as bad that I want a different version of them.

"It was nice to meet you," Charity says to me.

"You, too."

Caleb, Jon, and Matt are playing one of those games with a giant map and the little die-cast armies. There are soldiers and monsters. They're playing as if nothing happened last night. I try to go with that. "Wow, that's the least rock 'n' roll thing I've ever seen." I snap a picture though, and post it. People love when artists appear doing nerdy things.

"League of Empires," says Caleb. "Dragons, armies, dragon-armies."

"And damsels," says Jon in a faux British accent. "Damsel assassins. Want to play?"

"No thanks." I look at Caleb, trying to ask with my eyes if everything is okay.

"We're waiting for Randy and Val," he says simply.

Matt hasn't made eye contact with me yet. His hair is hanging down in his eyes, and he's wearing a vintage AtoN concert shirt, the iconic one that says "Follow Your Allegiance" with an arrow pointing up. He probably doesn't know yet the coincidence in his wardrobe choice. "Did things go okay with Maya?" I ask, figuring he won't like my asking but doing it anyway.

"Fine," he says grumpily, as predicted. "She's okay."

Jon glances at him sideways, then shares a look with Caleb, who rolls his eyes.

They keep playing, flipping cards and rolling dice, moving their little pieces around and erupting in swears now and then as one player's band of orcs decapitates another's cavalry, and so on.

Finally, a van engine rumbles outside and Randy bursts in, a tangled mass of technology cradled in his arms. "Found one that works, finally." He hurries over to the entertainment center, yanks it from the wall, and begins fiddling with cables.

I glance at Caleb. His eyes have followed Randy. Fret Face is back.

"So, now are you going to tell us what this is?" Jon asks. The shadow of last night crosses his face.

Caleb shakes his head and rolls the dice. "When Val gets here."

Randy curses at the web of cables behind the TV. "Why does your mom still have a VCR?"

The guys keep playing, but after half an hour, there's still no Val.

"What time did you tell her to be here?" I ask Caleb.

He looks at the clock. "Eleven." It's nearly twelve.

Finally, there's a knock at the door. Caleb heads up. I hear him talking in a low voice as he returns, with Val behind him. Not hiding his conversation, just one to one, and that of course is totally fine but the intimacy of it annoys me, and I tell myself not to stew, but then stew anyway.

Val is slouched in an oversized sweatshirt, her hair tied back and beneath an orange-brimmed hat that says "Reno" in script letters. Same jeans she's worn most every day. I even recognize the lavender socks. Her skin is pale and dark circles ring her eyes. She looks like she's barely slept. Her frown is apparently her default setting. I don't say anything to her, but I expect that, assuming she has some sense of decency, she'll offer me a hello or something. After all, she was the one all over Caleb when I'm pretty sure it was clear that he was spoken for. But no, she doesn't even look at me, just drops to the couch and tucks into a ball.

"Hey, Val," says Jon.

"Hey."

"You got it?" Caleb asks Randy.

Randy falls back on his butt. "Yes, finally. Welcome to the last century." He holds out his hand and Caleb passes him the tape.

"What's that?" Jon asks.

"So . . ." Caleb shoves his hands in his pockets. "I have some things to tell you, and after, maybe last night will make at least some kind of sense. . . ."

He does a good job with it, telling them everything

166

about Eli, though he doesn't read them the contents of the letter. And when he's done, they react:

Jon: "Holleee . . . shitballs."

Matt: "Wow."

Val: "Did your mom say why she waited until now?"

"She did," says Caleb, and then he doesn't add anything else. I wonder if this is partly for my benefit, drawing a line between what I get to know and what Val gets to know. If it is, I appreciate it.

I also expect Val to have some snarky response to the shutdown, but she just mutters, "Okay, then."

"So . . ." Caleb looks to Randy. "Let's see it, I guess."

"You haven't watched it yet?" Jon asks.

Caleb's eyes shift. "I . . . thought about watching it first but . . . I didn't really want to. The whole thing is so weird."

"We're here for you, man," says Matt.

Caleb joins me on the couch. Out of the corner of my eye, I see Val producing a Coke and a bottle of Tylenol from her bag.

"Here we go," says Randy. The screen turns blue. Then the videotape starts to play.

There's a wobbling view of a ceiling. Long fluorescent lights and then green walls. More shaking. A door comes into view. A hand reaches out and locks it.

Blur of movement. The camera slowly focuses. It's been placed on a surface.

A green counter. In a bathroom. Stepping into frame is

a tall, lanky guy. He sits on the edge of the counter, holding an acoustic guitar. He's in a skinny Weezer T-shirt and gray polyester pants. His hair is lighter than Caleb's and pressed this way and that with product. His eyes, though, the slope of his nose and the cleft of his chin . . . similar.

"Hey, Eli," Randy says quietly.

I squeeze Caleb's hand. He squeezes back weakly. I can't even tell if he's breathing.

"Okay, here we go," Eli says, waving, and there's something skewed about his movements, and I realize Eli isn't taping himself, he's taping the reflection of himself in the mirror. And the angle of the camera is just off center, which makes him strangely ethereal, ever so slightly disconnected from reality, and all the more like a ghost speaking from the beyond. It's a cool visual choice, and yet, isn't it strange to think about composition when you're making a video for a son you never knew? It seems oddly theatrical. "Welcome to the secret recordings of Allegiance's black sheep." He smiles to himself, but it looks halfhearted.

There are distant sounds behind him: thumps and muffled voices, like how the other bands sound through the wall at the Hive.

Eli glances off camera, a shadow crossing his face. When he looks back he says, "Nobody knows what I'm doing in here. . . . Well, they *think* they know." This makes him laugh again, but also shudder. He's twitchy. His eyes rarely stay in one place, and his arms and shoulders are alive

168

in constant, tiny movements. It seems likely that drugs have been on the menu, and will be again sooner than later.

"Those are the Hollywood Bowl bathrooms," Randy says, adding, "the backstage ones."

Eli takes a deep breath and steadies his gaze into the camera. "Hey, far comet," he says, looking through the screen and through time to his son. "Or whoever's found this. Maybe you're a worker at a city dump. Maybe you're an alien. Woooo . . ." He bounces his hand around on the air like it's a flying saucer. "Either way, welcome to my bathroom sessions." He starts speaking in a slightly British accent: "In which we secretly complete the last three songs we will ever write."

This makes Caleb release a tight exhale. I put my arm around him. This must be excruciating. As I do this, I hear a huff from beside me, but I'm not looking over at Val. She doesn't get to be part of this.

"Okay . . ." Eli glances at the door again. "I gotta be quick. Let's see . . ." His hands move over the strings, and he strums out a couple chords, not in any rhythm. "Yeah," he says to himself, "there it is. This is a new song I've been calling 'Exile.'"

"Dude," Matt whispers, and I can feel us all holding our breath as Eli starts to play.

"That was, D," Jon says, peering at the screen. "A minor . . . to F?" He's asking Caleb, but Caleb doesn't seem to hear him.

"F," says Randy.

Eli starts strumming. Slow and hypnotic chords in progression. Like when Caleb played "On My Sleeve," there is something solitary and almost more engrossing about a single guitar.

"That bathroom has awesome reverb," Jon says randomly.

Eli repeats the chord progression, head down. He's lost in it. Then he starts to hum, a wordless melody. It's lonely and searching, and . . . huge. Like if Coldplay had soul.

Then the chords change, slightly more busy, the tension higher, and Eli's head comes up. His eyes are still closed, his face looking pained, and he sings:

Living in Exile, without you . . .
Living in Exile, without you . . .

He hangs on a chord . . . "G," says Jon . . . then starts back into the verse. Humming again. There are impressions of words here and there, like ideas are coming to him.

But pounding on the door cuts him off.

Eli's reaction is sudden. His face contorts all the way to rage, and he shakes in an all-over tremor. "Motherf . . . ," he starts, mumbling a slew of swears to himself. It's one part deeply angry, and yet one part . . . well, a little crazy-person. Unstable. The other side of Eli. Or one of many.

There's a muffled voice.

"All right, already, fuck!" Eli shouts. "I'm coming."

He looks back to the camera. His face switches back to calm. It's unnerving how fast it happens, especially with the mirror skew. "Okay. I've got lyrics, just need to get them worked into the melody. I'll record more tomorrow night."

He reaches the camera. Sound of fingers on buttons . . . the screen goes blue.

We all watch the blank screen. Waiting for more.

After ten seconds, Randy starts to fast-forward. There's only the whine of spinning tape. "Huh." The rest is blank. He pops it out. "The next night must be on another tape."

"Whoa, okay, just hold on for one sec," says Jon. "Did we just see what I think we saw?"

"You did," says Caleb.

"'Exile.' One of Allegiance's lost songs," Jon breathes. "Do you think he recorded all three?"

"No idea," says Caleb. "His letter made it sound that way."

"Son of a bitch," says Val.

"You okay?" Matt asks.

I look over and see Val wiping her eyes. When she sees me noticing, she makes her deepest scowl yet. "Yes, fine. That's just, really freakin' sad, you know? That song was going to be amazing. That bastard had it all right there in his head . . . but he put it in the ocean instead. So self-destructive."

It's odd to me to hear this coming from Val, who seems

right on the edge of similar behavior.

"Okay, but," Jon wonders, "are we thinking there's actually another tape?"

"If there is, he would have hidden it," Caleb thinks aloud. "He said, 'tomorrow night.' Maybe at the next show?" He looks to Randy. "Where did they play after LA?"

Randy scratches his beard. "Can't remember. Their last show was in New York City, but that was about a week after the Hollywood Bowl. That's when Eli took off. Like, literally he went AWOL and the band had to cancel the rest of the tour. But after LA . . ." Randy sounds distant.

"Were you at that Hollywood Bowl show?" I ask him.

"No," he says. "Not any shows on that tour. It's just weird to see him now . . ." He trails off.

"I'll look up the tour," says Jon, his finger flicking over his tablet. "Mmm, late nineties are thin for detail online, like looking into ancient history . . ."

"Wait," says Matt. "Guys . . ." We find him turning around and pointing his thumbs at his back. "It's right here." The back of his Allegiance shirt has a column of show dates.

"Nice fashion choice, Matty!" Jon jumps up and runs his finger down the dates. "San Francisco," he reports. "They played the Fillmore."

"Would the tape be in a restaurant again?" Randy wonders. "The place they ate after the show? That was always Eli's favorite part, when the pressure of the show was behind him and he could just unwind."

172

"Eli's letter mentioned a Daisy," I offer. "Maybe that's the clue for the second tape."

"We're talking about this like it might be real," says Matt, sounding awestruck.

"That looked pretty real to me," says Jon. "And, if there really is another tape, and Eli wanted you to have it, shouldn't we *definitely* do that?"

Everyone looks to Caleb. He's been quiet. He seems so overwhelmed by all this. Finally, he says, "How are we even going to get to San Francisco?"

"I can take you guys," says Randy.

"My parents aren't going to let me road trip to SFO without a reason," says Matt. "I know, very *little brother* of me." He fires a glance at me.

I let it go, already typing in my phone. "What if we had a gig up there?" I have one idea in mind, and pull up the show calendar in the *SF Weekly*.

"They might be cool with that," says Matt.

I see two things on the calendar that could work, both on the same Friday night, in two weeks. One is an underground pop series called *Forecast: Sweaters!* that happens at an all-ages space called Tea & Crumpets. I'd wanted to book Postcards into it last year, and I still have contact info for Petunia, the girl who curates the show. I send a quick message to her.

The other opportunity would be the show happening over at the Rickshaw Stop that very same night: Sundays on Mars. Jason's band. There's only one opener listed so far. We could still get that show . . . but I can barely stomach the idea of Jason being near the band, or the secret we'd be carrying with us. If Eli really did hide songs, someone from Candy Shell Records is about the last person on the planet he'd want to get them.

"There's a pop showcase," I say. "It's supposed to be cool."

"Is that the weekend of the Harvest Slaughter?" Caleb wonders.

"Ah, yeah, it is. And I got you guys into that."

"Nice work," says Caleb.

"Thanks, but that's Saturday." Except I'm also remembering what else I said I'd do that weekend. The college visits.

Crap.

"I'm not seeing anything about what Allegiance did after that San Fran show . . . ," says Jon, swiping his finger back and forth across his pad, "or anything about a Daisy. No restaurants, nothing."

My phone beeps. A reply from Petunia. That was fast. "Okay," I report to the band. "Got the gig."

"Wow, well done!" says Matt, his eyes regaining their innocent sparkle for a moment.

"Cool," says Caleb. "We're going on tour." He sounds excited, but doesn't quite smile.

"Can I just ask," says Jon, "what are we going to do

with these tapes if we find them? I mean, besides geek out over them?"

I look at Caleb. He meets my gaze. "Summer thinks we should learn them," he says.

"And you?" Jon asks.

Caleb's mouth tightens into a knot. "What do you guys think?"

"Are you going to storm off again if we say something you don't like?" Val asks.

I have to give her credit for that one.

Caleb nods. "I'm sorry about last night. I didn't trust you guys, and I fucked up. But I'm trusting you now, telling you about all this."

Jon and Matt share a look. Val picks at her finger.

"I think Summer's right," says Jon. "If we find any songs, we should learn them. And then play them for the world."

"Yeah," Matt agrees. "That would be the biggest show ever. Val?"

Val just looks at Caleb. "It's your call. Eli chose you to give the songs to."

"I know," says Caleb, staring at the floor.

Still staring. None of us move.

And finally: "I don't know yet."

Jon sighs slowly, but no one says anything. I'm glad he heard it from everyone else, and that I wasn't the only one thinking it. But I think we all can sense that, now that he knows what we think, he still might need time to come around to it.

"Okay . . . ," Jon says. "But at the very least, we are going to play a gig in San Francisco, and if the next tape does exist, we're going to get a private concert of a never-before-heard song."

"Yes," says Caleb.

"I can live with that." He turns to Matt and brightens. "Road trip!" They high-five.

"Now that that's settled, can we please go practice?" says Val. "Hopefully nobody's forgotten that we still need to be, like, good when we go to San Fran."

"Let's meet up in an hour," Caleb says, and gets quiet again. "Randy, can you rewind that thing?"

"I'm not watching that again." Val is on her feet. "God-damn depressing. I'll be at the Hive. Caleb, why don't you just come now?"

"I'll stay with you," I say to Caleb. He's just staring at the blue screen.

Val mutters to herself and leaves.

"We'll meet you over there," says Jon. "Thanks for showing us this. Craziness."

As they leave, Eli's face appears on the screen.

"Hey, far comet."

Caleb sits on the edge of the couch. I sit beside him. We watch it again, saying nothing. And then again.

14

The band settles into daily practices. They are getting really tight, adding new songs. The only problem: Val is almost always late. She complains about the traffic getting up from Mission Viejo, but I keep an eye on traffic before the next practice, and it's totally fine. And she's still late.

On Thursday we meet up after school with Blaire Nolan, star video director in the PopArts visual media track.

"The song is so grand," he says of "On My Sleeve."

"Ear lube," I say, sharing a private smile with Caleb.

Blaire ignores this. "I wish we could film you playing by, like, a canyon, but since we can't do that, I'm thinking intercuts of facial close-ups, panning shots of a sparse

177

hillside from ground level, and then oversaturated footage of you guys eating ice cream."

"Can I spill some of the ice cream *on my sleeve*?" Jon asks. Matt cracks up.

Blaire looks away, scowling. "It's a tonal collage. If you want *literal*, go ask Wendy Morris to shoot your video."

"We'll be fine," I say.

Only Val never shows up.

"Does anybody have a number for her? Anything?" I ask as we sit in the Green Room drinking coffee.

The boys shrug.

"Well, has she friended you or added you on any sites?"

"Actually, no," says Caleb. When the others agree, he wonders aloud, "Huh. I did do a Twitter search for her once, but she's not on there."

I get out my phone. "What's her last name?"

The boys look at each other.

"You're kidding."

"I never . . . it never came up," says Caleb.

I start searching around. "Well, what do we actually know about her? She goes by Val, short for . . . Valerie?"

"Don't know," says Caleb.

"She's a student at Mission Viejo, her band in New York was called Kitty Klaws. She moved here in . . . June?"

"Maybe?" says Jon.

"And is she a senior? Do we know how old she is?"

More shrugs.

178

"You sound like a prosecutor," says Caleb.

"We should know who this person is," I reply, then lower my voice. "Especially since we're including her in something giant and secret, yes?"

"Agreed," says Jon.

"No, you're right," Caleb says, at least having the good sense not to disagree with me on this. "Let's just give her some benefit of the doubt, okay?"

"If she earns it." All my searches online, on Facebook, and on Twitter come up empty. Kitty Klaws had a Twitter feed—they are listed as being from Ithaca—but no one's posted since May 24, and all the posts around that time are cryptic conversations with other people. I scroll down and finally find a tweet about a gig at the beginning of the month. The band's website isn't updated either. That same gig is listed, but that's it. They just went to no signal. No farewell show, or mention of Val leaving. It's the kind of band ending that usually means there was trouble.

Still, I try to convince myself that Caleb's right. I should probably give Val the benefit of the doubt. After all, she's a kick-ass performer. And yet . . . I can't shake the mistrust.

After the coffees are gone and it's apparent that Val is never showing up, Caleb and I head to Taquita's to do homework.

"You guys can join, if you want," Caleb offers.

"Yeah, no," says Jon. "I've got a pedal to pick up at PRR." He means People's Republic of Rock.

"I'm meeting Maya," says Matt.

"Oh cool," I say, trying to sound enthusiastic. "How's that going?"

Matt's eyes dart past me. "Fine."

We get food and grab a table in the sun, trying not to get salsa on our calculus.

"Do you know what you're going to do about your dad and the college weekend?" he asks me.

"No."

"I'm sure he'll understand," says Caleb. "You could visit schools any weekend. This gig only comes up once."

"I think, to my dad, it's sort of the opposite." I can just hear his reaction if I tried explaining about the gig. And it ends with him saying no. And what do I do then? I've contemplated the drastic: but I'm just not the type who would ditch her dad for a gig, basically run away, no matter how much sometimes I wish I was. "My current plan is to eat enchiladas and pretend there's no problem."

Caleb kisses me, and taps his pencil against the calculus homework between us. "Should I use the chain rule here?" he asks from two inches away.

I kiss him back. "Sounds dangerous." Kiss again. Between each one, I stay close enough to feel his breath.

"Product rule then."

Kiss.

"Are you still talking about derivatives?"

Kiss.

"No idea."

Things continue, and then cool off, because we are in public. When I finally pull back and turn his notebook to see the problem he's working on, I can feel his eyes on me and I take a minute to imagine things that could happen in a less public place . . . and then briefly the same things happening in front of everyone, right on a food-court table, what the hell.

Then back to calculus.

But my head's not in it, not just because of all the kissing business, but because of the equation with Carlson Squared.

I've been trying to figure out my options with them. And there isn't one. I mean, there's the truth, but that doesn't seem like a good idea. And there's no scenario I could invent that's going to trump college visits. Thinking about it ramps me up, but when I try to think about something else, there's Val again. I need to know what her deal is. I tell myself that it's not just because I am trying to build a case against her. But I also know that I am trying to build a case.

"So . . . I'll just finish this," Caleb says about the homework.

"Sorry." I shake my head, trying to get rid of all the worries.

"Was that your phone?"

"Huh?" I realize that my phone just buzzed like I have a message. "Oh yeah." I pull it out of my bag.

(310) 271-1232: Hey there! This is Jason!

I just stare at the screen. What the hell? I try to stay calm, to not attract Caleb's attention. How did he even get my number?

Summer: Why are you on my phone?

Jason: I saw your SFO date! I'm hurt!

Summer: Gee, I'm so sorry.

Jason: I can't believe the band chose that little showcase over my offer. ;)

I can feel the sarcasm. I don't know how to respond. I just want him to go away. So, I don't reply, but after a pause, he writes again.

Jason: Come by my office tomorrow after school.

Summer: Why?

Jason: I'll tell you then. And I'll tell THEM if you don't.

Great. My nerves are ringing. Why am I even letting him hold this over me? I should just tell Caleb about the gig offer, and also tell them how Jason can't be trusted. Except I'm not sure they'll see it my way. Why would they not want to play a cooler gig in SFO? Not that my gig isn't cool but . . . am I really just holding out on them so that I won't lose them? I should give Caleb more credit than that. And, I'm sure my gig is the better move . . . aren't I?

Maybe I'll just meet with Jason. That can't be a good idea. What could he possibly want? But suddenly something occurs to me.

Summer: Deal, on 1 condition: You let me interview your dad for my blog.

There's no response for almost a minute. This was a risky thought, but since Jerrod Fletcher was Allegiance's manager, he would know about their San Francisco tour stop. He could fill in the details about where they ate and stayed and all that.

Jason: Deal. See you tomorrow, say, 4?

Summer: See you then.

I turn my attention back to Caleb, who is erasing fiercely. "Here," I say. "Let me see."

"Any good news?" he asks. As I take the notebook back, his fingers play with mine, and I feel a rush of guilt.

And then I say, "I'll be late to practice tomorrow."

"Oh yeah, what's up?"

I almost lie about the whole thing, but then realize that if my interview with Jerrod works, Caleb will need to know about it. "Actually, I got a meeting with Jason Fletcher at Candy Shell. He was asking me to be his intern when we were at the Trial. I don't want to, as he's slime, but I told him I'd meet with him if I could interview his dad." Only a lie by omission. But if I can unlock the key to the San Fran tape location, and convince Caleb that they should perform the songs, then one lost opener with Sundays on Mars won't even matter anymore.

"Good plan," Caleb says after I explain my reasoning,

183

"but remember we were going to go to find Pluto before our movie date."

"Right, yes," I say, and I hate that I momentarily did forget that. He smiles and we kiss, but instead of just being there in the moment, I spend the whole kiss chasing my thoughts and wondering if I'm doing the right thing.

15

MoonflowerAM **@catherinefornevr 45m**
There it is before you—smiling, frowning, inviting, grand, mean, insipid,
or savage, and . . . whispering, "Come and find out." #jconradFTW

Two buses take me across LA on Friday afternoon, to Santa
Monica and the sleek, coral white facade of Candy Shell
Records. I'm with Maya, who checks me in and takes me
up in the elevator to a waiting area, a dark, wood-paneled
room. The furnishings are sleek, with lots of chrome and
glass. Gold and platinum records line the walls, interspersed
with signed band photos and tour posters. The perky people
striding to and fro wear well-tailored skirts and tops, shirts
and ties.

"Isn't it cool?" says Maya. She changed before leaving
school, into a junior version of the power suits that glide
past us.

"Yeah," I say. It's my first time in a real record label, and it's not quite what I expected, or maybe not quite what I hoped. Maybe I wanted to see everybody dressed super casual or like they were going to a show, or to have there be wild art all over the walls, but this is all business. Big business. Part of me immediately wants to be part of it. Looking around at all these hustling people, you can feel the possibility. With this kind of machine behind you, man, you could reach so many people. As we've learned in class, there are whole departments here devoted to each of the things I have to do on my own: social media, creative development, branding and logos, booking, and on and on.

It also makes me feel hopelessly small. For as much as I like to believe that I can do it on my own, that I can get Dangerheart out there one email, tweet, or hashtag at a time . . . maybe this is what it really takes. Except then a band like Postcards is struggling to get anyone to their shows on tour.

Which makes me wonder: Do these people really see their bands for who they are? Or is Postcards just a commodity? Would Candy Shell love "On My Sleeve" because it's brilliant or because it could lead to brilliant sales? And what happens if you get hooked on all this big label stuff? What if you start to think of your art in terms of sales, too? Can you still be true to yourself?

But then I think of Carlson Squared sitting here in this expensive waiting area, as I walk down the hall in a pro suit to meet them for an expensive lunch. *That's okay, Dad*, I'd say, waving off his wallet. *It's on the company*. And I can see their opinions changing. There is no doubt they would be impressed by this.

Maya shows me her desk. It's tucked into a puzzle of cubicles. "Kinda sterile, I know," she says.

"Yeah, but, kinda fun, too," I say. The cubicle feels almost private, a safe space to get work done where you wouldn't have to fake doing homework. She has a big hand-drawn logo of Supreme Commander beside a spreadsheet of what seem to be email contacts.

She introduces me to her cubicle neighbor, Bev, a large older woman who's been at Candy Shell since its start.

"Bev knows all the dirt."

"A coffin's worth of it," Bev says. "You stick around bands long enough, it tends to pile up."

"I'm starting to learn that," I say.

Maya brings me back to the waiting area. "Good luck," she says, leaving me in a square of modern white couches and glass tables.

Two guys sit nearby in ripped jeans and T-shirts, their hair professionally messy. The first people I've seen who look like they actually play music. I'm guessing they do brat pop, the kind that's too whiny but always has really catchy melodies, even if they're always name-dropping corporate beverages and jeans. The kind of songs that are about rebelling but not against anyone specific. Twelve-year-olds can listen to them and parents can turn them up at barbecues in the Fronds while drinking pink margaritas. They probably sell a ton of records.

I wonder what it feels like to sell, say, a million copies of an album. Would it get to your head? Would it feel like pressure to sell more? At Postcards shows, we would sell ten copies and feel like royalty, and then be hopelessly depressed if at the next show we only sold six. Like we'd already peaked and failed.

An impossibly tall assistant strides up to me, heels clacking. She doesn't make eye contact, and delivers her greeting in a single exhale: "Hi I'm Royce right this way." She turns and starts walking like . . . she has no idea who I am. And I know exactly who she is. The one who got it on with Ethan last summer. I aim hate beams at the back of her head, but the sad truth is she probably never even knew about me.

Royce leads me down branching hallways, and we leave the shimmery entry spaces and enter grid after grid of cubicles similar to Maya's. Charts, graphs, a drab kitchenette with a stained coffee machine, a stark conference room.

We pass through a graphic design department and briefly everything looks like I had imagined and I am in love: everyone's workspace is cluttered with posters, sketches, album covers, and they're dressed in jeans and T-shirts and sundresses, with stubbly chins and barrettes and thick glasses. After that it's back to crisp shirts and graphs and charts.

Finally we reach a closed office door. Royce knocks.

"One sec!" the voice calls from inside.

Royce checks her watch. She has astonishing eyelash extensions and a body like a comic book character, all straining against a tweed skirt and blouse. Her face seems to have no pores, no hairs. Is she even a mammal? Also: this is what Ethan was into when I wasn't around? Gross.

She has yet to look at me and she pops open the door in spite of Jason's request and ushers me in wordlessly.

I'm expecting to find Jason kicked back at his desk, feet up, but he's hunched over a chaos of papers, his neck kinked to hold his phone. "I know, right just . . . um—one sec." He glances up. "Thanks, Royce," he says sarcastically. "Stick around to bring her back out, 'kay?"

"Mmm." She nods icily and closes the door. I hear her heels clicking away.

Jason gestures to the single chair in front of his desk. It's a hurried motion, not the cocky guy from the party. I don't sit right away.

The office is barely wider than his desk. There's a skinny window behind him that looks out on another wing of the building, a small couch behind me, and a bookcase to my left that houses a mishmash of CDs and books. I notice some rock biographies, and also some business-y books, with titles like *Spotting the Talent Within* and *Predict the Next Big Thing!*

On the right wall is a collage frame: photos of Jason with various celebrities. I see Jeff Tweedy and Katy Perry.

In the one of him and Michael Stipe from R.E.M. he must be, like, thirteen. And in that shot and many others, Daddy Jerrod is never far away.

"I understand that, Mel," Jason is saying back into the phone. "Pre-sales aren't my problem." He taps his pencil rapid-fire against the clutter of papers on his desk. "I get that the promoter is unhappy, but honestly, it's freakin' Memphis. Where does he think he—no, I . . . yeah. Of course distributors matter. Listen, I gotta go. Okay—no, I will. Definitely."

He hangs up and for just a moment, I see what is maybe stress on his face . . . but then he looks up at me with a jackal's smile. "Hey, intern."

"I thought someone as successful as you would have a bigger office." It doesn't feel like the best barb, but I can't think of another.

"My office is in here," Jason says, tapping his eraser against his temple. "Besides, when you're the boss's son, everyone expects you to take a big office upstairs. But I have no intention of just following in Daddy's footsteps."

It's the first thing he's ever said that I can relate to. I nod to the phone. "Sounds like trouble in Memphis. That's where Postcards's next show is, right?" I've been tracking their tour online.

Jason shrugs. "The record's not hitting there. What can you do."

"Why did you send them there before you built a fan base?"

Jason wags his pencil at me. "See? This is why you'd make such a good intern. My job is talent, seeing it, knowing it, and bringing it in. You could play the role of the plucky whiz kid, and we could own this label in a year."

The vision of me, professionally dressed buyer-of-lunch-for-impressed-parentals, flashes across my mind again. I do my best not to show it. "Am I supposed to swoon?"

"Summer," he says, "look, you can't take it personally that you got cut out of Postcards from Ariel's contract. You're a kid. This is a grown-up's game. Nobody is going to take you seriously as a band's manager, because you don't know how the game is played. You can't. You're too busy being this little idealist, which is totally fine—hell, necessary. This place could use more of it. But you're not a shark. You're more like an adorable parrot fish. You're not meant for the big open sea—"

"Okay, I get the analogy already." I know I should know this. That it shouldn't hurt. But it does anyway. And yet also, I've spent so much time loathing Jason that it's surprising to me to hear that, of all people, he sounds like he's taking what I do seriously.

This internship might be enough to reschedule a college trip, too . . .

But I still have this deep, whirring feeling inside that somehow this would be wrong, that it would be putting Caleb and his music, the whole band, and my soul, at risk. Last year we read *Animal Farm*, and isn't this it? The pigs become the men, the parrot fish becomes the shark, or whatever other unappealing metaphor you want to use. Maybe I could resist it. Or maybe I'm being horribly naive to think I could, or that I even should.

There's a knock at the door and Jason stands. "Ah, good." A gruff-looking girl in goth makeup, a tank top, and jeans comes in and hands him a printout. "Thaaank you, Carla," says Jason, then to me, "Had my graphics girl whip this up for you."

I hear her sigh as she walks back out the door. So far it seems like nobody working here likes Jason. This makes me laugh to myself.

"What?" Jason asks.

"Nothing. Just . . . I don't think Carla liked you calling her your graphics gal."

Jason glances at the door as if this hasn't occurred to him. I wonder if his biggest problem is that he just isn't that aware of how he comes across. "See how valuable you are?" Like that, does he mean it to sound as slippery as it does? "Anyway, check this out."

He hands me what I now see is a poster. It's got a cool, spacey design, and reads:

THE RICKSHAW STOP

presents . . .

SUNDAYS ON MARS

September 29, 10 p.m.

with special guest opener

DANGERHEART

featuring Caleb Daniels,

son of Allegiance to North's Eli White

I read that last line and my breath catches in my throat. Jason steps back and leans against the window, arms crossed, and he grins and I realize:

The trap has been sprung.

Think fast. Sound casual. "Oh," I say, "so, you know about Caleb's dad."

"Surprised?" says Jason. "You shouldn't be. Everybody knows. Well, I mean, everybody connected to Allegiance."

"Caleb didn't even know, until a month ago."

"Nope. After Eli died, Caleb's mom was adamant that he not be told. She wanted him to grow up out of the spotlight. Everyone honored that. But we've of course had our eye on him. And I mean, I can't put Dangerheart on a bill of this magnitude just based on that performance at the Trial."

"Caleb doesn't want to make it on his dad's name," I say.

Jason laughs. "Is that the career advice he's getting from Moonflower Artist Management?"

"It's— They're going to be great on their own," I say.

Jason shrugs. "Maybe. But . . ." He points back to the flyer. "Come on. Ask me how I knew."

"How you knew . . ."

"How did I know that Caleb knew? That's the question, isn't it?"

He's right. It is my question. I just didn't want to ask it.

Jason doesn't wait for me to ask. Cue full-on shark grin, multiple rows of jagged whites, as he says, "You told me."

I feel a flush of nerves, heart scrambling, and I try to think of what I could have done. I haven't posted anything about it. . . .

"Or I should say, you gave me the hint. Let's see . . ." Jason is searching on his phone. "Here: 'People have this idea about LA. I have that idea and I live here. But then there is this other LA . . .' You posted that on Friday night to Twitter and BandSpace."

"So what? And also, it's creepy that you're looking at my posts."

"Not really. Like I said at the Trial, your band made an impression, and so later that night I was sussing them out online, and conveniently, BandSpace automatically includes location tags on all posts, which is a very nifty feature for fans to find a gig. And that's how I knew this post was from Canter's Deli."

Location tag. Dammit! I knew they weren't on Twitter, but it never occurred to me to check BandSpace.

"I've heard all the stories about Canter's," says Jason. "My dad went there with the band all the time. I'd seen you leave the party with Caleb, and it was so curious to me that you went there with him, not to mention his uncle Randy. He was tight with Eli, back in the day."

"We were hungry," I say weakly.

"Of course you were. But I stopped by Canter's the next day and talked to good ol' Vic."

Oh no.

"He told me you guys were there. That it was Eli's son. He even put you in their old booth." Jason nods to the poster. "So I figured Caleb must have known about his dad, and you've now confirmed to me that he does."

I look at the poster, trying to keep my breathing calm. Waiting. Does Jason know anything else? Vic had been helping Eli keep the secret of the tape for fifteen years. He wouldn't have told Jason about it, would he? He hasn't mentioned anything about the tapes yet. I try to steer us away from them. "Caleb wants it to stay secret."

Jason smiles. "I bet you've tried to convince him otherwise. Obviously, it would be *the* thing to say about Dangerheart, wouldn't it?"

This makes me flush. It's one of the first things I tried. Ugh, but I am not like Jason! "I respect his decision," I say. "And we already have a gig in San Fran." I have the overwhelming urge to get out of here. "So . . . about that interview with your dad."

Jason grimaces. "Yeah, about that. I don't know, you won't be my intern, you won't let Dangerheart open for my band . . ."

"You said all I had to do was come down here."

"The first rule of negotiation is get the band through the door." Jason looks at me and suddenly his face is serious, a gleam in his eyes, and though I've been making shark jokes all along, this is the first time that he looks truly predatory. "Summer, I can't help but think . . . Caleb finds out about his dad, you guys visit Canter's . . . the very next thing you do is book a gig in SFO, which, don't think I don't know, was the next stop on the band's final tour."

"Was it?" *Stay calm, stay calm.*

"I'm pretty sure it was, considering I was there. I was only twelve when Dad took me along for a few shows and I mostly had to hang out in the hotel, but I still remember the route."

"We're only going to San Fran because it makes sense as a first tour from here. I was trying for San Diego, too, it just didn't come through."

Jason continues as if I hadn't spoken. "And to top it off, then you want to meet with my dad."

"Well, just because Caleb has some questions. He just wants to know Eli better—"

"Or . . ." Jason pauses. "There's something else." *What*

does he know? It's making me crazy. He turns and looks out the window. "Everybody was really mad at Eli on that tour. Even a twelve-year-old could tell. He was erratic, tanking shows, not to mention holding up the new album, and that was before he blew the whole thing up and took off. There was even talk that he was holding back his new songs, the ones that never got finished."

"I was never a big Allegiance to North fan," I say.

"Strange circumstances around his death, too," says Jason.

That's a comment I can't ignore. "What do you mean?"

"Just, all the legal battles at the time. Complicated stuff. Dad doesn't like to talk about it. You should ask Randy. I'm surprised he's never told any of it to Caleb. Maybe he feels guilty."

"And why would he feel guilty?"

Jason shrugs. "Second rule of negotiation. Never play your whole hand. Last chance to be my intern, get your interview."

Whatever part of me thought coming here or even interviewing Jerrod Fletcher was a good idea now just wants to get . . . out. Fast.

"Sorry," I say. "I guess I'll just go."

Jason sighs. "Okay, then. Have fun on your little tour." I expect more, like that he's going to tell the band about the opening slot, but instead he just sits down and starts looking at his laptop like I've already left.

I let myself out. Royce is of course long gone, so I text Maya. People hurry by me in the hall. If I'm not invisible to them, I'm a nuisance. Standing there, the enormity of my failure starts to sink in. No meeting with Jerrod. No info on the second tape. And, if anything, I only raised Jason's suspicions.

Finally Maya shows up. "Hey! How'd it go?" she asks as she leads me back through the cubicles.

"Like the Cold War, more or less."

"Aww. I guess I was hoping to have you on board, but I know Jason's a jerk. Nobody here likes him. Do you have time for a snack?" Maya asks hopefully. "I have a teensy expense account at the cafeteria, at least enough to split a chocolate croissant."

"Okay." I'm in no rush to get back to band practice with all this on my mind.

We head down a few floors to the cafeteria. While Maya goes through the line, I text Caleb that I won't make practice. I suggest meeting up after to go see Pluto. He doesn't respond. They're probably running the set.

Maya's a few people back at the register, and I notice that the walls are lined with framed black-and-white photos. I see pictures of Candy Shell's biggest names, all caught in candid moments.

I walk the perimeter, and find shots here and there of Allegiance to North. There's one where the band is standing in a Dumpster, wearing suits, visible only from the chest up. There's a small accompanying photo from above and behind, revealing that they're wearing no pants. I snap a photo to show to Caleb. He and his dad both with Dumpsters in their past.

The next wall is somber: tribute photos to those who've died. Most are serious, reflective shots. I find Eli's, and expect the tortured artist, but his is actually kind of playful. He's crouched down on one knee, hugging a grinning golden retriever. He gazes up at the camera, his eyes in dark circles, stubble on his face, but lit by a weary grin. It twists me, and I fight back tears.

"Okay, finally." Maya arrives beside me. "Oh . . ."

"It's okay," I say, brushing at my eyes. "This wall is just a bummer." I take one last look at the photo, my eyes dropping to the tiny card beneath it that reads:

Eli White 1976–1998

And I've almost turned away when the text below stops me in my tracks:

With Daisy at Ear Socket Records, San Francisco

16

MoonflowerAM **@catherinefornevr 32m**
This traffic knows we have planets to visit. Oh, it knows, and it grins its chrome grin and we go nowhere. #LAsubway

I miss the ideal bus by mere seconds, watching it pull away as I wait to cross the street, and the second one is late, and then the 405 is a mess, and by the time an hour has gone by I'm reconsidering everything. Catherine, sitting in her own car, could exit and try another route. Hell, she wouldn't even be in Malibu at all this afternoon. She wouldn't miss the Pluto expedition.

But then she'd never know Caleb in the first place.

I text him.

Summer: Traffic fail.

He doesn't reply, and hasn't to my earlier text yet either. When he finally does we're moving, but it's almost six and so what he says doesn't surprise me.

Caleb: It's all good. Pluto another day. Things came up anyway. Rain check on tonight?

Summer: Absolutely not! Will be late but not missing our date.

We've had this plan all week, first Pluto, and then Sacred Cow, and then the Prism, a second-run theater in the little downtown of Mount Hope that operates on an arts grant. This month they're showing the early works of the Coen brothers and tonight it's *Barton Fink*.

Summer: Just go ahead and order when you get there.

Caleb: Do I know what you like?

Summer: Pretty sure you do. ;)

Caleb: Ha. See you then.

The texts make me smile but cause a squirm of guilt. I'm still on edge after the cloak-and-dagger routine with Jason. I'm not sure what from the meeting I'm going to tell Caleb. I can't really tell him that Jason is on to us without also telling him about the gig offer. But I know Caleb wouldn't want to do the show if it was advertised with his connection to Eli. So why not just tell him everything? Maybe I will. I'm sure I could convince him that Jason is not to be trusted. That we're better off on our own. Though the band as a whole might not agree. And Caleb would wonder why I didn't tell him until now. But since Jason seemed far more concerned about finding out what we were up to regarding Eli, maybe the gig offer was bait and will just fade away anyway. I'll see how the night goes. Luckily, I have the info on Daisy, which is all we really need.

I spend part of the bus ride looking up Ear Socket Records, but find that it closed five years ago. There is contact info for the owner, Carter, who says that he and Daisy will be looking to open a new store. A few searches indicate that they haven't done so yet. I send a quick email, claiming to be a fan of the old store and asking if there's any news on a new location.

My second bus connection is delayed, and by the time I arrive home, freshen up, get Mom's car, and race downtown, I'm half an hour late to dinner. Parking takes even longer. I'll have fifteen minutes to eat, tops.

When I rush into the dimly lit, crowded restaurant, I look for Caleb at one of the tiny tables for two by the windows. Not that I told him to sit there, it's just where I've pictured us being. But instead, he's in a semicircular booth near the back.

And then I see why.

Val is with him.

She's sitting at girlfriend distance again, both hands cupping a mug of chai, leaning in his direction and talking. Caleb is listening, nodding as he gazes into the table and once again, there is something so intimate and exclusive feeling about their interaction. I may be in detective mode, but I can't just be making this up, inventing the chemistry. It's so obvious even from twenty feet away.

He catches sight of me first, and straightens, even flinches slightly away from her. Val makes no such move.

202

She just scowls, her dark-shaded eyes narrowing. I more than kinda want to let her have it. Except I put on as much of a smile as I can for Caleb. She's in the band. This could just be band business. But I know well enough that those lines get real blurry, real fast.

"Hey," says Caleb, in that I-know-but-please-be-cool tone. A replacement basket of naan arrives just as I do, and I sit to his right, and hate this positioning, Caleb in the middle, me just one of the girls.

"What's up?" I ask, and by *What's up*, I assume Caleb will know that I mean *What the hell is she doing here on our date?*

Val and I don't even pretend to say hi to each other. It's her job to say hi to me, isn't it? She's the one who's added herself to our equation. But she just looks down into her mug like I'm irrelevant.

"Val needed a place to hang for a bit," says Caleb, "so I invited her along."

He gives me another look that seems to say *Can this be cool?* I'm not sure. Val, meanwhile, is tearing off some naan.

But I don't really feel like being cool. I lean around him and ask, "What happened?"

"Stuff," she says without looking at me.

"Same stuff that made you miss the video shoot? And half of every practice this week?"

"Summer . . . ," says Caleb.

"What?" I snap at him. "Oh, did you ask that already?"

"Well, not like that . . ."

"Okay then."

"He doesn't have to," Val mutters.

"Why?" I feel myself winding up. "Because you're *connected*—"

"Because he gets it."

Oh man, I want to unload right now. The feeling is so strong though, that it's overwhelming me and all I can manage to say is, "Right."

"Okay," says Caleb. "Listen, Val's having trouble with her stepdad. He's a real . . ." He glances to Val.

"Asshole," she offers, shoving in another bite.

"It's bad," Caleb says to me, and I suddenly feel embarrassed because, okay, that is serious, and probably has to do with so much of how she's been acting.

"I just can't be there tonight," says Val.

She sounds wounded. I try to push the whole snuggling-up-to-my-boyfriend thing out of my mind, at least for a minute. "Do you have somewhere to go?"

Caleb shifts in his seat. "She's gonna stay at my house."

"Oh." I go for some naan too, thinking, *You've got to be kidding me*. On the other hand, maybe what I should think is, Caleb is amazing, and generous, taking care of his band mate, of course of course of course.

And yet instead I'm thinking: pajamas, Val sneaking in while Caleb's asleep, more bonding for the burdened lead singers, their connection inevitable. I hate that I'm thinking that, what a ridiculous scenario! I know Caleb. . . .

"Is that a problem?"

I look up and see Val finally gazing at me.

Dammit. What am I supposed to say? Obviously I should say no but . . . does it have to be Caleb's house? Don't I trust him? Pretty sure I do, but her? And then there's how she acts toward me . . . and so instead I say what I shouldn't: "What's your last name?"

That makes her look away. "Why do you want to know?"

Gotcha. "It's just a last name."

"Exactly," she says, tearing more naan.

"What if someone wanted to friend you online?"

"Who, you?" Val shrugs. "I don't do that stuff, anyway."

I look imploringly at Caleb, trying to say, *See? What about this?* I don't trust her. I just don't. How can he?

He makes an almost queasy face. "Summer, come on. I just want to help."

"I know." And then I don't know what else to say.

Food arrives. Caleb ordered just what I like: chicken korma and channa masala, and this should be cause for a kiss in acknowledgement of such chivalry, and yet, also arriving at the table is saag paneer for Val, which is gross, and she's probably judging my enjoyment of meat from an animal, and honestly whatever. I hate feeling this way. I hate all of this right now.

205

We eat in silence, and after a few minutes I'm so mad that Caleb hasn't thought to ask me about my meeting with Jason that I want to leave. Of course I could always tell him. It's not fair of me to make it a test. But who's on his mind more, his girlfriend, or his needy band mate? Maybe I'm a bitch to expect it to be me. Fine, I'm a bitch.

But then he asks.

I fill him in, almost mention the gig but skip it, and explain that Jason wouldn't go for the interview with Jerrod unless I agreed to be his intern. "But we don't really need the interview anymore, because I found Daisy." I explain the photo and location.

"Wow, cool," says Caleb. "Do you think Jason suspected anything?"

"He was a little suspicious for sure," I say.

"I suppose Candy Shell technically has the rights to any songs by Eli," says Caleb.

"I think so."

Caleb's face darkens. "So what did my dad think I was going to do with them?"

"Maybe we should ask Randy," I say, thinking of Jason's comment about how they were tight.

"It's not fair," says Val.

"What?" asks Caleb.

"Your dad putting this burden on you," she says. "He could have left you the songs when he died, like in a will or something. Or given them to your mom. Why put you through this ghost hunt? And make you do something illegal?"

"It's not illegal to find the songs," I say, though I agree with her point about Eli.

"But it will be illegal to play them without Candy Shell's permission." Val's right about that.

"Which we might not even do," Caleb reminds us. "But it's probably also technically illegal to keep them a secret."

"So, what do we do?" I ask Val. "Do you think we should tell Candy Shell?"

Suddenly Val smiles. "Hell no."

"No way," Caleb agrees. "I really want to hear the rest of that song. I have to."

"Definitely," says Val, and then she . . .

literally . . .

reaches out and rubs his arm.

And I lose it. "Do you not see me right here?"

"What?" she nearly snarls. "Why are you like the most overprotective bitch ever? We're friends. What's the problem with that?"

I look to Caleb. Oh, boyfriend, this is one of those moments where you have to step up and not let the band girl hit on you with your girlfriend right there. . . .

He looks back at me with an expression that is honestly pathetic, as if he wishes the situation would go away or fix itself. *I'm still trying to figure out what to do about it*, is what he said at the beach. I get that it's complicated, kinda, but . . . if he's not going to do anything, then what choice does that give me?

"The problem, right now, is you," I say to Val, and as the words leave my face I'm pretty certain that I'll wish for a hundred years that I had a do-over to say something smarter. But honestly, whatever. I start to scoot out.

"Where are you going?" Caleb asks.

"Can we go to the movie?" I ask.

Caleb flashes a glance at Val.

"Just the two of us," I add. "Val can handle herself for two hours." I know I'm probably being unfair, and I sort of hate myself for feeling like I need to do this. To ask Caleb to choose between us. To choose me.

"But," he says queasily. And he glances again between Val and me and doesn't get up. It's an impossible position for him. That's how he feels. Fine. But that leaves me feeling like I only have one option. "I'm gonna go."

"Summer . . ."

My name just infuriates me. "Stop." I look to Val. "I'm sorry about what you're going through. I am. You guys just go to the movie. Have a sleepover. I'm going home."

It's my turn to storm off even though I'm already regretting it as I do it. But once you set your exit into motion, you've got to stick the landing. "I'll see you tomorrow at practice." I keep walking. I hate it. I feel tears coiling, ready to spring free. Not doing that. Walking out. Holding my breath.

I'm outside, halfway up the block, when I exhale and

the tears pour out. My phone buzzes.

Caleb: Come on. I'm sorry. Come to the movie.

I keep going, and as I drive home, I hate everything. Hate hate hate. To myself: "Real mature, leaving like that. Playing right into her hands." To Val, via the window: "Where do you get off thinking you can just get that close to him?" To myself, via the dashboard: "You don't own him. You didn't need to put him in that position. Can't you just be confident?" But I remind myself of the lessons that feel all-too-recently learned: "Fine line between being confident and being oblivious."

When I get home, I go straight online. I do searches for Val, or Valerie, in every location. Nothing. No photos of her or mentions with Mission Viejo, and nothing before the six-month stretch from last winter to spring when she appears in photos and gig listings in Ithaca with Kitty Klaws. It's like she's only ever existed in New York and our practice space.

Around midnight, my phone buzzes.

Caleb: Movie was amazing. Wish you'd stayed. Val is just a band mate. That's all. I felt like she needed help. Maybe I messed up.

Summer: Thank you. Sorry I missed the movie.

And before he can say anything else:

Summer: Good night.

I just want today to be on the other side of sleep.

But first, back to the search. In all the listings and bios for Kitty Klaws, she's only Val, even when the other two members have last names. They have prior projects listed, too. Val doesn't. There's no information about why they broke up, or contact info either.

Nothing, nothing, and nothing . . .

Until finally, around two a.m., I am looking at the comments beneath one of the band's YouTube videos, and I find an old post:

> **Darren_Peters39:** Looking good, Cassie! Love the new band. I won't tell, but drop your mom a line so she knows you're okay.

The other members of Kitty Klaws are named Sarah and Cooper.

I click on Darren Peters's profile. He's from Princeton, New Jersey. . . .

And ten minutes later, I find her.

Cassie Fowler.

A picture of her at a high-school battle of the bands. Her band then was called File Under Tragedy.

Another where she's standing with the cross-country team last fall, looking very un-Val-like in a powder-blue uniform.

And then something else.

A police log in the Princeton newspaper, from last Christmas:

*Police were called to investigate a domestic violence call in
the 800 block of View Crest Lane. Officers arrested Melanie
Fowler for drunk and disorderly conduct. Police are looking for
the suspect's daughter, Cassie Fowler, age 16, who made the
call but fled the scene.*

And she's been running ever since.

Val doesn't go to Mission Viejo.

Val's not even Val.

You might put your head on someone's shoulder when
you have no one else to turn to. You might crash somebody's
date when the alternative is sleeping . . . where? In her car?
She wears the same clothes nearly all the time. I thought it
was anti-fashion politics; it's probably because she doesn't
have anything else. I realize that I've been basing all of my
opinions about Val on the assumption that she's another
middle-class kid like the rest of us. But it's not even close.
Not that she's let us in on any of that, except Caleb.

I think about texting him, but it's late. Val is probably
asleep, and now instead of imagining her sneaking into his
room, I see her getting one of the only good nights of sleep
she's gotten since . . . when?

And it almost makes me love Caleb more that he's the
kind of person who can be there for her, while people like
me are so quick to judge. Sure, the question of whether she's

into him is still there, but it pales in comparison to what she needs. Friends. Safety. To hide. Oh, man. I know I couldn't have known, but I feel like an idiot.

And yet . . . as I lie in bed turning all this over and over in my head, there is still one question that's unanswered. If Val's not from Mission Viejo, and her asshole dad is a lie, what exactly is she doing here?

17

Even though I don't fall asleep until nearly four, I'm up far too early, whirring with anxious energy. I lie in bed, listening to my parents bustle, wondering what I'm going to do about Val, about San Francisco. At one point, the phone rings. I hear the murmur of conversation, then footsteps up the stairs, to my door . . . and away again. My dad saying, "She's still asleep."

I keep hoping that will be the case, just for a little while longer, but finally accept that sleep is not coming back. I get up and trudge downstairs to find Carlson Squared eating on the deck. It's one of those warm, seasonless LA mornings, the sun scorching the patio, the nearby lemon tree fragrant.

"Hey, I made eggs," says Dad. "And Aunt Jeanine

called about shopping. You should call her back."

Aunt Jeanine has been taking me shopping since I was little. I'm the surrogate daughter she gets to dote on. It sounds like the perfect distraction for this morning.

I call her back, and down a bagel in my room while doing some basic band business. I post to our Band-Space forum about the *Forecast: Sweaters!* show. One fan, *TooSexyForYourShirt*, has a cousin in South San Francisco, and soon we are chatting about putting up posters. I contact *SarahFromTheValley*, who's been designing buttons, and ask if she can make a poster. I get Petunia to give us five free show passes to give away and then I start a contest on LiveBeat.

When all that is done, I find myself back in Val's world. A quick search, and I find Melanie Fowler's Facebook page.

Since we're not friends, all I can see are her basic stats and profile picture. She doesn't have an employer listed. The picture is a self-portrait with a bad, bright flash. She's smiling but it's hazy, her eyelids kinda half asleep, dark circles beneath. It looks like a photo from the bleary end of a long night. There's a dude in a cowboy hat grinning around a beer beside her, a cigarette in his fingers. He doesn't look all there either.

She has her photos locked down for Friends Only, but I can see her Likes. I click there. Nothing remarkable. Bands, movies, restaurants—

And Candy Shell Records.

Their page has fifty thousand likes, but . . . it seems like an unlikely coincidence. I do a search for Melanie and Candy Shell.

A few pages in, I find results. Melanie Fowler worked for a publicity company called Ultra-Lozenge. And they ran some promotion for Allegiance to North. Candy Shell bought them up in 2000. All of this suddenly seems too coincidental.

I text Maya.

Summer: Can you do me a secret detective favor?

Maya: Yes, please!

Summer: Can you ask your coworker Bev about Melanie Fowler and Ultra-Lozenge Publicity and see if there's anything scandalous there?

Maya: Sure! Do I get to ask what it's about?

Summer: Not yet. Soon. I'll owe you many chocolate croissants.

Maya: OK!

Aunt Jeanine picks me up at ten thirty and we head for Bloomingdales and its surrounding mall. Her little vanilla-colored Pomeranian, ironically named Cocoa Bean (or maybe a subtle hint from Aunt Jeanine to the world that someone's appearance does not necessarily dictate who they are inside) yips from her shoulder bag/kennel in the back-seat. Aunt Jeanine works for a clean water nonprofit, and travels to West Africa a few times a year to manage well projects. I take care of Cocoa Bean when she's gone. I call the dog "the weasel," but it loves me.

"*Sanu ki*," says Jeanine as I get in the car. "*Ina aiki?*"

"*Aiki da godia*," I say, humoring her with the one phrase of Hausa she's taught me. It always feels forced, these greetings, as they're so different from how Carlson Squared operates, and yet I do think it's cool that Aunt Jeanine has this solo, world-traveling life, even if it leads one to get a weasel dog instead of a proper canine.

I ask Jeanine about work so she'll talk and I can just gaze out the window, answering her questions in *mmm*s and one-word replies. It's all Val in my mind, and as Jeanine goes on about next month's trip to Niger, I try to make sense of what I know:

Val, formerly Cassie, runs away from New Jersey on Christmas and goes to Ithaca. She must have had someone to stay with. And after being there for six months, she comes here. I wonder if her mom tracked her down in New York state. But even if that's the case, why come here? Why Caleb? Is that coincidence? Did she just happen to know someone out here and then wanted a band to play in? But then why not change her name again? And, is it also a coincidence that she shows up and auditions for Caleb's band right around the time that Caleb is finding out about these hidden songs? But it's ridiculous to think she could have known about that, isn't it? Except her mother has old ties to Candy Shell and Allegiance to North . . . and something about all that makes her purpose in the band potentially . . .

what? Sinister? Could she be after the songs? It seems unlikely. How could she have even known about them?

I need more information, but it's going to be a long wait for Maya to get back to her internship and get the gossip. Despite the suspicious mom connection, at least I now half believe Val's story last night: her home life is more than a mess; she has no home. And no matter what wild plots I might suspect, I have to try to remember it's innocent until proven guilty. I can't let my own issues with Val get in the way.

Also, the fact that Val's mom was arrested and Val ran off isn't something I can discount. There was a real police report. Real danger. Real pain. I can't let my snooping lead to Val's mom finding out where she is.

"Brunch first?" asks Jeanine as we park. "I'm starving."

We go to the outdoor café and both order Belgian waffles. As we are digging in, Aunt Jeanine says, "So, your dad tells me you're going on a college trip next weekend."

Crap. "Yeah."

"Let me guess: that lack of enthusiasm is because you don't actually want to do law and he's totally jumped on it?"

"I don't know that I wouldn't want to do law someday, but yes, that's part of it."

Aunt Jeanine smiles. "Your father has always been like that. And is your lack of enthusiasm also because you have plans to go to San Fran?"

217

I swallow a rush of anxious energy. "How did you know about that?" I wonder if she, too, is following my movements on Twitter. I keep all this stuff off Facebook, because I know most of my family is there. I thought Twitter was a family-free zone.

"Actually, I saw the listing in the *SF Weekly*," she says. "I wasn't looking for it, I just happened to be reading the last bit of an article and there were gig listings on the facing page, and there was Dangerheart."

"There we are. . . ." I feel myself deflating. At least obsessing about Val had kept my mind off this. "I don't know what I'm going to do about it."

Jeanine nods. "Donald is probably not going to go for the idea of you trading college visits for a band gig. He still pictures you as the twelve-year-old with braces who hangs on her father's every word. He's not quite ready for you to be your own person."

"Especially if that person isn't the one he was picturing."

"I'm assuming that you plan on there being other gigs," says Aunt Jeanine. "Is this one really so important? Couldn't you just miss it and be at the next one?"

"It's kinda the opposite," I say. "This gig is more important than any future ones."

"I see." Aunt Jeanine feeds a chunk of waffle through the top of her bag to Cocoa Bean's snapping jaws. Then she places her purse on the table. It's a woven bag from Niger.

It's gorgeous but the leather was cured in camel urine, a very distinctive smell that tends to linger. She shuffles through the contents and produces a thin red envelope.

"What's this?" I ask.

"Somebody's favorite aunt happens to be going to San Francisco this weekend. She's going to see an opera. Puccini's *Tosca*. And she has an extra ticket."

I kind of gape at her. "You . . ."

"Are providing the perfect alibi, yes."

I slip open the envelope. "These are two-hundred-dollar seats," I say.

"Yes, and I have the perfect date to take."

"Um," I say, trying to keep up, "but I'd be at the show. . . ."

"Not you," says Jeanine, batting her hand playfully at me. "I have a long-time 'what-if' in Berkeley. She and I have been on four well-installation trips together. And on this last one we realized our shared love of *Tosca*, among other things."

"Oh," I say. I smile, wanting to add something about this news, about this *life* that Jeanine has kept completely under wraps during all family get-togethers ever.

Jeanine seems to read my mind. "Something else that Donald isn't ready for, despite the changing times."

"This is . . . amazing." I'm nearly crying with relief. "Thank you."

"You just do your thing, and we'll educate your father

at another time. But, keep my cell at the ready, in case we need to coordinate. We'll tell them that you're coming to my place the minute school ends Friday, and that we're grabbing the five-p.m. shuttle from Burbank."

"Sounds good."

"And, now that that's settled, you have to humor me and let me buy you something to wear to the opera."

When we enter Bloomingdales, we are greeted by Franca, Aunt Jeanine's personal shopper. She's a stout, peppy little thing in a black sales suit, her red-dyed hair back in a severe bun, exposing her gray roots. "Ahh, there you are, and oh . . ." She smiles tenderly and rubs my forearm. "You brought my Vivien."

"Hi, Franca," I say. Franca says I look like Vivien Leigh, an actress from the golden age who was in *Gone with the Wind*. I'd say the resemblance is a stretch but I haven't spent much time comparing the finer points of our features. And I haven't ever yearned to be one of those movie stars with the soft filter around them.

"Me first," says Jeanine, "and then Summer needs something for the opera."

I spend some time hating everything I try on: jeans, boots, sweaters. The world is fitting wrong today, despite the good news about San Fran. Maybe I don't like looking in the mirror and seeing the girl who jealously stormed out last night. Of course it's not my fault I didn't know the whole story. I still feel like my anger was valid. Maybe I'm just exhausted.

By the time we meet back up, I've managed to pick one cardigan that I can live with. It disappoints Aunt Jeanine if I don't find something. She's chosen a very classy sweater and skirt combo and some killer black boots for her date.

"And now, Vivien's turn." Franca takes my arm with her ring-covered fingers and leads me toward the escalator. "We will make you look so elegant."

I have to talk Franca down from getups with no back and no shoulders and all kinds of frills, eventually settling on a black thing that's formfitting, with a shimmer but still seems like me. Not that I'm even going to wear it, but still . . . Franca seems satisfied. She says it's a great brand.

"You would of course want to perm your hair," says Franca.

Has anyone gotten a perm in thirty years? "Maybe I'll just put it up," I say, piling it atop my head and flashing a stylish pose at the triple mirrors. I do look pretty good. I think for a moment that I could do this, be a dressed-up classy girl, but would everyone still see me? Or would they automatically assume I'm Catherine? Maybe, on occasion, I'd like to be both. You should be able to be both, but it never quite feels like an option.

Still, mugging in this thousand-dollar dress makes me wonder: last year, Ethan and I shunned all things prom.

221

But what about this year? With Caleb . . . Except I'm still wounded from last night.

"Okay, this will work," I say.

"Of course it will, but you must let me dress you up in some more things, Vivien."

I smile. "Fine." Some more time before Caleb and I see each other is probably best anyway. I text him that I can't make practice, and then for the next two hours allow the ridiculous pleasure of shopping to take over.

18

MoonflowerAM @catherinefornevr 3m
We have entered the Red Zone. #ROCKreferencenotJOCKreference

It's Monday before I see Caleb again. I have my cousin Mike's birthday on Saturday night, and Caleb is busy Sunday doing a day of house projects with his mom. We've texted enough since the failed Friday date that everything seems cool, and I guess it is, but I've still been avoiding him. I'm going to have to tell him what I found out about Val, both the serious facts and the suspicions, and I can't shake this worry that he's not going to listen to the second part. So, I've been holding back, wondering when the right time to tell him is.

I enter the Hive churning about that, and also wondering how I'm going to deal with Val herself, how I'll keep my mouth shut when she gives me her usual scowl, but when I walk into the room, I realize that none of it matters, because we've entered the Red Zone.

There is something delicate about the week before a show. Any slight conflict can get totally blown out of proportion and lead to someone either bailing on the gig, or playing poorly, or worse, quitting altogether. The day after a gig? Great time to talk about anything complicated, as there's still success right there in the short-term memory, keeping everything in perspective. But right before is the most dangerous time. If you're lucky, everyone in the group senses the Red Zone, and sets aside their annoyances, mistrusts, and fears. I can feel the eggshells when I arrive, and hear the short, quick cadence of everyone's voices. So, all these things I've been fretting about? Post-gig.

Practice is usually a wave form, oscillating from funny highs with jokes and great takes of songs, to intense lows when parts aren't working or somebody's just off. But tonight, everything is tight. For Caleb, the pressure must be double. Not only is there the gig, and the desire to make amends for what happened at the Trial, but there's also the anticipation of what we might find in San Fran. So I do my best to stay out of the waves. When Matt still isn't quite there with the beat on "Chem Lab," I decide not to mention it.

Unfortunately, Val does. The bass suddenly drops out midway through the song. "Can you straighten out the chorus?" she asks with typical Val severity.

Matt flashes a glance at me, then sends his gaze to its

usual space by the kick drum. "I did."

"Maybe, but it's still busy and it's losing me. What does everyone else think?"

"I hadn't noticed one way or the other," says Caleb. "I'm still trying to make sure I've got the lyrics."

"Still trying to get my delay right," says Jon.

Both classic Red Zone answers.

Val looks at me and asks with her eyebrows.

"Well," I say carefully, "I mean, I think maybe you could try it a little more straightforward."

"You could just say, *Matt, you suck*, already," Matt suddenly snaps at me.

Shit.

"Matt, that's not at all what I'm saying."

But Matt is getting up. "I need a soda." He storms out.

"Well then," says Jon, and fiddles with his knobs.

"I'll get him," I say.

I find Matt at the machine one floor down, slamming the Fanta button. "Why is there always no fucking Fanta?" he says.

"Listen," I say as calmly as I can, "you have to remember that Val says everything with claws out—"

Matt slams the machine and a Sprite rolls out. He just stares at it for a second, as if that Sprite sums up the indifferent nature of the entire universe. "It's not what Val said."

Great. So this is still about me. "Hey, you know I think you're a great drummer."

He sighs. "You think I'm your little brother. You think I'm cute."

"Matt, what does this have to do with—"

"The night I came up with that drum part, the first thing I thought about was how it might impress you. And then when I changed it after you didn't like it, the first thing I thought was that you'd be really impressed at how I changed it. But . . . you never even commented."

I rack my memory. Did I really not comment on the fix? I meant to, but there's been so much going on. "I thought I said the song was sounding great," I try.

"But you still didn't think the beat was good enough, obviously."

"Matt, there are like ten songs, and we are talking about one beat. I don't think it's a big deal."

Matt's eyes meet mine for a split second. "Fine. Then it's not." He starts back up the stairs.

"Then are we cool?" I ask from behind him.

He turns. "Do you think Val is right that I should straighten it out?"

"Well, yes."

"Then I will."

Matt doesn't even look at me the rest of practice, but given that it's the Red Zone, it could be worse. All that matters is that we're still a band and the gig is not in jeopardy.

"He just loves you, that's all," says Caleb after practice,

as we scoop week-of-the-gig-plus-secret-songs-plus-high-stakes-lying-level toppings onto our frozen yogurt.

"I know. I don't know what to do about it."

"Maybe you should accidentally make out with him on tour."

I raise an eyebrow at him. "That would be okay with you?"

"Not at all."

"Yeah, me neither. Besides, the last thing he needs is hope." Though we're joking, I do have a flash of when Caleb didn't know what to do about Val, but let her get almost-make-out close. I remind myself that the situations are different. I do wish there was some way I could help Matt, but I don't know what it would be other than to just keep being honest with him.

And besides, I've been waiting all night to ask Caleb about Val. I do my best to sound casual: "So, how was having Val stay over?"

"Fine," Caleb says into his yogurt. "She was actually there all weekend." His eyes flash to me and away.

Remain calm. I let him continue.

"Well, not really. We didn't, like, hang out. But she stayed over Saturday and Sunday. My mom made up the basement couch for her, and then kept inviting her to meals and stuff. They actually really get along. Val thinks Mom's counseling work is cool, her cases—"

227

"Caleb." I just want him to stop sounding so guilty. "It's okay."

"You sure?"

I'm not, but at least during the Red Zone, I can focus on the fact that Val needs safe haven. "Yes, unless you're going to tell me that you two accidentally ran into each other in the bathroom and shirts came off and toothpaste went everywhere or something."

Caleb's face is stone serious . . . then Fret Face cracks into a smile. "No, no, nothing like that."

I smile too, but add, "Did she try?"

"Summer, no! I'm pretty sure it's not like that."

"Pretty sure?"

"It's NOT."

"Okay." Then I say, "Listen, I did some research and . . . she's actually a runaway." I'm still unsure if I should have even brought this up, given the Red Zone.

But Caleb says, "I know."

"You do?"

Caleb kind of shrugs. "It was one of the first things she told me. That she ran away from home in New Jersey. Then to her stepdad out here. Her mom's ex. She swore me to secrecy but I was planning to tell you, I swear. I'm sorry."

"It's okay, I get it," I say, and I probably do. It doesn't excuse Val rubbing his knee or arm or trying to make a clearly exclusive connection, but it does complicate Caleb's response to that. "She dumped a lot on you."

228

"Yeah."

"But I don't think there's even a stepdad. Did she tell you her name was Cassie?"

"What? No." Caleb's face tightens. "If there's no step-dad, where is she living?"

"I don't know. Friend? Car?"

"She didn't tell me that."

I consider bringing up the trust thing, the coincidence of her showing up right when we're finding out about Eli's songs, her mom's connection, but it feels like too much. Instead, I kiss him and shift to school-day drama, and try to just be easy.

The week goes by. I walk the eggshells at home and with the band, hoping this will all go okay. Catherine is in full effect in school and around the house. Part of my act involves seeming almost disappointed that I have to go to the opera instead of the colleges. Jeanine's plan worked perfectly, my dad not only agreeing that high culture could trump the visits, but also glad to see me bonding with the sister he worries too much about.

Meanwhile, Summer is working the social media over-time, and making sure everyone survives practice, and researching the whereabouts of Daisy, or the backstory of Cassie, if there is one. . . .

It's not until Thursday, between econ and calculus homework, that I finally find a lead on Carter and Daisy.

In an obituary.

He died of lung cancer a year and a half ago. I find this remembrance in a music zine, and it says Carter's *famed record collection, along with its faithful watchdog Daisy, will now be housed in the Vault at Space Panda.* A search reveals that Space Panda is a club, owned by a DJ named Claro, and the Vault is an ultra-hip vinyl listening room. Images of the Vault reveal that Daisy is indeed there: stuffed, and keeping watch over the door. It's a ritual to pet her on the way in.

If we needed to talk to Carter to get that tape, then we're screwed. But if the tape is hidden in the vinyl, like the last clue, then we still have a chance.

And then much later that night, after I pack my bag with gig clothes hidden beneath the shimmery black opera-dress decoy, my phone buzzes with a text.

It's Maya.

Maya: I found out something. Debated telling you while you're in the Red Zone.

Summer: SPILL IT.

Maya: Ultra-Lozenge went under when Allegiance to North fell apart.

Summer: Anything else?

Maya: Yes: That Melanie person was briefly engaged to Kellen, the bassist. Apparently it fell apart right around when Allegiance did, too.

Luckily you don't need to breathe to text.

Summer: OK. Thanx.

Maya: Can I ask what's going on?

Summer: Not yet.

Maya: Boo. Good luck tomorrow!

Summer: :)

Worry creeps up my spine. Add to Val's coincidental arrival that her mom was not only connected to Allegiance to North directly, but engaged to the person in the band who hated Eli the most, who tried to sue Eli for all that money.

Innocent until . . . more evidence. Could Val really be after the songs? Did she know the drama from her mother? Is she hoping the songs can get her out of her situation? Or . . . is her mom somehow involved in this? What if the running away is a lie, and she's actually a plant for Kellen, Candy Shell, even Jason? Could that actually be possible? Or am I completely insane to be thinking of these things? The police report and the little time I've spent with Val do not point to such an elaborate conspiracy. I'm taking it way too far . . . unless it's true.

I want to call Caleb, want to tell him all this, and yet . . . Red Zone. More than anything, this band needs to play this next show. And we need to find those tapes. Derailing the whole thing now just can't happen. Have to just survive one more night. And yet this night just spins on and on, the questions like moths in my brain.

19

Friday drags, everything in slow motion.

"Excited?" Caleb asks as we finally meet up after school.

"If by excited you mean are all of my atoms spinning too fast and are my palms oddly cool and damp? Yes."

We drive to Caleb's, debating the finer points of the Modest Mouse discography. We're both trying to keep things meaningless and light, but I feel like we're just filling time until hours from now, when we may have answers.

We find the back doors to Randy's van wide open. All of his painting supplies are strewn haphazardly across the driveway, and he's trying to shove a couch into the back.

"Um," says Caleb, "that's not at all going to fit."

232

"But it's so ROCK"—he shoves the couch—"AND"— shoves again—"ROLL to have a couch in the van!" He slumps against it, sighing in defeat.

"Why don't we just take the cushions?" I say.

Randy considers it. "Less rock, but also less roll for you in the back. Deal."

Soon, everyone has arrived, we've piled in, and we're off. As we wind over to the 405 and merge onto the highway, I feel the inevitable flutter of guilt, the lie to my parents, even though it's aunt-approved. Still, I can't help but wish there was another way, that I had parents who understood me, that I could just be who I really want to be around them.

And I'm basically avoiding all eye contact with Val. I can't look at her without total distrust. It makes me dig my fingernails into my palms. Luckily, she's not looking at me either.

Still, all the worries do get briefly swept away as we leave the city limits: by the hum of tires on highway, the glare of afternoon sun in our eyes, even the worrisome creaking and vibrations of Randy's van as he careens through traffic. For four years, maybe for my whole life, I have dreamed of actually being out on the road, on tour with a band, with *my* band, and this is it! We are going! Out into the unknown to do our thing. All of us are buoyant, fired up. Behind us is what we were, somewhere ahead of us is where we're headed, and right now, we're free and on our way. It feels like this van could be going anywhere, it almost doesn't matter. But it does. We're on the road to play a show. On a mission.

Everyone takes turns swapping their playlists on the stereo, and at one point Caleb and Jon get out their guitars and there's an impromptu run-through of the set. We all sing along in golden afternoon light. It sounds like freedom.

The miles of vacant central valley slide by, cooling orange sun lighting the tops of row after row of almond trees. After a stop for an ill-conceived mash-up of all the available rest-area snack genres that leaves the van smelling like Cool Ranch and mint, I recount my findings about Space Panda and Daisy.

"Stuffing a dog is barbaric," Val mutters. It's the first thing she's said in over an hour.

Jon asks, "So do we actually think the tape is even there?"

"It's all about the vinyl," says Caleb.

"Yeah, but," I say, "Carter's record collection is massive, and now it's been added to an even more massive collection. How will we know where to start?"

"What did the letter say again?" Randy asks.

Caleb reaches into his jacket pocket and unfolds the paper. I didn't know he'd been keeping it with him. Was it just for this trip? Or has he had it along every day since he found it? "'Get a kiss from Daisy and search for a hidden yesterday,'" he reads.

"Hmmm . . . ," says Randy. "That almost sounds familiar, but . . . I don't know."

"Space Panda is twenty-one and over," Jon reports from his phone.

"Sounds like a solo mission for me," says Randy.

"I can go, too," says Val.

We all look at her. She's typing busily into Caleb's phone, which she asked to borrow. "I have a fake ID."

"Cool," says Matt.

I resist the urge to comment on this, that it doesn't surprise me, that her whole ID is actually fake, or isn't it, or what? But I remind myself, *Get through the gig, get through the gig*.

Except I can't resist asking, "Who are you texting?"

Val's eyes don't leave the screen. "A friend of mine who's coming to the show. Weezil. He goes to Berkeley."

"Cool," says Caleb, probably thinking like I am that we'll need every head we can get in that club tonight. It's just too bad I don't even remotely believe her.

The sun slips behind the mountains, and the sky darkens. Quiet settles over the van. With each mileage sign, our anticipation builds.

Then, Randy says, "This is déjà vu, like being on tour all over again."

I think of my own feelings of circular motion. Randy's comment sounds like an open door. "Did you tour up here a lot?" I ask.

"Only once. Should have happened a thousand more times, but . . . something always screwed it up."

"How was it?" Jon asks.

"So amazing," says Randy. "Junior year of high school, Savage Halos opened for Allegiance to North, actually. They were just about to blow up; it was right before they signed with Candy Shell. It was the first time Eli and I had really gotten to hang out since Poison Pen broke up."

"That was your band with Eli?" I ask.

"Yeah."

"What were you guys like?" Caleb asks.

"We were pretty good. Our lead singer was a guy named Zane. He went Ozzy, though, like literally brought a mouse to a gig and bit its head off."

"You're kidding," I say.

"I wish. Hormones, man. Anyway, that band fell apart. I kinda thought Eli and I would put a new band together, but . . . he'd met Kellen and their songwriting styles were really perfect for each other, at least at the beginning. Eli and I were compatible players, but not writers."

"Savage Halos were better, anyway," says Val, not looking up. "*Sear My Face* rules."

"You found our album?" Randy asks.

"Sure did," says Val.

"Well, thanks." Randy sounds sincerely touched. "But, no way. Allegiance was so great. And Eli's songs ruled. But anyway, we toured up the coast with them that spring, and we got to play the Fillmore, opening for the Dave Matthews Band."

"That must have been huge," says Jon. "Those guys can play."

"They overplay," says Caleb.

"You've lost your mind," Jon replies like a stodgy Englishman.

"It was a sick show," says Randy. "I remember standing onstage at soundcheck, and Eli and I were both testing guitars, and we looked out at the room. I mean, this was a place where Hendrix, the Doors, Cream, the Who—they all played, and we used to geek out about all those classic bands, man, back when guys really *played* rock, not just rehashed it, and there we were. . . ."

Randy trails off. A second of silence. I wonder where he's gone . . . then he's back.

"And Eli, he was always thinking big, such an idealist. He was like, *We'll headline here someday*. And I was like, *Maybe* we'll *headline*. And he said, *You guys will open for us*. He meant it as a joke, except that's kinda how it turned out."

"You guys opened for them at the Fillmore?" Caleb asks.

"Well, no. Other places, but not there. Savage Halos was never exactly mainstream. Eli promised me he'd get us an opening slot on that last tour, and I'm sure he tried . . ." I sense some doubt in whether Randy actually believes that. ". . . but Candy Shell had up-and-comers they wanted on

237

board, and you know, a promise in the music business is rarely a real promise."

Caleb and I share a look. Randy's putting fifteen years of perspective on it, but we can still hear the hurt.

"That's too bad," says Val. "Record labels are bastards."

Randy shrugs. "Sometimes. Anyway, like I said, Eli was a dreamer. He said a lot of things, just, idealizing, that was what he did, thinking of what would be awesome. Start his own label, write three albums a year, open a rock club in London . . ." Randy trails off. After a pause, he adds, "Everybody always knew better than to believe him, but, you kinda couldn't help it."

The van returns to silence.

"There it is," says Matt from the front seat a little while later. We all look up and get our first glimpse of the San Francisco skyline.

"Here," Caleb says, handing his phone to Randy. "Put this on."

The song that comes on is Allegiance to North, the big hit off *The Breaks*, a song we've all heard a billion times called "Excuses in Technicolor."

"Nice," says Randy, rolling down the windows.

He cranks it ear-bleeding loud.

Jon grabs his guitar and calls out chords, as we all start to sing:

It's all black and . . .

238

"A!" calls Jon.

whiiiiiite with you, And when I . . .

"E!"

tryyyy to prove, That I'm . . .

"G, B minor, E!"

different and debonaire

"G, B minor, D!"

In my tuxedo and greased-back hair

"Hits on E!"

The PER. FECT. Gen-tle-MAN.

"F sharp minor!"

But oh no, Just when I

"A!"

thought that I knew

"G, B minor, E!"

Your excuses in Technicolor, Make me blue

"F-sharp minor!"

Oh no, No matter what I do

"G, B minor, E!"

Your excuses in Technicolor, Paint it new

"D to E!"

Your excuses are mixing me u-uuupp!

"This is going to be awesome," Caleb shouts over the guitar solo. A minute later, I feel my phone buzz.

Caleb: Don't tell them yet, but I'll play the songs, if we find them.

Summer: We HAVE to.

I feel a thrill at reading this, and flash him a quick smile before singing along with the next song.

We light into the Mission, buzzing, free, alive, far from home, and ready for anything—

Until Randy pulls up at Tea & Crumpets.

"This is it?" says Jon. Before us is a tan brick building, a Masonic temple. Dead fluorescent light spills out the front door. There is a gathering of people visible inside, milling around. They all look old.

"It's in the basement," I say. "Petunia said to go in around back. It could still be cool." But inside I'm knotting up with worry. There is nothing worse than showing up for a gig and finding out it's lame. Especially when you've driven six hours and spun lies to get there.

There's a back door down concrete steps. A hand-made sign announces the TEA & CRUMPETS ALL AGES SALON. It's exquisitely made with lace doilies and script letters hand cut from gold foil paper. There is a teacup on one side, and a unicorn reading *Alice in Wonderland* on the other.

"Danger," says Jon. "This is not looking very rock 'n' roll."

"It's supposed to be a good crowd," I say weakly.

We enter into a storage area that's dank and smells like old towels. Through the next door, we find ourselves in a low-ceilinged basement with cement poles here and there. There are speakers and mics, a crooked house drum kit, and frayed amps set up beneath two harsh yellow lights in the corner.

"Ouch," says Matt, eyeing the drums like he just witnessed someone wiping out in the school hallway. "Good thing I brought my own cymbals."

Across an empty sea of concrete floor, lit only by strands of multicolored holiday lights strung around the poles, is a little sitting area, thrift-store furniture and floor lamps arranged on a patchwork of threadbare oriental rugs. Past that is a counter with a popcorn machine and a cooler of sodas and fruit.

There are five people sitting in the chairs. A wide-framed girl stands up. She's wearing a magenta polyester dress that is straining to fit her. "Hey, you must be Danger-heart," she says. She's got thick glasses with pointed frames, like something a grandmother in the fifties would wear. She has a triangular handbag that matches. Her friends are a collection of sweaters, polyester pants, hipster sneakers, more thick glasses, and retro hairstyles.

"Hi," says Caleb.

"I'm Petunia. You guys can unload by the stage and when you're done, we have tea sandwiches and Dandelion made her signature crumpets."

"That sounds adorable," says Val with a spoonful of sarcasm, except I probably agree with her.

We drop our stuff, get our paper plates of crumpets, which are dry and made from whole wheat and likely flax and who-knows-what-else, and then sit on the couches. We take up two, and Petunia and Dandelion and their other friends sit on their side and it feels like the worst social event ever.

"So glad you guys could make it up," says Petunia.

"You're from LA," says Dandelion. She's dressed in a similarly retro lime-green housedress, with a thick strand of costume pearls. "Do you know the Lapels?"

"Oh, not really," I say, "are they new?"

This seems to offend one of the boys, causing him to get up for more tea.

Petunia is about to answer when there is a huge sound from above, like twenty cases of grapefruits just got dumped on the floor. Then there is a long scrape, followed by another chorus of thumps.

"Oh God, they're at it again," says Dandelion.

"What's happening?" I ask.

"There's a monthly African dance class in the hall upstairs."

The sound of hundreds of feet thumping and sliding continues over the next hour, as the first band of the showcase, New Erasers, plays. It's a three-person band in matching black V-necked sweaters, two boys and a girl, drums, bass, and accordion, and they are all equally hunched in half as they play. The girl whisper-sings her lyrics and the drummer plays with brushes and it is barely possible to decipher their songs with the dancing horde from above.

Halfway through the set, Val springs up from the couches and hugs a tall, pencil-thin guy with frizzy hair who just entered. So, Weezil exists.

By the time New Erasers finishes, there are only about fifteen people in the room, just enough for it to feel even more empty. They stand in clumps, far back from the stage. Dangerheart starts to unpack, and I begin to feel the sinking certainty that this is so lame, and what are we doing here? Why did I think this was a good idea? And I can see the same solemn disappointment on the band members' faces. They're all staring quietly into space as they swap places with New Erasers. So, so disappointed.

And then I hear a clap of hands from behind us. A slow, sarcastic clap.

Jon turns, and squints. I hear footsteps striding toward us.

"Isn't that Ari's brother?" Matt wonders.

Oh no. I turn, and before he even steps into the stage light, I can see the pro teeth, gleaming from behind their predatory smirk.

"There they are!"

"Shit," I mutter to myself.

"Hello, Dangerheart. Jason Fletcher, associate talent scout for Candy Shell Records. I'm sure Summer's told you all about me."

20

"She hasn't, actually," Val says immediately.

"Oh no? Ah, no big deal." Jason smiles broadly. "Well," he says, "I didn't realize you'd scored such a cool gig." He looks directly at me. "Now it makes sense."

The band looks at me quizzically, but Jason is on it before I can even speak.

"I saw your set at my brother's party. Not bad. I told Summer, with a little polish, you guys could really be something."

"Summer didn't mention that," says Val. I can feel the glare.

"No? Well, it probably slipped her mind."

244

"What do you want?" I ask him. "They're just about to go on."

"Just came by to say good luck." Jason looks around at the sparse crowd. "I get it. You guys want to keep your indie cred. Start small . . ." I can hear it coming, and I'm thinking, *Don't say it, don't say it*, but I understand that of course, he's going to. Of course this was when he was planning on telling them all along. "That crowd I would've had you in front of tonight is at least five hundred, but, I suppose that's *selling out*, or something. Also, no crumpets."

"What crowd?" Caleb asks.

Jason's smile is enormous, and all I can do now is watch.

"You know," he says, "opening for Sundays on Mars over at the Rickshaw Stop? I wanted you guys, but . . . like I said, I get it. And it worked out anyway. Your pals Freak Show were available."

Unbelievable. He brought in Freak Show? That had to be just so he could twist this knife. I want to scream at him. I want to cry. Both feel impossible. I'm frozen.

And the band's eyes have all turned to me.

"Ooh." Jason is checking his watch. "Gotta get back. Anyway, good luck." He looks pointedly at Caleb. "Summer's got my number if you guys want to come by the club after the set. I put you on the list. We could talk about the future. I've always got more dates." He takes one more theatrical look around the basement. "Adorable." Then he turns and strides away, leaving us in stunned silence.

"Um, so, are you guys ready to go on?" Petunia appears at the edge of the stage light.

"It's going to be a few minutes," says Caleb slowly. "Sorry."

"Okay," says Petunia with a sigh, "well, but our sound curfew is at nine forty-five, so . . ." She heads back to the couches.

"Curfew," mutters Jon, pointedly staring at the floor. "WOW."

I feel Caleb's eyes on me. I can't believe I let it come to this, and I don't want to look, but I force myself to. "True?" he asks.

I nod. "He treats bands like crap, guys. He put Postcards out on tour and they're totally flailing now. We don't want him involved in our business. I didn't know this gig would—"

"What, completely suck?" says Val. "But you knew, you *had* to know it wouldn't be as good as playing the Rickshaw."

"I wasn't sure," I say, and it sounds oh-so lame.

"This is because of what happened to you with Postcards," Jon adds. "That's why I'm playing under a *curfew*."

"You should have told us," says Matt. "So at least we had a choice." Even Matt . . .

In my mind, I'm thinking about how I know I have to take this. That I deserve this, for keeping the gig from them. But I also need them to know that it's not that simple. "Caleb," I say. He's looking near me, but not at me. "Jason wanted to advertise the gig using your connection to Eli. I knew you wouldn't want that."

"I'm not sure the rest of us wouldn't want that," says Jon. He looks at Caleb. "We wouldn't be *here* if people knew who you were."

Oh boy. I figure this will ignite Caleb, but Val jumps in before he can respond.

"That's not the point," she snaps. It's hard to tell if she's meaning to defend Caleb or not. "We could've still taken that gig under the condition that he not use Caleb's background."

"But if we *did* use his background, we'd probably get a huge crowd," Jon says.

"You were fine with this before," says Caleb quietly.

"That was before we ended up here, at a dumb gig, on a wild goose chase after songs that we're not even going to play!"

"I was going to play them!" Caleb whisper shouts, glancing around. The sparse crowd is definitely noticing. We're violating the dirty laundry rule so badly. "I decided you guys were right, but hell, maybe I was wrong."

Jon holds up his hands. "Okay, cool, but still, the Rickshaw . . ."

"He probably wouldn't have given it to us without using Eli's name," I say, but hearing the club name makes me picture the five hundred people, the lovely stage framed by red curtains (I stalked it more than once online). Sure, Jason

247

would have been there somewhere, but . . . I feel sick again.

Val pounces, like she's been waiting for this. "Did you *ask* him?"

I bite my lip. "No."

"I'm not saying I'd want to work with Jason," Val continues, "but you just thought about yourself and not about us."

"I did think about you guys," I say weakly.

And then Val looks at Caleb and says, "I told you."

Caleb doesn't respond; he's lost in the spiral of this mess. But I can't help it, that comment sends me over the edge. "You *told* him?" My voice rises despite the crowd, who are definitely all curious onlookers to this car crash. "You know what I *haven't* told him? Haven't told anyone?"

Val looks like she's about to respond, but her secrets make her hesitate.

And now it's my turn to jump, even as a part of me feels like I shouldn't. "I could have told Caleb about your mother, about how she was engaged to Kellen, and Candy Shell! You've been lying this whole time. And I think I know why."

As the words are coming out, an equally loud voice is screaming inside me: *Wrong place! Wrong time! The most dangerous moment of the Red Zone is right before taking stage when nerves are at their highest!* But, no. I have to fight back. Val does not get to tear me down when she has secrets of her own, far bigger ones.

Her face is frozen in a lethal stare, but as if to prove my point, she has no response. Except then her eyes tremble, and a tear falls free.

Then another.

That's not what I expected.

"You think you know what my life is like?" she says quietly, her voice shaking. "You think you know what it's like to sleep in your car every night, trying to avoid police and freaks, to eat at kitchens and shoplift bags of chips? You think you know about . . ." Her voice thins to a sliver. "My mother? My mother who likes to use her fists when she's drunk? Who likes to take her shit out on me? Over . . . and over?"

"Jesus, Summer," Caleb says.

"No, I—I don't know," I say, backpedaling pathetically. The sight of Val's crying face has ground my thoughts to a halt. What have I done? But is this even real? Or an act? Except, I can feel the sadness from her. It's real. There's no way she's faking it. And her tears unlock floodgates of guilt inside me, no matter how she's acted. "But how can I know anything about you when you won't tell us?"

Val keeps staring at me through glistening eyes. "There's a difference between my secrets and yours. Everything I've done has been in the best interest of this band." She takes a step back, wiping her nose. To the floor between us all: "I'm out." To Caleb: "Sorry." To Matt and Jon: "Sorry, guys." To me: not even a glare. Then she picks up her bass

249

and she and Weezil head for the door.

"Val," says Caleb, "wait." But he doesn't follow her.

I call after her. "How is this best for the—"

"Summer, stop," says Caleb.

I do. I'm glad he said it. Whatever pathetic thing I was going to say would've just made things worse.

Val slaps the back door open and she's gone.

We all just stand there, a circle with a hole in it, gazing at the floor.

"Band member storming out . . ." Jon holds up an imaginary pen and paper. "Oh, we already checked that one off this list at our last gig. Guess we get bonus points!"

"Is every gig going to be this intense?" Matt wonders hopelessly.

"I don't know," Caleb says, and I find him looking at me. "Is it?"

"Um . . ." It's Petunia again, her hands folded in front of her. "If you guys, could, um . . ."

"There's no show," says Caleb, pulling his guitar off his shoulder. "Our bassist had an emergency, and, we have to go. Sorry."

"Oh my God, are you serious?" says Jon. "Really? We're just leaving?"

Matt sighs. "We're bailing on a set again?"

Caleb looks stuck. "What are we supposed to do?"

"Whatever, fine," says Jon, "but no gig, no band."

"Caleb," I say, my voice wet with the tears I'm fighting

250

back. I meet his cold gaze and flash my eyes at Matt and Jon. "You should still play the set," I say. "Make it short, and stripped down——"

"Why? What's the point?" Caleb shouts, and it kills me to hear the same words he used last summer. "This is all destined to fail anyway! It's obvious. I can't——"

Randy appears; he's been hanging back, listening, but staying outside the band circle. He puts a hand on Caleb's shoulder. It's fatherly, and Caleb pauses. Breathes.

"Hey, I can sit in," says Randy.

"You know the songs?" Jon asks.

"Yeah. I've heard you guys a bunch. And it's rock, not rocket science. I got it."

Caleb doesn't react for a second. He's processing. Then he looks to Jon and Matt. "What do you think?"

Jon doesn't need to answer. Matt looks around like he'd almost prefer to go home. "Well, I guess we're here . . ."

"Okay," says Caleb. "Thanks, Randy." He calls to Petunia: "We're going on."

Everyone moves to their spots. I'm planning to just let Caleb go, and then to slink away to a safe corner until the set is over. But as he passes, I can't resist touching his shoulder. He pauses . . . but it feels like most of him would rather keep moving.

I want to just say *Have a great show* but then my stupid heart is throwing out words. "I'm sorry," and, "Are you okay?"

Caleb's eyes flash to me, then return to distance. "No . . . but, the show must go on, right?"

"Yeah. Good luck. Break a leg, except, don't actually . . ." As the words are tripping out, I suddenly know that I need to kiss him. I need to stop failing with my voice and just kiss him so he knows, he has to know how much I love him and believe in him and hope for him—but I can't quite move my body. Because would he even want a kiss from me now? After all that just happened? *Who cares? GO!*

Yes—but I miss my chance. He's turned around into the glare of the stage light, facing the crowd. The house music fades out. And so I slide off the stage, back into the shadow beyond the speaker stack. Caleb is alone in the naked spotlights. I am alone in the dark. But at least he has the guys, just out of sight around him. For me, there's only empty floor and knowing that I have messed this whole thing up.

Caleb tunes, and then waits as Randy finishes negotiations with the New Erasers' bassist to borrow his gear.

"Hey, we're Dangerheart from Mount Hope," says Caleb to scattered applause. "This is our first gig on tour, and some of you may have noticed, we just had a bit of drama." This line gets a few knowing laughs, and only one snicker. "But, we came all the way up here, so . . . is it all right if we play for you anyway?" This line gets sympathetic applause, a few shouts of approval. I'm proud of him, knowing he must be wound so tight.

"Thanks." Caleb checks his guitar one more time,

turns and locks eyes with each band member. They share little nods, their game faces on, and then Matt counts off with his sticks.

They open with "Knew You Before" and Randy was right, he's got it. Caleb, Jon, and Matt are all eyes down, but after a few bars, I can see the music freeing them from all the drama. They start to move, heads bobbing, coming alive.

The crowd stays. Applauds. It's polite, but curious.

I check the set list. Second up is "The Spinelessness of Water," one of Val's. Third is "On My Sleeve." But Caleb skips to "Chem Lab," instead. Thing is, that's the only other Caleb song on the list. It was supposed to be a thirty-minute set, with three Val songs and three Caleb. They sub in "Artificial Limb" after that.

The applause has gotten bigger with each song. They definitely need to do another. I see Caleb glancing at his set list. Randy appears at his shoulder and says something quietly. Caleb doesn't react immediately, and Randy steps back. Then Caleb leans to the mic. For just a second, his eyes find me in the shadows.

"Okay, well, we only have one more song for you. It's called 'On My Sleeve.'"

He stares down at his fret board, his fingers settling into position. He's nervous, but so brave, and right now I'm so proud of him. In spite of losing his bass player, being let down by his manager, and his own fears, he's going to put himself out there, tonight, to this skeptical crowd in a place so far from home, put his heart on display. I wish I was that brave. Wish I'd done the same thing weeks ago. I could have told them about that other show, and made my case for how I thought it was a bad idea. But if they wanted to do it anyway, I could have sucked it up and been brave and trusted that this time it would be different.

And maybe that's the secret: Maybe we do go in circles, but they're orbits, created by the gravity of our hearts and hopes, and so if we stay true to ourselves, we will face the same situations again, but each time we come around, we know more, we've grown, learned, and this time we can get it right, or at least a little better.

Caleb starts the slow jangling chords. A few people in the crowd start to chat quietly, as any ballad always causes them to do. I see Caleb noticing this, and I hope he doesn't doubt himself. He puts his head down. Starts to sing. The words are raw as ever, even though he's gotten better at performing them. I fall for him all over again, and around the room, I can see others doing the same, eyes widening, hearts breaking. It's perfect: an honest response to an honest song. Just people, connecting.

Jon and Matt and Randy bring in the crescendo for the second half of the song, and it lifts off, starting to soar. If I'm honest with myself, I'd admit that while Randy is doing great, Val really had a certain presence, maybe just from playing the songs so many times, but also from being her black hole swirl of intensity, gravity so absolute that no light escapes. In a few minutes, this set will be over and we're going to have to reckon with that loss. Among other things.

But for this moment, in the spare stage light, beneath the zombie-like scraping of the dancers upstairs, Caleb is performing amazingly, beautifully. So is the whole band. And my heart nearly explodes for him, for them all, for being amazing in spite of everything, for making something beautiful in such a meaningless corner of a vast and dark universe. For a moment, I forget the silly politics, the cat-and-mouse emotions. Given everything, there is no reason for Dangerheart to be doing something this beautiful here, now. And yet, they are, and this moment *is*, for them and for all the people here. Right now, there is just music and I am happy to be in it, like that autumn sky ceiling at Canter's, it just is and we are and that's enough.

They finish, and the applause is full-on. "That's all we've got," says Caleb. "Thanks."

I see them all allowing a moment to smile and soak it up. A gig completed, at long last, even if under ridiculous circumstances. I watch them pack up and as they move off-stage, my stomach flips with anticipation about how our next interactions will go. Maybe having played a great set will make things easier. Or maybe, now that they know they can do it, they'll feel like they're better off without my drama.

"That was excellent," I say to Caleb.

"Thanks," is all I get, head down.

I let him put his guitar in its case, then try, "What did Randy say to you?"

Caleb stands. He glances at me for a moment, our eyes finally meeting, but he looks away. He does smile, but it's into space, not at me. Still, it's something. "He said, 'There's always another gig, and this is it.'"

"'On My Sleeve' was pretty amazing."

More relief from Caleb. "Yeah. It felt good."

I want to hug him but instead I sort of pat his shoulder. His shirt is cool with sweat. He doesn't move, but he does smile at me. Getting warmer.

"So," Jon says after packing up, "do we want to go over to the Rickshaw?"

"Let's go to Space Panda first," says Caleb, "and see about the tape. After that . . ." He glances at me. "Maybe."

I don't respond. If we are meant to go to the Rickshaw, I will face it. But I'm glad we're going after the tape first.

We thank Petunia, explain that we have a bunch of driving to do, and duck out as the last band is playing. It seems clear from her frown that we won't be playing *Forecast: Sweaters!* again anytime soon. We can probably expect some snarky comments online about our behavior, *typical LA drama queens*, that kind of thing. But hopefully there will also be a mention that the set was great.

We get in the van, and after a couple blocks of silence,

Caleb finally turns to me. "Was that true? What you said about Val? That her mom was engaged to Kellen?"

"Yeah, all true," I say. "But I don't know what it means."

He shakes his head. "I don't know what to make of it."

"Of all the things she's ever said," I admit, "I felt like I believed her last statement, about how she's done everything in the best interest of the band, most." The more I think about it, the more I can't believe how I rushed to judgment, how easily I let myself believe in conspiracies without actually finding out the truth, without trusting the people around me.

"She doesn't seem like the sleeper-cell type," says Jon. "Though if she is, storming out on us would have been the perfect time to go get the tape."

"Shit." All my thoughts reverse. Val and her fake ID. Her friend Weezil, who could drive her there . . . and she's got a half hour head start. . . . Suddenly, I'm right back to fearing the worst.

21

We barely speak for the next mile as Randy muscles his way through traffic.

"Even if she is after the tape for herself, or for her mom, or even Candy Shell," says Randy, "she doesn't know where it's hidden."

I imagine us all in the Vault searching, her on one side, us on the other.

"Neither do we," says Caleb.

"Yes, we do," says Randy as we sit at a red light. "*Search for a hidden yesterday.* That's what we do after we kiss Daisy, right?"

"Right."

"Well, it's obvious," says Randy. "Okay, not *obvious*, it did take me a little while to figure it out, or I should say to remember it."

"What?" Caleb asks.

"He's talking about one of the greatest rock 'n' roll cover controversies ever. I remember going with Eli to vinyl shops and he was always looking for it."

"Randy!" Caleb nearly shouts. "For what?"

"Do a search for *Yesterday and Today*, by the Beatles."

"That's not one of their albums," says Jon. "I have the whole box set."

Randy groans. "It's not one of the *digitally remastered* albums. The iTunes versions are the British versions. This was an American release. They did the albums different in the US and England back then."

"Got it," I say, clicking on a link. There is a photo of the Beatles sitting on a luggage trunk, like the kind people would have taken when traveling across the Atlantic on steamships. "What about it?"

"Look for the picture with the babies."

I scroll down and there it is. Another version of the cover, with the Beatles all dressed in white smocks, and covered in baby-doll heads and pieces of meat. "Gross."

"But kinda awesome," says Caleb, leaning over.

"Exactly," says Randy. "The reaction to that cover was so bad that Capitol Records recalled all the copies, and they pasted a new cover over it, but then word got out, and lots of people tried to soak off the new cover to get to the old one. Lots of warped copies out there. My dad had one. But Eli and I were always looking for a perfect original cover that escaped the recall. There were very few."

"So, if this Carter guy had one," I say, "that's where the tape is."

"That's got to be what he means," says Randy.

Caleb has leaned away and is typing into his phone. When he feels me looking, he says, "Weezil's number is in here from when Val used my phone. I'm trying to get in touch with her."

"She's not going to respond if she's after the tape," I say.

"But if she's not, and she cools off and realizes she needs a ride home, she will."

By the time we park ten minutes later, Val hasn't replied.

We end up a few blocks from the club, and when we round the corner we find a giant snaking line to get in.

Given that I will probably live my life without ever boarding an intergalactic starship or meeting alien races in far-off nebulae, this may be the closest I come to experiencing alien life. It's group after group of spindly club girls, all twenty-something (if not teens with fake IDs), dressed in shimmery short skirts with strappy tops, hair in spirals, glitter everywhere, multicolored eye paint, impossible heels, and most (and often too much) of every thigh. The dudes who surround them almost look like they should be on chain leashes fastened to metal collars. They loom with

260

rounded shoulders in their baggy dress shirts, profession-ally torn jeans, and gelled hair. They speak in grunts. The women answer in high-pitched roller-coaster voices, twit-tery laughs with wide mouths. They're constantly preening. A part of me wants to understand their customs, their lan-guage, and yet I might as well be an astronaut in a baggy white suit, except an astronaut would be noticed. Here I am invisible to them.

Caleb, Jon, Matt, and I stand off to the side while Randy gets in line. In his flannel, jeans, and beard, he looks like someone who's come to fix the plumbing.

The walls thump, deep waves of bass washing over us. Through the high windows of the two-story brick façade, we can see wild lights spinning. There is a bar up on the roof, edged in palm fronds, and laughter spills down from it like rain.

The line barely moves, as groups keep strutting right up to the front, checking with the burly black-suited bouncer, and then walking right in.

"This is going to take forever," says Caleb.

"Hey! Hey, you four!"

The shouts of the bouncer get our attention. And he's looking at us.

"Yeah, you!" He waves us over.

"Um . . ." I glance at the band, and we make our way to him.

The giant man leers down at us. He has two fingers to a

Bluetooth device in his ear. I notice a camera keeping watch from over the door, silhouettes up above, possibly looking down.

"Which one of you is Caleb?" he asks in an impossibly deep voice.

"Me."

"The manager says I'm supposed to let your party in. IDs."

"We're not twenty-one," says Caleb.

The bouncer exhales, so bored by this. "They're minors," he says into the Bluetooth. "Uh-huh . . . we're going to need a chaperone."

"Kill me," says Jon.

Caleb motions to Randy, who pushes out of line, causing huffs around him.

The door opens and a tall, professionally dressed woman with jet-black hair and giant brown eyes steps out. "Right this way."

"Any idea why the manager is letting us in?" Matt wonders from behind us. "Do you think we're in trouble?"

"Stay cool, Matty," says Jon. "They obviously knew we were coming."

"Yeah, but *who* knew?" Randy wonders aloud.

"Maybe the DJ got word that we were coming somehow," I say. "Maybe he knows to help us."

Caleb just shrugs. He's deep in Fret Face.

We enter a world of dark and pulsing light that smells

almost tropical. We have to walk single file through the tight crowd. The music hammers at my chest and saws at my ears. No melody, just urge and overkill. We pass a bar gleaming in red and amber, lined to the high ceiling with sparkling bottles, and a dance floor that is literally crushed with people.

"Whoa . . . ," Jon breathes. He's pointing to a platform along the far wall, where a line of girls wear identical skimpy silver dresses wired with white LEDs. They look like androids and dance with stiff movements. I wonder if they are paid to do that, or if that is really their idea of fun.

Caleb's hand slips into mine as we thread through the shoulders and hips, as if our troubles are less important than getting through this zombie horde alive. Ahead I see a staircase to the balcony, where a couple DJs spin. The one in the center is lit in red and wearing a welder's visor. The disco ball reflects in it. Something tells me that's Claro.

We're led up the stairs to the balcony. More stairs lead up to the roof. We're behind the DJs now, where two minions scramble back and forth to crates of vinyl.

Our escort proceeds to a huge metal door with a heavy spinning handle, like a bank vault. We push through and find ourselves in a high-ceilinged room. When the door seals behind us, there's a whoosh of air and the thump of the club is extinguished. The assault is replaced by whispers of tinny music and I see that it is coming from headphones. Everyone in here is wearing them. They sit in leather chairs, plugged into stereo systems on low tables between them, each with a turntable. The walls are lined with dark wood shelves like we're in an old library, complete with ladders that slide along, only the shelves are filled with records. The clientele are all hipsters in fashionable vintage attire, cool hats, flouncy dresses or jeans and sneakers, thick glasses and beards and scarves. Or maybe they're all time travelers from the sixties. They talk quietly about records by the walls, or bop their heads along to the headphones. Waitresses dressed in tweed skirt suits bustle in and out of a door on the side, delivering cocktails and coffees.

Daisy sits obediently by the door. We all pet her head lightly. It feels like sandpaper.

"Okay," says Caleb, "wow."

"Oh, oh, oh," says Randy. "There is a god."

"Must resist . . . the urge to find . . . all Ramones records," says Jon. He vibrates like he's hooked up to electrodes.

"Are you kidding me?" says Matt. "*Zeppelin II*, and *2112.*"

"I thought drummers had to choose sides in the great Bonham versus Peart debate."

Matt shakes his head. "That's like debating pancakes and waffles. Totally different. Both awesome."

"And both need the maple syrup goodness of lead guitarrrr!" Jon air-guitars.

"Sshh!" One of the tweed librarian-waitresses holds a finger to her lips.

I am busy scanning the stacks. They are organized by genre. Rock, jazz, R & B, and soul.

"This way." Our escort leads us across the thickly carpeted room, stopping at a set of chairs by the high back windows, which look out on a collage of back porches and windows and layers of city. We find ourselves standing before two older men.

The man on the right has a badge pinned to his tan jacket. He's not wearing headphones, but the man on the left is. Seeing us, he slips them off his bald head. He's wearing a slim black suit and looks like he just stepped out of a casino in a James Bond movie. I feel like I almost recognize him. He smiles, eyes on Caleb, and he and Randy seem to know exactly who this is.

22

"Hey, Randy," the man says over tinny headphone music. "Caleb, it's nice to meet you." He reaches over and carefully lifts the needle off the spinning vinyl. As it slows, I see it's the Doors's *L.A. Woman*.

The man puts out his hand. "Kellen McHugh." In his other hand he holds a thin black cylinder.

Caleb shakes, manners taking over. "Nice to meet you."

"Hey, Kellen," says Randy, and it doesn't sound friendly. "What brings you to San Fran?"

Kellen holds the cylinder to his mouth and inhales, and I realize it's an electronic cigarette. It lights up blue at the tip. Kellen has thin features, kind of hawk-like, and small glasses. He looks more literary than rock star. When he

266

exhales, the cloud of steam smells like mint.

"Same thing that brings you here, I'm thinking." Kellen motions to the man beside him. "This is Detective Saunders. He made the trip up with me."

I suddenly have that feeling of being in detention (only happened once), or grounded (a few times). Both Caleb and I are silent.

"I've heard you're a great musician," Kellen says to Caleb, "and I also know that you recently found out about your dad. That was probably kind of a shock."

"Yeah," says Caleb tightly.

"I'll be honest," says Kellen. "I don't really know why you're here, but based on what I've heard, I suspect that maybe it has something to do with Eli's lost songs."

Caleb just shrugs.

"Look," says Kellen, "I don't want this to be complicated. I always suspected Eli was working on those last songs. I'm sure they're genius. When he never delivered them, not to mention bailed on the band, it really messed things up for all of us."

"You make it sound like none of that was your fault," says Randy, his tone frigid.

"We all play our parts," says Kellen. Back to Caleb: "I completely understand you wanting to find your dad's lost songs, but I also don't want your life to get messed up by Eli, like mine did."

"What's that supposed to mean?" Caleb asks.

267

Kellen produces a fold of papers from his jacket and hands it to Randy. "That's a copy of the contract Eli signed with Candy Shell Records. You saw a contract at one point, with Burn Bottom Records, right?"

That last comment feels like a slight. "Yeah," Randy grunts, leafing through the pages.

"So you can verify that it's the real thing. Any songs that Eli wrote during the time that he was in Allegiance to North are technically the property of Candy Shell," says Kellen. "The fact that he passed away doesn't change that."

"No thanks to you," Randy mutters, and I'm startled by the venom in his voice.

Kellen winces, and flashes an almost annoyed glance at Randy, but he doesn't bite on whatever Randy is referring to. Instead he looks back to Caleb. "Look, the world should hear your dad's songs. He was a genius. Legally, though, they're Candy Shell's. I know that may not sound right to you, but that's the deal he made."

"He wouldn't want *you* to have them," Randy adds.

"Maybe not, but that's not his call to make. Caleb, you probably feel torn about this, but I'll make you a deal. Show me the songs, and I'll let you play on the record when we release them. Everybody would love that."

"Can it be my band?" Caleb asks. I'm proud of him for thinking of that.

Kellen shrugs. "I don't think so. They're Allegiance

songs. I think the rest of the band would want to get together and play them."

"You don't deserve it, Kellen," Randy says through clenched teeth.

"Randy, come on," says Kellen. "These kids are in over their heads with this. You knew Eli; isn't this all classic *him*? I don't want there to have to be legal awkwardness, talks with all your parents . . ."

This point spears me, as it was probably meant to.

Caleb stands there, hands in his pockets. I wish I could talk to him telepathically. I don't want him to agree, and yet I don't know what else he can do.

"Think about your mom, too, Caleb," says Kellen, "having to hire lawyers . . ."

"Okay," Caleb snaps. "I get it." He starts to reach into his pocket.

"What are you doing?" Jon asks.

"Caleb . . . ," I say, but I don't add *don't*.

"He never bothered to send me a letter, or even call, while he was alive." Caleb produces the tape. I didn't realize he'd been carrying it with him. Kellen leans forward when he sees it.

Caleb turns the tape over in his fingers. "I was happier without him. All this has done is remind me what's missing. What I can't ever have." He turns to me. "Even playing the songs was never going to bring him back. Never going to give me a dad."

He's still holding the tape close to him. His eyes lock with mine. He looks like he might pass out. I don't want him to hand it over, but I don't see what choice he has. I nod slightly.

And Caleb holds out the tape. His hand is shaking as Kellen plucks it from his fingers.

"Thanks, Caleb. This was the right choice. And I'm guessing you're here because there's another one?"

Caleb nods. "Hidden in a Beatles record."

Kellen turns the tape over in his fingers. "Go ahead. I won't steal your chance to find it."

"Come on," Caleb says to me. We cross the room, reading the labels. Caleb is silent, his face stone.

We stop at the "B" section.

"I don't think you had a choice," I say to him. He doesn't respond.

Then his hand shoots out, and his fist slams into the back of an empty chair beside us. It makes a loud smack—Caleb was probably aiming for the padding but it sounds like he hit the frame—and the chair wobbles. Caleb shakes his hand, wincing, and lets out a slow, crushed sigh.

"I'm so sorry," I say. I move to hug him whether he likes it or not, but he lets me.

Caleb sniffs, maybe fighting tears. He's so still, I can't tell. As we hold each other, I hear urgent voices from behind us. We turn and see Randy talking angrily to Kellen. Jon and Matt have stepped away awkwardly. A librarian-waitress swoops over and shushes him.

Caleb takes a deep breath. He makes his best attempt at a smile for me. "Look at the bright side: we can wake up tomorrow, and just focus on having an awesome band. On having fun and being great. Doesn't that honestly sound like a relief?"

"Yeah, kinda." I wonder if he will still feel that way tomorrow. I point to a nearby shelf. "There."

Caleb climbs a ladder. The Beatles records take up nearly an entire floor-to-ceiling section. There are imports, mono editions, all kinds of things. They're alphabetized, and Caleb runs his finger over the spines. "I don't see it."

I catch the eye of a librarian and wave her over. I explain what we're looking for. "Oh, yeah," she says, "a classic. Of course we have one. It's so rare that we keep it on the side here—" She's points to a vertical line of records displayed face out between this section and the next. Each record is on a stand in its own little alcove. A sign between them says, "These rare covers are for viewing only." One of them is empty. "Oh my. It should be right there. . . I'll be right back." She hurries off.

Caleb climbs down. "It's gone?"

I gaze at the blank spot and all I can picture is Val. "Gone."

Both our heads turn as Randy's voice swells again. Now a pair of nearby listeners joins in shushing him. The anger on Randy's face is obvious from here.

"Here it is." The librarian returns, the record held like a

plate of hot food between her hands. "Phew! Someone slipped it out of there, and left it over at a listening station. All the records are tagged; it would have set off an alarm if it left."

"Can I look at it for a sec, and show my friend over there?" says Caleb.

"It's not a handling copy," says the librarian.

"That's Kellen McHugh from Allegiance to North," I say. "He'd really been hoping just to see it."

"Well . . ." But the librarian gets a little starry look in her eyes. I want to tell her he's not worth it. "Okay," she says, and we bring it over.

"Success?" Kellen asks, leaning forward.

Caleb feels around the outside, pressing the cover flat in every spot. After a moment, he hands the record to Kellen. "It's not there."

Kellen does the same. "Are you sure there was a tape?" he asks Caleb as he hands the record back to the librarian.

"Not completely," says Caleb. "I mean, he made it sound like there would be."

Kellen shakes his head. "Caleb, I don't mean to speak badly of your dad, but he was in a pretty bad way on that tour. I'm surprised to hear he could get it together to make even one tape, never mind a second one." He stands up, flipping the first tape in his fingers. "Thanks for this. And I'm sorry. You probably got your hopes up. I think he'd be proud if he knew you. But . . . this is kind of what it was like working with Eli."

"That's enough, Kellen." Randy is still fuming.

Caleb just stares into space. "No, it's cool." Then, more bravely than I can imagine being, he meets Kellen's eyes. "Thanks for the offer to play on the song. I'll let you know if anything else ever turns up."

Kellen smiles. It's impersonal, like business, but still a smile. "I hear you know Jason over at Candy Shell?"

"Yeah," says Caleb.

"Good. I'll make sure he hooks you guys up with some great shows."

Kellen and the detective get up and head for the door.

I watch them go. "What are the chances they're going to meet up with Val somewhere? That she got the tape out of here before?"

Caleb shrugs. "I don't even know if I care. Maybe it's better there's no second tape. I never wanted this. That gig tonight? It was fun. It should just be about that. The music." He turns to Randy. "Can we go home? You up for driving back?"

Randy is distant. "Oh yeah, I'd be awake all night anyway."

"I'll text Weezil again," says Caleb. "Just in case."

I wish I could share his optimism. Caleb thumbs his phone as we make our way out of the Vault and back down through the seething club.

"Anything?" I ask as we emerge from the dancing horde in the welcome cool of night.

"She says to go without her," Caleb reports.

"Are you going to ask her if she has the tape?" Jon wonders.

Caleb shakes his head. "Not tonight."

We walk silently back to the van, and go.

23

MoonflowerAM @catherinefornevr 45m
Yoo hoo. Any other space travelers awake out there?

Hours pass in the infinite dark. Despite the swirl of the evening, exhaustion takes over. Caleb, Jon, and I lie on the floor in the back of the stalker van, the gear precariously stacked to either side of us. Our only contact with the outside is the retreat of taillights across the inside of the roof from the windshield, and the advance of headlights from the two tiny back windows. Randy is driving fast, always in the passing lane, eating up the late-night drivers and trucks.

"Randy," Caleb asks, after a rest-area pit stop an hour into the drive. "What was going on with you and Kellen at the Vault?"

"Well, for one, I think he's a dick." He's quiet for a minute, but we can feel that he's got more to say. "I always thought it was bullshit that Kellen and Jerrod were trying to sue your dad for lost money and royalties. They were basically trying to get him to forfeit his rights to Allegiance money. After your dad got his head on straight, he was actually going to give them the rights. Void his contract. I told him I thought that was crazy. That what he needed to do was worry about fixing his drug and depression problems, and then get back to making music again."

"What did he say?"

"He didn't. We talked about it the last time I ever saw him. The afternoon before he died."

"So, you blame Kellen for all that legal stuff," I say.

Randy is quiet again. "There's more. When Eli left me that afternoon, he said he was going to go see Kellen, to talk it out. Next thing I know, I'm standing over a casket."

"Wait . . . ," says Caleb. "Are you saying you think Kellen had . . . something to do with it?"

"Not exactly," says Randy. "Kellen had a rock-solid alibi. He was at a party at Jerrod's house. A big Candy Shell anniversary event that Eli was not invited to. So Kellen was never a suspect. But Eli apparently stopped by there. A friend of mine said he saw Eli early on at the party, and he seemed fine, but he wasn't when he left."

"How did he leave?"

"Shouting, screaming, and stumbling. Basically a wasted mess. Security threw him out. I don't know if he got high before he went there, or while he was there, or what. He was fine when I saw him, and had been sober for a couple weeks. But after the party, he drove down to the beach, and took that swim. But . . ."

"What?"

"I shouldn't even be saying this," says Randy. "It was so long ago and there's no proof. It's not doing anyone any good."

"Jesus, Randy, just say it." I can hear the tension in Caleb's voice.

"Well, if you're Eli, and you went to talk to Kellen, and it didn't go well, why would you get high at Jerrod's house? If you hated all those people and were in legal battles with them. It just seems like Eli would have left, and done whatever drugs or booze he was going to do somewhere else."

"What exactly are you saying?" I asked.

"Nothing, I'm not saying anything," says Randy. "I just wonder if Kellen, I don't know, drugged him or something, even just put an extra shot in his drink. It didn't take much to get Eli started, and once he was going, then he went all the way. I know that sounds all conspiracy-ish, but . . . ah, it doesn't matter now anyway."

"Drugged him why?" Caleb asks darkly. "So he'd kill himself?"

"No, I don't think it was *that*. Maybe just to make him make a fool of himself at the party, to create a widely witnessed scene of Eli acting out of his mind. That would have helped with the legal stuff. They were trying to prove that he was responsible for their loss of tour money and royalties, and also irresponsible when it came to himself, and the party would have been full of credible witnesses."

He's silent, and so are we.

I reach over and take Caleb's hand. He responds, but there's a guitar case between us and eventually our hands are cramped and he pulls his away. I try not to take it personally that he's the one to retreat. I know he's still hurting about the tape. But is he still hurt about me? What I kept from him about the gig and about Val?

With his hand gone, I fold my arms like I'm in suspended animation, nothing to do or be or even think until we arrive.

My thoughts run in circles anyway.

So, now what, then?

It's a three-ring circus spectacle. Tonight was a failure, or was it? I try to remember that even just the act of throwing yourself out into the universe and playing a stupid gig to twenty people is still participating, still practicing the routines that might someday get you to the place you want to be. I don't have cliché notions, like that I regret not going on the college trips, regret lying to my parents, regret not telling the band about the better gig. I did what I thought was right for everyone. Except maybe when I thought *everyone* I was thinking more of me, of keeping myself safe.

Meeting Kellen has sparked a curious sensation in my

head. We think of ourselves as the center of our universe, the star of some universal play, and that everyone else is in some way in this galaxy to act out a role in our story. And yet the more you see the world, the more you realize how silly that is. We are all planets, far comets, asteroids, and suns, inhabiting a shared universe, acting on one another. Eli is a force acting on Caleb, and yet he is a force acting on me, but then there is Kellen, or Randy, orbiting the Eli system, and on and on beyond that. All of us rotating around each other, sometimes feeling the heat of a sun, sometimes colliding and killing off the dinosaurs, sometimes just glimpsing one another across the void, barely realizing the effect we had on one another.

Somewhere tonight, the members of Freak Show are all sitting around a San Francisco club living it up, orbiting Jason, who is orbiting us. Somewhere in Memphis, Ethan and Postcards from Ariel are learning about the real life on the road, somewhere my aunt Jeanine is on a date, and on and on, the universe expanding in overlapping circles, bigger and bigger, rendering you smaller and smaller, and something about it is terrifying and sad.

But something about it is also freeing. If we are not the center of a grand story, then the pressure's off. Dangerheart can *not* release Eli's lost songs. Dangerheart can just be Dangerheart. Caleb can just be Caleb. And I can just be Summer. I can look my parents in the eye and read them

Catherine's eulogy. Then just focus on being the best version of me I can be, free, but the world doesn't depend on it. Only I do.

Maybe it's all okay.

We can be the moments in basement clubs playing beautifully.

We can be autumn ceilings.

We can just be.

Or maybe these are just the thoughts that three a.m. in a windowless stalker van inspire.

It's the cool blue of predawn when we pull back into Caleb's driveway. Jon and Matt head home. So does Randy. I can't go home yet. Not when I'm supposed to be sleeping off an opera.

Caleb and I stand by the garage. I just want to grab him and lean against him, but we stand like neighboring trees instead.

"You should probably get to bed," I say to him. My body is whirring from the complete lack of sleep, making edges fuzzy, so completely shot, and it makes me feel forward, like Caleb could say anything at that moment, after all these strained hours, and I would fall into him, or vice versa. It seems like such a dumb time to be flooded by desire, maybe all the valves are just too tired of being wound too tight. I look up and he's looking at me . . .

He says, "I've had something on my mind to show you. Now's as good a time as any." He reaches out and takes my hand.

"You should still be mad at me," I say.

"Summer."

"Caleb."

I step toward him, probably to smash my face against his, but he's starting down the driveway. "Take a drive?"

Right. I shake off the woozy desire. "Sure."

24

We drive for fifteen minutes, through still-asleep streets, getting stopped at lights with no one else around.

"Man, I hate the traffic in this town," says Caleb.

I answer in a craggy old lady's voice, "Things aren't the way they used to be."

The sun, who we said good night to so recently, returns, blasting through the windshield as we weave through the silent mallscape, and then up into hills of sleeping houses. Finally, we arrive at a fenced-off lot. There's a stone sign for TERRACE MUNICIPAL PARK, but behind that, a high chain-link fence holds a sign reading NOTICE OF PROPOSED LAND USE ACTION, and beside that, COMING SOON: ETERNAL HOPE! SEVEN NEW LUXURY OUTLET STORES! This little park, which

I remember had a splash park and a great spiral slide, is the next victim in the zombie retail apocalypse.

Beyond it I can see a geometric footprint of concrete, stuck through with metal support beams.

"Come on." Caleb grabs the links and starts over the fence. I follow, dropping down to the dirt on the other side. He leads me between the unfinished foundations. There are four around a central hexagon, a patch of dried-out grass and shrubs, leftover park that hasn't yet been landscaped.

In the center is a pedestal.

Caleb stops beside it. "Say hello to Pluto."

The pedestal is the same size as the others I've seen, but the model of Pluto itself is no bigger than a marble. It's coated in a film of dust. I brush it off with my thumb. "Hello, little planet," I say.

"Dwarf planet, technically," says Caleb.

"I really like when you get astronomical with me," I say. This makes him smile. "Are they going to keep it here?"

"I don't know," says Caleb, looking around. "It's no longer a planet. And besides, it's taking up valuable smoothie space."

"But it's lovely."

I reach for Caleb's hand and instead he puts his arm around me. "I wanted to wait until we had like, a big date, or homecoming or something, to bring you here."

I glance back at the fence. "That would have been tough in a dress."

"Oh. Didn't think of that."

He hugs me, and I push my cheek against his neck.

"Thank you," he says.

"For what?"

"For believing in me. For trying. Even with the Jason thing. You believed so much in our stuff, in my songs."

"Don't say 'believed.' We're just getting started." But then a flash of nerves shoots through. Did he bring me here for some other reason? "Unless . . ."

He looks at me and is surprised by my worry. "Oh, no! Yeah, I mean, believING. Sorry."

"Okay, good."

He buries his face in my hair. "Thanks for everything with the tape, too."

"I'm so sorry you had to give it up. I'm sorry we didn't find the songs."

"It's okay. Or, it sucks. I don't know. We were going to get in huge trouble if we tried to play them live. And anyway, the second tape was just as much of a ghost as my dad." He laughs darkly. "He couldn't even come through on that."

I rub his arms. "You came through last night. You played 'On My Sleeve.' You nailed the show when things were at their worst. You came through for Matt and Jon. And for me, not that I deserved it."

"Stop. But thanks." Caleb sighs. "Maybe it's better there's no big lost song. Just us. We can just do our own thing, our own way. Just be what we are."

I love hearing how his thoughts and mine from last night are on the same wavelength, so much so that I have to resist smothering him with kisses. "Like Pluto," I say instead.

A smile cracks through. "Yeah, we can be the Pluto of bands. Out here, doing our thing, not giving a damn what people think, or if anyone notices us at all."

"People *are* going to notice," I say. "But yeah, our thing. That's all we can do, right?"

A minute passes. The bird sounds increase, as does the hum of cars in the distance.

"So," says Caleb, "now what?"

"Oh man, that's what my dad asked me," I say, yawning.

"The boat for Palau probably casts off soon," says Caleb.

I fall into his shoulder. "Days of sleep in a cargo hold. We'd need immunizations. Passports. SPF 6000."

"Not if we're stowaways. And we could sleep under palm trees all day."

I point to the little planet. A sunbeam is just painting its top. "Maybe after we watch sunrise on Pluto."

We kiss sleepily, and then watch the golden light crawl across the surface.

I doze off on the drive back to Caleb's. When the bump of the driveway stirs me, I feel like I'm made of lead, and so, so brain dead.

"Can we have pancakes?" I mumble.

Caleb stops the car, but instead of replying, he says, "What the hell?"

I look out the window, and have to squint hard against the reflection of morning sun blasting off the back bumper of Randy's van.

And the bumper of another car beside it.

A little blue hatchback, all beat up.

My eyes adjust to the glare and I see just about the last person I'd expect leaning against the back bumper, right beside the New Jersey license plate.

And of course, Val is scowling.

25

"Hey," says Caleb as we get out of the car.

"Hey," says Val.

Our eyes meet for the usual second, in passing only. She looks like she hasn't slept either. What does it mean that she's here?

"Why didn't you tell us you were coming back?"

Val looks around warily. "Can I explain inside?"

"Okay."

We go quietly down to the basement. Sit on the couch. I end up on one side of Caleb, Val on the other again. She looks really down, but maybe it's just the exhaustion.

"Look," she starts, "I haven't been totally honest with you."

287

I refrain from comment.

"Okay," says Caleb.

"I . . ." and suddenly her eyes start to tear up. She looks at the ceiling. "Things have kinda sucked, you know?" She looks past Caleb to me. "Caleb knows a lot of it. I guess in a way you know more. About how I ran away, how my name is really Cassie. But, you don't know what it's like having a family that fucked up. That's so . . . MIA, except it's even worse when they're around."

"I'm really sorry," I say.

"I know you think it's more than coincidence that I'm here, now, that maybe because of my mom, I've got some . . . agenda or something."

"I think you should just tell us," says Caleb. I'm relieved that he says *us* even though I know it's selfish.

Val holds out a clenched fist and uncurls her fingers.

In her palm is a tape.

It's identical to the other one. I look at her but her eyes are fixed on Caleb. And tears are just pouring out.

"I went and got it when I split last night. Fake ID. I even saw Kellen from Allegiance to North come into the Vault. But he wouldn't know me like he knows you."

"The tape was there," says Caleb. He's looking from it, then back at Val, back to the tape. And I think he's not grasping what suddenly I feel like I know, what is kind of making my brain melt . . .

"I knew you were having a hard time," says Val, "and

288

I didn't want to overwhelm you, so I thought if I just got in with the band, then I could tell you over time, so that when I did, you'd already kinda know." She sniffs hard.

"Know what?" Caleb asks, his voice caught in his throat.

Val continues like she hasn't heard him. Maybe she rehearsed this in the long dark and needs to say it in order. "And when I saw things getting crazy last night, partly I was mad about the gig and stuff, but partly, with that Jason guy on our tail, I had to make sure . . . make . . ." She chokes up. Presses her mouth against her fist.

"Go ahead," I say.

Val looks at the tape, wiping at her eyes. "Make sure we could hear from our dad again."

Caleb gazes at her. "Our dad . . ."

And suddenly everything is different.

Val tries to speak again but she can't. Her rail-thin frame quakes. She rubs at her eyes almost angrily. I get up and kneel in front of her, and for a few seconds she lets me hug her. Then she pulls away, wiping at her nose.

"You never could have known," she says, crying. "He never knew. Eli. He didn't know about me, ever."

"You're . . . ," Caleb stammers. "My sister."

"Half sister," she says, and her eyes track up to Caleb, wide, clear, guard completely down.

"Really?" he says.

I punch him in the shoulder and hiss, "Yes, really."

"Oh my God, okay." He reaches over and rubs her shoulder stiffly.

Ugh, boys sometimes. I clear my throat and when he looks at me I motion with my eyes. He gets it, and wraps her in a hug. She sinks into him, while I burn the last silly shred of jealousy.

He pulls back after a minute, and Val smiles at him. "Weird huh?"

"Weird," he agrees.

"Eli and my mom started hooking up on that last big tour," she continues. "She was actually engaged to Kellen at the time, but she was also engaged to heroin, and she and Eli used to get high together. It's all so completely gross to talk about."

"You don't have to," I say.

"I want to, though," says Val. She takes a deep breath and continues. "Kellen found out, and that was part of what destroyed that tour. Eli and my mom shacked up in New York for a few months, just using together, and sometime along in there, I happened. Didn't turn out too bad, considering the drugs. They broke up, no surprise, and Eli moved back to LA and Mom moved back to Princeton. Mom, and her addiction, were convinced that Eli was the love of her life. After a few months apart, she was going to go see him and try to make up, tell him about me, but the doctors wouldn't clear her to fly. And then he died. She blamed herself, felt like she should have taken better care of him.

Like she ever could have. And so, especially when the supply would run dry, that would give her an excuse to blame me for just about everything."

I'm crying, too, now. And feeling like an idiot. Not that I could have known. But still.

"When did she tell you all of this?" Caleb asks.

"She told me years ago. She doesn't have a very good filter, especially when she's using, which she manages to keep out of sight . . ." Val's voice lowers. "Most of the time. She also told me never to tell anyone. But she told me all about Eli, her great lost love. She even told me about his other kid."

"You knew about me. Why didn't you get in touch sooner?"

"I've been watching you for a long time. And I knew you didn't know about him. I could just tell. But then I saw your freak-out, those tweets . . . I felt sure you'd found out. So I came. The timing was good. Mom had tracked me down in Ithaca anyway, and I needed somewhere else to go."

Val pauses, wiping her nose. Caleb just looks blown away.

"I know it's a lot," says Val. "I know . . ."

Caleb shakes his head, like he's returning from far away. "It's okay." He hugs her again.

When she sits back, I ask, "How did you know about the tape location?"

"One of my mom's stories, the ones she loves to repeat whenever she's in a stupor, is the time she went record shopping in the Village with Eli and he found a copy of a particular album that he'd always wanted, only they were out of cash at the time. So Mom went back, and . . . God knows what she did to get that record, but she brought it home and surprised him. I guess he was really excited. But it must have been some fight when they broke up, because Eli stormed out and never came back for any of his stuff, even his records. So, his collection ended up at our place, including the copy of that dead-baby Beatles record. I've been looking at that cover all my life. Freakin' disturbing. But, anyway, I got the reference right away."

"Val, geez . . ." Caleb searches for what to say.

"Don't worry, bro," she says, cleaning off her face with the dirty sleeve of her sweatshirt, then surveying the stains of tears, snot, and eyeliner. "Okay," she says. "This is getting gross. Want to watch this tape?"

We put it in the camcorder, still set up but hidden behind the TV, and after a moment of blue screen, Eli appears again. It's a weirdly similar scene, this time a blue bathroom instead of green, a red T-shirt instead of black. His movements are twitchy and he's got a cigarette between his lips.

"Allll right," he says around the cigarette as he positions the camera. "Spent the bus ride today putting these lyrics together. It still needs a second verse, but it's almost done. Man, these songs have been coming so easy, finally."

He starts strumming guitar, same as last time, and now sings:

Somewhere you are dreaming
While I'm chasing silly dreams
Learning firsts in everything
While I am stuck repeating,
the same . . . old . . . mistakes

Can you miss someone you never knew?
Do you feel the space I should have occupied?
I'm watching from a distance
Trying to hear you through the breeze
When you laugh, when you cry
I want to know why . . . but I'm too far
Living in Exile . . . without you
Living in Exile . . . without you

The guitar rings in the hollow bathroom when he finishes. When Eli finally looks up at the camera, there are tears.

"Travel day tomorrow," he says, "but I've got the other songs dialed in."

There's a knock at the bathroom door.

"Okay then." His smile at the camera is tender, genuine. "More from the next show."

The video clicks off. Caleb keeps staring into the blue.

He blinks. I wonder if he will have tears, too. Then he shakes it off and asks the obvious question: "Where was the next show?"

"We can search, or check Matt's shirt," I say. "But, then what do you want to do?"

Caleb and Val lock eyes. "What do you think?" she asks.

Caleb glances at the blue screen again. "I told Kellen I'd let him know if we found anything else. . . . But then Randy said some interesting things about Kellen on the way home. I think there's more to all this than we know. So . . . keep the tape to ourselves, for now."

"I mean about the 'next show,'" says Val. "The next tape."

Suddenly Caleb breaks into a wide grin. "Are you kidding? We're going after it."

Val grins, too, and holds up her hand. "That's the right answer."

Caleb turns to me. "You think?"

My heart is racing, because here we are again. *Now what, then?* But Summer knows the answer. "I think." I hold up my hand, knowing it's corny. Caleb smiles like he agrees, but we all high-five anyway.

"Ohhh-kay, now that that's settled . . ." Val leans back on the couch, yawning. "I think I will now sleep for a week."

I check my phone. "We've got a Harvest Slaughter to

rock in just about thirteen hours."

"Okay, bed," says Caleb. He looks at me. "Upstairs couch okay?"

"Sure," I say. We stumble up the stairs, and he kisses me in the kitchen before I collapse on the couch. Woozy feelings are gone now. There is only the desire to be unconscious pulling me under. And also the sense that I will need as much sleep as I can get, because this . . . is only the beginning.

26

I wake up to a busy kitchen and the smell of frying foods. The complete lack of adequate sleep is partially made up for by mugs of coffee and faces full of pancakes and eggs from Caleb's mom, whose first reaction to the news about Val seems to be a determination to set the world record for number of pancakes made in a morning.

I find her by the stove as I'm getting thirds. Val and Caleb are immersed in a conversation that has something to do with whether Dave Grohl is a better songwriter or drummer. Charity is dabbing her eyes with a kitchen towel.

"This is probably hard for you," I say, more because it seems like something you'd say than anything else.

She sort of nods and shrugs at once. "It's a lot," she

says. "But I'm happy." She glances back at Caleb and Val. "It's always just been the two of us here. For a lot of years, I made sure of it. This wasn't what I was planning on, but . . . it's good. It's right."

I feel a squirm of guilt hearing this, thinking of how dissatisfied I always am with all the family I've always had.

Her hand falls on my shoulder. "I hope you'll be part of it, too."

I'm completely unprepared for such a not-typical-boyfriend's-mom kind of thing, but I find myself saying, "That's the plan." We share a smile and I bring a stack back to the table, where Val and Caleb are bickering like I used to with my brother. For the first time in a couple years, I miss him.

Later, at the Hive, the band takes it well, too, Jon's only comment being, "Cool, just now please don't do any Luke-Leia Hoth action or I will slit open a tauntaun and crawl inside."

"Technically Luke and Leia didn't know they were siblings at the time," Matt points out. "But yeah, what he said."

"Except we're only *half* siblings," says Val. She says it with all the blank stoicism that she's always had, but this time, I can actually detect the joke, and laugh and be cool with her. Well, mostly.

After practice, I have to return home. Caleb gives me a ride to Aunt Jeanine's, where I wait until she pulls in, looking exhausted and delighted. "Wonderful," she reports of her weekend. "I will be making many more weekend flights north. And you?"

"All kinds of amazing," I say.

"Excellent. I'll tell you all about the opera on the way, what we ate after, where we stayed."

"Jeanine, thank you," I say seriously as we drive.

Her smile fades for a moment. "Long-term, we should make it our goal to be truthful with your father. He does deserve that. And so do we."

"Yeah," I say, the guilt returning.

"But for today, we are just two ladies full of thrilling secrets!"

My parents buy the story.

"Both schools were delighted to reschedule for a girl to see *Tosca*," Dad reports. "We'll go up on Thanksgiving weekend?"

"Sounds good," I say, flipping to the calendar on my phone.

"Maybe we'll make a whole long weekend of it."

"Well, I'll have had midterms all week and I might be exhausted." I say this as I am noticing that the big Homecoming Concert is the Wednesday night before Thanksgiving. "Could we wait to leave until after the holiday?"

This of course works, and yet, it makes me sad. After all this, I find myself back in the same role, lying to keep my parents satisfied, with bigger lies than ever before, rather than being seen for who I really am. . . . How much longer can I keep doing that? How much longer can I survive it?

Luckily, my eye notices two other words on my calendar, for the weekend before: Homecoming Dance. I'd been planning to ignore that with malice . . . unless Caleb wants to go. I could actually wear the opera dress. We could be fancy and not care what anyone thinks.

But for tonight, I need to tear up the hideous pink prom dress I bought last week at Goodwill, cover myself in brown, black, and red makeup, and make my hair stick this way and that. My costume is basic zombie princess. It never gets old to imagine a Disney princess as a devourer of brains. It works on so many levels.

Dangerheart is on third at the Harvest Slaughter. They've kept it simple with a unified zombie prep school theme. Shredded jackets and ties, faces painted, and all in the shorts and socks like Angus Young from AC/DC. Val looks the best of course.

Freak Show will close out the night, and I see them strutting around the cafeteria bragging about their gig the night before. And when I say cafeteria, I mean Mount Hope's version, as in, one that has a wall that slides back to reveal a complete stage with professional lights and concert-quality audio. Supreme Commander is playing when I arrive, and the crowd pulses in a frenzy of bizarre costumes.

Right before Caleb goes on, I grab him around the neck and plant my lips against his, right there in the green-and-blue light in front of anyone who might care to notice. I may still be in hiding at home, but not here, not anymore. I know him, I know it's right, and I know me.

Then I pull back and we bump fists seriously. "Give 'em the ear lube," I say.

"Pluto strong," he replies.

And then we kiss again.

"Please stop!" Jon calls from the stage.

Caleb leans his forehead against mine. "Gotta go play a show."

"Gotta go check out a hot new band."

"Summer."

"Caleb."

Encore kiss. And Caleb bounds up onstage.

"Hey, everybody," Caleb says, sounding as free and easy as I've heard him. "We're Dangerheart. How's everyone doing?" He smiles, no Fret Face, and the band proceeds to kill.

Maya appears beside me mid-set. "Hey!"

"Hey! Awesome costume!" I say of her Matt Smith outfit. Always a great look on a girl, and her bow tie and swoopy hair are perfect.

"You, too!" she shouts back. "They sound amazing!"

"Yeah!" I agree. Something about the trip has made the band gel. Exhausted and painted gray and black, you can feel the internal steel of the group. They don't need to glance at each other anymore. Don't need to check the songs. Don't even need to take deep breaths. They just are.

I hear a couple things that could be better, of course. But I'll save them for a while.

"I just sent you a link!" Maya shouts.

"Oh, cool." The band is midway into "On My Sleeve." The room is on pins and needles, the lights orchestrated perfectly to the swells of sound. I don't know why she's telling me this now.

Then I feel her leaning toward my ear. "You should probably take a look at it ASAP."

"Um, okay." I try to keep an eye on Caleb, singing tenderly, sounding lovely, as I open my phone, find the link and click. But as soon as I see the first words that load, my eyes are glued in disbelief:

VINYL CUFFLINKS Where We Are / Music Infinite

Allegiance to A Secret
—posted by ghostofEliWhite on September 30

Friends, you absolutely will not believe this. A friend just sent me this copy of an unused poster from last night's show at the Rickshaw Stop in San Francisco. And if you look at the bottom of the listings, you will see something that will blow your tiny minds. ELI WHITE HAD A SON.

A quick scouring of the internet seems to confirm it. These pictures below show them side by side. Caleb

Daniels of Mount Hope, CA, and lead singer for a band
called Dangerheart, is the secret child of Eli White!
Apparently Candy Shell has been keeping this secret
for over eighteen years! Caleb, if you're out there,
please write in and tell us your story!

Below are the poster Jason had made up, side-by-side
photos of Eli and Caleb, as well as over fifty comments
going crazy about this news.

My heart sinks. This is going to suck for Caleb. And I
have to wonder: Did Jason leak this? Was this his way of
forcing Caleb into the spotlight, to shine on his terms? I
wouldn't put it past him.

"It's true, right?" Maya asks in my ear.

"Yeah."

"People are going to freak!" Maya says. "I won't
though, promise, especially not now that I've seen your
reaction!"

"Thanks." I want to tell her to keep it quiet, but there
will be no keeping this quiet.

Up onstage, Caleb sings:

I wear you on my sleeve
Always waking from some silly dream

Damn, Caleb, you're going to be wearing this way more
than you ever wanted.

"Can I help at all?" Maya asks.

The song is coming to an end. "Yeah," I say. "Go crazy for the set."

We applaud and scream, as does the rest of the room. Out of the corner of my eye, I see people swaying to the final chords. The song will capture hearts. But now people will figure out what it's about.

And Caleb won't be able to hide it anymore.

Of course, this is probably going to be a good thing, in terms of exposure. The problem is, everyone will have their angle, will try to define Caleb in terms of Eli. What if they never see him for who he really is?

But then I remember that we have the ace up our sleeves. The lost songs. We can show the world how Caleb and his dad are connected. *We* can set the terms, not the bloggers and music critics and commentators. And once we find those songs, we will.

We just have to hang on until then.

For now, I try to put it out of my mind. At least for a few more minutes.

The band breaks into "Chem Lab," and I try to be content to watch Jon dance over Mission Control, arcing his guitar around his body and spinning crystal notes, to watch Matt bob and weave to the rhythm, his sticks a blur, to watch Val shake and hop onstage, like a boxer just waiting to hit you with the next note, the next brazen lyric, to watch Caleb lose himself in a song, and look up like he's just

303

returned from somewhere far away inside his heart, and to every now and then glance at his band mates, at his sister, a far comet found, and between songs, at me.

I wish they could play all night. Never come offstage and face reality, the future, any of it. I wish we all could just stay in this moment, in beautiful light, lost in music, free to play and dance. But the song ends.

"Thanks!" says Caleb as the crowd erupts in the wake of "Chem Lab." "We've got a couple more. Does that sound cool?"

Yes, Caleb, it definitely does.

Continue the Journey
in Book Two of the

Trilogy

ENCORE TO AN EMPTY ROOM

Acknowledgments

I would like to acknowledge John Bonham's drum fill at the 3:33 mark of "The Wanton Song" by Led Zeppelin, side B of *The Joshua Tree* (on CrO2 cassette), and the exquisite melancholy of Rosemary Clooney's performance of "Sway" with Pérez Prado. These and a million other moments make music the thing. I would also like to acknowledge my wonderful editor, Katherine Tegen; the ultra-creative Patrick Carman; my wise and valiant agent, George Nicholson; the Seattle authors, booksellers, and librarians who make me feel like a rock star; my family and friends who keep me sane; and, of course, Steve Perry.